UNTOUCHABLE

AN UNTOUCHABLES NOVEL

CINDY SKAGGS

Entangled Publishing, LLC
2614 South Timberline Road
Suite 109
Fort Collins, CO 80525
Visit our website at www.entangledpublishing.com.

Ignite is an imprint of Entangled Publishing, LLC.

Edited by Alycia Tornetta and Lucy Clark
Cover design by L.J. Anderson
Cover art from iStock

Manufactured in the United States of America

First Edition July 2015

ignite

To Brianna and Noah, for understanding what it means when I say, "do not disturb except for blood or fire." Also, to the neurotic dog for entertaining them when I'm in my writing cave.

"No one leaves the family, except by way of a body bag."

Chapter One

The deal with the devil hadn't been signed in blood, but Sofia was certain that breaking it would bring bloodshed. As long as it wasn't her blood, she didn't have a problem with it, because today, one way or another, she was breaking the agreement she'd never wanted to make.

She couldn't think about the risks. Win or lose, everything would change and she needed change almost as desperately as she needed freedom. She glanced in the rearview mirror at her half-sleeping son. Her heart squeezed at the thought of all she would do today, but Eli was worth it. She tossed another glance in the mirror to see a car slip in behind her. Her hands flexed on the steering wheel.

Let the games begin, she thought sourly as she made a sudden right that took her off the main street and into a maze of a suburban neighborhood. The white sedan followed; hugging her bumper so tight she didn't have room to breathe. She braked hard so the sedan had no choice but to back off. She eased her foot back on the accelerator and considered her options. Eli was safe enough. They were headed to a public place. Later in the day a tail would be deadly, but right now, it wasn't her primary concern. She made a swift turn into a cul de sac and followed it with a rapid U-turn before circling back. The white sedan continued in the opposite direction. Sofia wiped damp hands on her workout pants.

Maybe she was just paranoid. Knowing that didn't keep her from checking the mirror every few seconds for the rest of the trip, but the white sedan didn't reappear. When she made it to the gym, she grabbed a parking spot close to the door and released a pent-up breath. She could do this.

Today was about taking back her freedom.

She grabbed Eli from his car seat and gave him a swift hug. With a chubby little hand, he shoved a cheese cracker shaped like a goldfish into her mouth as they walked toward the daycare area of the gym. The salt had been licked clean, but she smiled at her son. "Mmm," she said, raising her eyebrow to cover the grimace.

Eli giggled.

She checked him into the daycare and made small talk with the workers before sparing a glance at the camera behind the counter. The gym's video surveillance amplified the feeling that she was under near-constant watch. She stepped out of the daycare and onto the weight room floor. She knew without looking that the bodyguard was in place to her left. Tall, blond, built, and unseasonably tan, he was the epitome of everything she had left behind.

She walked past, heart pounding, before taking her backpack to the locker room and heading upstairs to the cardio floor. The treadmills were her torture of choice, so she found an empty one with a view of the yoga studio. The familiar whir of the belt calmed her nerves. She'd lost count of the times she had run on one of them like a hamster in a wheeled cage.

The cage was nice, for a cage. A two-story health club, it boasted 70,000 square feet dedicated to the pursuit of health and wellness. Happiness was optional. Sofia tuned into the pulse of the sterile space, her nerves hyperalert to the labored breathing of the runner next to her, the pervasive smell of sweat, and the hum of energy that flowed through the machines and the people who went nowhere on them.

Anticipation mixed with adrenaline to send her pulse into the red range on the treadmill's heart rate monitor.

The target would arrive any moment. Sofia searched for the man in the pre-work crowd. He blended into the backdrop of the morning drudge. She liked that about him. A person accomplished more in the background. She knew that firsthand. Two years she'd spent playing nice; all while hatching a plan that hinged on an anonymous tryst with an unsuspecting target. This morning was phase one.

The erratic beat of her heart told her she wasn't as blasé about this experiment as she wanted to believe. Admitting it cost her a few confidence points. She tapped the buttons on the control panel, forcing herself into a faster sprint designed to increase the adrenaline and decrease the doubts.

Doubt accomplished nothing. The plan was solid. The bodyguard wouldn't follow her to yoga. No need. The weight room was downstairs near the daycare, so he had a solid view of the lower level. If she left the building, he'd know it. If she went to the locker room, he'd see it. He couldn't see if she went to the mind and body studio so it was the perfect place to start.

The clock on the far wall showed five minutes to the hour and a new class was about to begin. The bodyguard was still on the bench press. Sofia slid off the end of the treadmill and reviewed the plan.

The target—she still didn't think of him as a man, and that could pose a problem—was at the gym nearly as often as her. He'd joined last spring, so not long enough to be one of her watchers. He didn't limit his time to bulking up with weights. He ran, like her, but not as fast or as long, and that was important.

She didn't trust a man who could chase her down, if it came to that.

The rush from her final sprint filled her with toe-bouncing energy. Sofia Capri did not bounce. She did nothing to stand out in the crowd, but inside, energy mixed with nervous excitement as she waited several feet from the man who could help her more than he would ever know. As the previous class left the studio, she eased through the doorway, waiting to see where the target landed. She stretched her calves while watching in the mirror.

He wore navy sweats and a matching T-shirt, sleeved. No jewelry. No flash. He was of medium height and build, tended to blend into the crowd, and his face was not unattractive. He was honest looking. She could spend time with a man like that, in theory. He swiped a sanitizing cloth across a green mat at the back of the room. She strolled forward to stand next to him and smiled when he looked up. His eyes widened a second before he smiled back.

Yes, she thought, he was just about her speed. He would keep her proposition to himself. If not to himself, he wouldn't blab about it to every man in the locker room before lunch.

As the class assembled, warmed up, and moved from one asana to the next, Sofia hoped her luck would hold. There was defeat in her past and fear in her present, but the future? It had potential.

The music hummed through the floor like an embryonic heartbeat as they moved into quiet meditation at the end of class. Her body stilled, absorbing the thrum of the music.

Now or never. Now or never, her brain chanted.

Not the best mantra to calm her nerves, but it was the truth. Time was not her friend. Already the next group lined up outside the door. She caught the target's gaze in the mirror and smiled. The look of confusion on his face matched the trepidation in her heart. She turned to grab her shoes from along the back wall. Clumsy, her fingers fumbled with the laces as she tied her shoes.

The new class moved into the studio, making the room more crowded as Sofia took the plunge. Now or never. "Would you like to get some coffee?" she asked.

When he didn't answer right away, she smiled and rose to her feet.

Mr. Average was gone. In his place stood six feet two inches of the wrong man.

• • •

Logan Stone had had his eyes on Sofia Capri for two years and counting. The woman commanded the attention of anything male within her sphere of influence, including him, but she'd never so much as acknowledged Logan's existence. She wasn't supposed to. He was supposed to be invisible.

The direct approach robbed him of all powers of conscious thought. Or maybe it was the smile that managed to convey mystery and uncertainty. And trouble. Trouble he couldn't afford and didn't want. He reminded himself that he was a professional. It took more than a disarming smile to counter years of training.

"Coffee?" He smiled, or tried to, and nodded in agreement. So much for training. His answer should have been a polite "no thank you," or a firm "hell no," but instead, he left Body Combat class before it began.

The cardio room was a maze of silver and black treadmills she navigated with a familiar speed before descending the stairs. The hum of ESPN on a nearby television did little to distract him from the woman in front of him. Runner lean, she packed an extra dose of curve. Despite an hour of yoga, her body was strung tight, with her back as stiff as that of any soldier, but she couldn't keep the sway from her hips. Two years of watching had done little to dull his body's instant reaction. Logan figured he might as well enjoy the view, because the cost of this little diversion was high.

An untrained observer wouldn't notice the slight pause at the bottom of the stairs as she turned her gaze to the right. The glance-and-pause lasted mere seconds before she walked briskly past the membership desk and into the café. She went straight to the coffee counter. "A tall, non-fat mocha, no-whip, with half the pumps."

Coffee drinkers had their own code and hers was high maintenance. The woman didn't disappoint. A smile thawed

Logan from the shock of her invitation. He ordered a coffee, black, and when she reached to pay, he swiped his card first. "I got it," he said.

"Thank you." The coffee machine sputtered as the barista worked on Sofia's latte. She stared at the backside of the industrial coffee machine with a neutral expression. As often as he watched her—and he did watch—she maintained this disturbingly placid look. She never looked hurried or flustered or happy.

The woman was aloof; as starched and tailored as the clothes she habitually wore. The fact that she was elusive made her damn near irresistible. As evidenced by the fact that he hadn't resisted the urge to go with her. He hadn't even tried.

He couldn't think of a single thing to break the ice. They called her the Ice Queen. In two years, she hadn't dated, flirted with, or talked to a man. At all. She was socializing now, with him, and that made it news. Any witnesses, and the gym was filled with them, would note that it was unusual. It would stick out in their minds.

Logan glanced around to count the potential problems. A plump man fighting with a toddler near the restrooms outright stared as Sofia tapped her red fingertips against the coffee counter. Others were less obvious, like the two kitchen workers who came out from the backroom, one at a time, to talk to the guy making coffee. The sideways glance they gave to Sofia was anything but disinterested.

They might as well post the news on the member bulletin board. Logan had captured the attention of the Ice Queen. Yee-haw. Now all he had to do was figure out how he'd said yes when his brain had definitely said no. His boss had given him a direct no-contact order—observe and report—and he was breaking that because his brain had gone AWOL.

The bitter smell of espresso woke him from his Sofia-induced haze. He couldn't afford to get lost in her spell. He needed to focus on damage control. How could he keep five days administrative leave from becoming permanent? Why had she singled him out? Did she know who he worked for or was he just the unluckiest schmuck in town?

By the restroom, the altercation between the dad and the little boy escalated so that the kid's wails were heard across the cavernous space, drawing more unwanted attention. A few weightlifters glanced across the room toward the kid, but stopped when they saw Sofia. The Ice Queen accepted her coffee with a small, polite smile and headed for a table away from the crying child. The spot put her behind a pillar that blocked her from view.

"I'm Sofia." She extended a narrow hand toward him.

A wave of cold rippled from her hand to his and then instantly heated. She broke contact with a barely audible gasp.

"Logan," he said, and made eye contact with the most complicated woman he'd ever met. The brown eyes that didn't quite meet his gaze were set deep and clouded with an emotion he couldn't read. Dark shadows that spoke of sleepless nights rimmed dark-lashed eyes, giving her another layer of mystery, yet something in those eyes told him more about her than any two-inch thick file ever could.

She was beautiful, but not in a conventional sense. The beauty was in the pale skin and dark hair that gave her an exotic appearance. Up close for the first time, he noticed a slight overlap in her front teeth that made her seem less perfect and more approachable, and full lips, soft pink, that spoke of an innocence at odds with her history. Her hair was a warm chestnut that she pulled into a silky tail. Tiny bits of hair tore free in what he considered a practiced look.

She glanced at the wall of glass on the east side of the room and rubbed her arms, despite the glow of the June sun. "I'm glad you joined me. I've seen you at the gym before. How long have you been a member?"

Small talk from anyone else, but he knew she was fishing for answers. He went with the truth. She'd probably done the research. "Two years."

"So this will be your second summer enjoying our great pool."

"Third," he said. "I joined in May."

A muscle in her jaw twitched. It didn't take a genius to know she was running the dates and not liking how it fit her timetable. And she was absolutely right. He wasn't here by accident.

"Is something wrong?" he asked. The woman was a pawn, a weak link in a game where she had no power. Her jitters had him wanting to take it easy on her. It had nothing to do with training and everything to do with his upbringing.

"No." She shook her head, her eyes focused in the distance. "I'm sure this is all very cryptic. Or not. Unless you're used to women asking you for coffee? And then—"

He reached for her hand across the table, a move meant to soothe her obvious nerves. "It's just coffee."

She pulled her hand away and slid it onto her lap. "My…" She took a sip of coffee. "My work keeps me busy forty-six weeks a year and I don't get much time for coffee with… Well, for just coffee. My six-week…"

Fingers shaking, she took another sip from the plastic-lidded cup. "My mandatory six-week vacation is coming up, and I thought maybe, that is, I was hoping…"

Sofia set the coffee firmly on the table and met his gaze for the first time. Her wide, espresso-colored eyes mesmerized him. The sincere expression startled him. A soul-deep sadness reflected in their depths.

"Honestly, I was hoping this year I wouldn't have to vacation alone."

• • •

The conversation continued along the script she had rehearsed, while inside she fought back panic. The script would have played better to the plain-Jane man upstairs who had left her in the lurch. There was such a small window of opportunity that she rushed blindly forward, playing out the scene she had practiced more times than she could count. In her exhaustive planning, Sofia had compiled a list of best and worst candidates for the job. Logan was number two on the worst list. Number one was at the free weights with the bodyguard.

The reasons were too numerous to ignore. Logan had joined the gym when she joined and she had every reason to believe that was not a coincidence. Yes, she knew how paranoid that sounded, but that didn't make it wrong. It was possible he joined the gym to keep an eye on her. He wouldn't be the first. That was a problem, as was the fact that she often caught him studying her when he thought she wasn't paying attention. She always paid attention. Sofia didn't like being watched.

But more than the worry of who he might be or whom he might work for was an underlying threat. The man was built like a bodybuilder. He was taller than her, stronger than her, he ran farther and faster, and had the unfortunate distinction of being standout handsome. This was not a man that blended into the crowd. Worse, something about him sent feel-good shocks coursing through her like waves in a tranquility pool.

What in the name of all that was holy had she been thinking?

"Let me get this straight." He rubbed a thumb along the rim of his coffee cup. "You want me to take a vacation with you?"

The judgment in his tone made her want to slink out of the room in disgrace. She forced herself to tune back into the conversation that had gotten so far out of her control.

At the counter, the barista joked with a mom and toddler while another worker disappeared into the back freezer. Sofia shivered, the cold caressing her skin. "I'm not talking anything inappropriate, Mr.–"

"Stone. Don't you think you should know the name of the man you want to take on vacation?"

No, she thought. She hadn't wanted to get that close, for the person to be that real, and while Sofia acknowledged her mistake, she moved forward with the plan. Forward. It was the only direction she knew. "I don't like traveling alone. My job keeps me busy forty-six weeks a year, and I have—"

"Six weeks mandatory vacation," he finished.

Sofia clenched a fist under the table. "I must have said that already."

"And you want to leave tomorrow. To Europe? What

makes you think I have a passport?"

Good question, Sofia thought. The people in her life—the people surrounding her the past several years—had passports. Two or three apiece. She'd assumed and that had been a mistake.

Her gaze shifted to the other tables in the café. Tables where people had normal conversations. A college-aged couple chatted two tables away. Maybe they flirted. Nothing wrong with a harmless flirtation. Closer to the barista, a couple fed dry cereal to a toddler. The husband reached over and brushed something from the woman's cheek and she leaned into his hand, smiling.

The pain stabbed at her, the deep and unsatisfied longing for the normalcy this couple had. Tears threatened, but she pushed them down with the ruthlessness of a despot. It did no good to want what she couldn't have. She turned her gaze back to Logan. She felt like a schoolgirl in front of the principal. "I didn't think about that."

"And what kind of person can take a vacation without notice?"

Someone with no discernible income and plenty of money. In short, the kind of people she knew. She pushed the coffee aside and swallowed what remained of her pride as she stood. "This was a mistake."

"I didn't say no."

Her vision shimmered, but it could have been the glare from the morning sun. "You didn't say yes."

The Ice Queen—yes she knew what they called her—didn't run from the café. She marched, shoulders back and head held high. The desk clerk looked up, but Sofia didn't meet his gaze.

The cavelike entrance to the women's locker room beckoned her into its camera-free zone. It wasn't safe, no place was, but it offered fewer witnesses than the public spaces beyond. It gave her a moment to regroup.

She'd been so desperate for the plan to work that she hadn't considered any of Logan's logical questions. She'd wanted it too badly to think straight. The plan was ill conceived, she could see that now, and she was rusty. She didn't remember how to have a simple cup of coffee with a man. The idea of weaving a web of seduction around him was ludicrous. She'd failed before she'd even begun.

She leaned against a locker. Her shoulders falling against the hard wood as she blinked away anger and frustration and hopelessness. The soothing music from the overhead speakers made her want to bang her head against the wall. She didn't want to be soothed. She needed to focus. Compartmentalize.

She should have made contact earlier, to make sure the target had a passport and the freedom to travel, but that would have broken the agreement. And her ex would have known. The man had more informants than the FBI.

The buzz of a blow dryer reminded her that she wasn't alone, even in the ladies' room. She grabbed her backpack from the locker and tried to find a silver lining. At least Logan didn't appear to have a connection to the inner core of gossip that ran through the gym like the backyard of a small town. It was one small blessing. Sofia tossed the backpack over her shoulder. All she wanted now was to get past the café without seeing Logan. Following the straight line of the beige tiles, she kept her gaze forward, shoulders back, as she made the march of shame to the daycare.

Taking a deep breath before entering the kids' area, she opened the door and plastered a smile on her face. The list of mistakes she'd made in this life was long, but her son wasn't one of them. She never let him see her upset. She gave her name at the counter and asked for Eli.

The young blonde gave Sofia a practiced smile. "Your husband already picked him up."

"My husband?" Sofia didn't soften the hard edge to her tone.

The girl smiled and tilted her head. "I'm sorry, your *ex*-husband already picked him up. You did tell us this morning that Eli would be gone for six weeks while he visited his father."

Panic blew through her body like an explosion.

"Is everything okay?" the girl asked.

"I—" Sofia sucked in a lungful of air. "I didn't realize we were doing the swap here, that's all."

Hadn't she paid her penance a hundred times over?

As if the failed plan wasn't bad enough, now any hope she harbored of recovering it was shot to hell. Leave it to Nick to alter the arrangements at the last minute. She pivoted on one foot and went back the way she'd come. She peered into the weight room. Eli's bodyguard was gone. There was no way Nick had come to the gym, but maybe he'd had Vince act as go-between. It wouldn't be the first time, but why hadn't the bodyguard said anything?

Nick had no right. She could accept the fact that the plan failed straight out of the shoot. She could accept that she didn't have anyone to use as cover to get out of the country. What she couldn't accept was what this did to Eli. He didn't have his clothes. Or the elephant he slept with at night. She didn't get to say good-bye. Her throat constricted. She coughed to break off the tears before they started.

The one lesson she'd learned above all others was to control any visual clues of her emotions that someone could use to manipulate or control her, but inside, she seethed. It had been one hell of a bad morning. Nick would not get away with this autocratic bullshit. Not today. She marched to the courtesy phone and punched in her ex-husband's cell phone number.

"Who is this?" he answered.

"Classy, Nicky," she said with the sweetness of a honey-bee. "Is phone etiquette beneath you?"

"What do you want, Sofia?"

"We had an agreement. Thursday at six o'clock. I have nine hours left."

"What are you talking about?"

"Don't play games, Nicky. Why did you take Eli early?"

"I didn't."

Good God, that couldn't be right. "Yes. You did."

"You playing games with me, Sof? 'Cause I think you know better. I warned you before. You try to take my kid, I'll kill you."

No doubt he would do it. Her hands shook. She couldn't help Eli dead. "I'm not playing, Nicky. I'm at the gym. Eli's gone."

"Prove it."

If Nick didn't have Eli, who did?

"Call Vince," she said, her voice rising. "He's supposed to guard Eli. Where is he?"

"You trying to make my guy take the fall?" he asked. "Bad move."

"I'm trying to find our son," she hissed.

"That's my job. And when I do, we're going to adjust this little custody arrangement of ours." He clicked off without warning.

Sofia dropped to the chair beside her, her mind going back to the last time she'd seen Eli, to the soggy goldfish and his innocent giggle.

Did Nick have Eli? Was he finally following through on his threat to take him full-time?

No, she thought. *He won't take my son.*

She took a deep breath, then another. Yoga had been an escape at first, but she'd learned to appreciate its calming effects. She used it to temper her emotions and regain control over her body. At the moment, she willed her breath to counteract the panic that sent adrenaline through her fight or flight system. While her body stilled, her mind replayed the morning. Eli had been grouchy. He didn't want to get up. To avoid a fight, she'd promised him pizza at Chuck E. Cheese and all the arcade games he could play. Their last day together would be special, she'd promised him.

At 6:40, she'd left Eli with a daycare worker who'd led Eli to the little kid room. He galloped like a horse down the hall and asked about craft time. Only after he was out of sight did Sofia go into the gym proper. Then what? She closed her eyes and rewound the day step-by-step. The "what" was what had happened to Vince? He'd been there when she'd gone to yoga, but after? Sofia hadn't looked, too absorbed in avoiding him. The pulse in her neck jumped. He'd definitely been gone when she'd tried to pick up Eli.

The clang of weights falling into place acted like an alarm. She opened her eyes and glanced at the television monitor above the desk. This wasn't an ESPN/CNN TV. It was the split screen of all the rooms in the daycare that parents used to keep an eye on their kids. If there was an upside to the privacy invasion of the ever-present video surveillance system, it was that nothing happened that wasn't on record. She rose and walked back to the daycare.

The young woman at the desk glanced up. Her nametag said Tamara. "Is everything okay, Miss Capri?"

"Fine, Tamara. I'm just being an overly cautious mom." She smiled, thankful for the years of practice at masking her emotions. "I couldn't reach Eli's father. I was hoping you could show me the video footage of him picking up Eli so I won't worry."

"Certainly." Tamara rose. "If you'll follow me to the office, I'll have one of the managers bring that up for you."

Following the girl out the daycare door and into the gym, Sofia felt the tingle of exposure tickle her nerves. She was being observed. She often felt that way. The trick was learning to ignore it. She lifted her chin in defiance. Let them watch.

Sofia followed silently while the girl explained the situation to shift manager James. He was a big man, a former football star who'd put on a few pounds since the glory days. He'd been with the gym since it opened four years ago, which only meant he wasn't a Calvetti plant. That didn't mean he wasn't on Nick's payroll now.

James led her to a small office adjacent to the membership desk. It housed a row of three computers with requisite black chairs and an indistinct painting. The chair groaned when he sat. He motioned for her to take the seat next to him, but the proffered chair put the big man between her and the only exit. That was a rookie mistake. She took the seat nearest the door and waited as he rewound the security footage. Even on the exit side of the room, the office walls closed in on her. The manager wasn't as large as one of Nick's associates, but he was tall and broad and filled the room in a way that made her twitchy. Her heart skipped and jumped like a kid on too much sugar.

The manager rewound to the time Eli was picked up. As he pushed play, someone paged him on the radio he habitually carried. "I'll be right back, Miss Capri."

She didn't know if his departure was a blessing or a curse. She felt safer without his linebacker presence, but for all she knew, Nick was the one calling. A phone call like that wouldn't bode well for her. She watched the silent tape as a harried young mother picked up an infant, and then watched Vince pick up Eli. The boy went without a whimper. Why not? Vince was his bodyguard. Vince was always there. And Vince now had her son.

Sofia slammed a fist onto the counter. The sting of it made her angrier. Nick had to be behind it and he sure as hell wasn't going to get away with it. On the desk next to the computer sat a box of empty DVDs. She grabbed one and put it in the computer's DVD drive. There were advantages to having lived where she'd lived with whom she'd lived. Burning a copy of a video was only one of her many hidden talents. She slipped the copy of the DVD into the waistband of her sweats as the manager swung the door open.

"Did you find what you needed, Miss Capri?"

She smoothed her T-shirt over her hips to soothe her nerves, but inside, her stomach churned. His body blocked the light and made the room feel more enclosed than the door had. She nodded, her mouth too dry to speak. Squeezing past him, she all but ran from the room and out to the parking lot. The sun and the open space eased the panic. She pulled out sunglasses; not to block the glare but to hide the emotions that played out in her eyes.

Sofia Capri was in full-blown panic mode.

As her mind raced, she forced her body to slow down, to make every movement precise and unhurried. Until she saw the car. The flat rear tire on the Volvo was no less than she'd expected and everything she feared. The backpack dropped from her numb fingers.

Whether she called the auto club or changed the tire herself, it was time that Vince would use to get farther away from her.

"Problem?" Someone asked behind her.

She whirled to confront the voice.

Logan. His dark hair was damp from a recent shower, but he hadn't bothered to shave.

"Your car?" he prompted.

"Flat tire." It came out glum, despite her best effort.

"Not the end of the world. I can change it for you?"

"I was just debating that myself, but I really have to get home. I have an appointment…"

"I'm happy to give you a lift." He smiled and waited for her response. The smile warmed his face and lit his eyes. Genuine, she thought, a little surprised by the way it hit her deep in the gut.

An hour ago this man had intimidated her. *Ridiculous.* What power did he have over her? The power to say no? So much the better for both of them. The rejection didn't matter. It was a pinprick to her pride. She'd forgotten real terror, the kind that crawled under her skin and leached it of warmth, but she could always count on Nick to remind her.

"It's really not a problem." Logan waited beside her as she stared morosely at the flat.

Rejection might humiliate her, but it couldn't kill her. She needed help and Logan had offered. "I'd appreciate a ride."

He picked the backpack off the ground where she'd dropped it and led her deeper into the asphalt jungle. In a parking lot filled with SUVs and four-wheel-drives, he led her to a midsized gray sedan. It surprised her. He was a tall man and would certainly look at home in a big, black SUV. He held the passenger door for her, which unsettled her more. It had been a long time since anyone had treated her like a lady. Longer still since she'd believed it.

The parking lot faded in the rearview mirror before he asked where to drop her. He didn't engaging in small talk. He asked where she lived, then left her alone. Traffic on the divided highway was light, with plenty of maneuvering room. It took her five minutes on a good day. Right now, it took an eternity as Sofia wondered which direction Vince had taken when he'd left the gym, wondered if he'd taken his car or another, and worried if Eli had had a car seat. Was there an accomplice traveling with them?

She glanced at the speedometer. Logan drove the speed limit. Sofia pressed her foot into the floorboard. No matter how strongly she wished otherwise, their speed remained too slow.

The dark grey interior of the car was quiet and climate controlled, like the man behind the wheel. He didn't tap his fingers on the steering wheel or curse at traffic or listen to the radio. It was all she could do not to slide her leg over the console and press her foot on the gas pedal. As they turned into the gates outside her neighborhood, she tossed him the electronic key card that opened the gate. Every delay sent Eli farther from her. She directed Logan to the right and around the bend to her house.

He whistled when she pointed it out. "Nice house."

"It's just a house." She shrugged. It was nice, from the outside looking in. Like its neighbors, the two-story stucco home stood back from the road on a half-acre lot that was manicured to the Homeowner Association's specifications. Two large oaks framed the front entry and provided shade for the wall to ceiling windows in the living room. A long stone drive led to a three-car garage and its loft apartment.

Logan pulled into the drive, stopping near the walkway to the front door. "*I* live in a house," he said. "*This* is more."

She shrugged. Her love-hate relationship with it had nothing to do with appearances. "It's just a house," she repeated.

"If you say so. Something like, 'it's just coffee?'"

The irony wasn't lost on her. This morning's coffee was supposed to be more. She smiled sadly. This morning her only worry was how to lure an unsuspecting sap into a plan that now seemed ridiculously out of reach. How on earth could she live the rest of her life without her sweet baby boy? She closed her eyes to block the thought.

Logan walked around and opened her door. "You know," he said, "I never said no."

She waved her hand dismissively as she climbed from the sedan. "That's the least of my worries. Thanks for the ride."

Taking her backpack from Logan's large hands, she

ignored the sizzle of his touch as she climbed the front stairs to her house. Sizzle was dangerous.

At the door, the *click* as she turned the key wasn't the lock turning, but the *click* of something far more deadly. A woman in her position knew better. She dropped the bag, jumped the steps to the walk, and dove behind Logan's car the moment the entryway exploded.

Chapter Two

The shockwave from a bomb lifted the front tires off the pavement. Seconds later, debris sandblasted the windshield. Logan reached for his weapon and came away empty. *Damn.* Five days administrative leave. He cursed again.

After the initial blast, a vacuum sucked all sound from the air and all air from his lungs. The moment stilled around him as Logan tried to clear the ringing in his ears. He didn't have time to recover. A bomb could be the opening salvo in a much larger battle. He was unarmed and in the company of a woman on the FBI watch list. Not his finest hour. Logan opened the driver's side door and rolled to the driveway.

Sofia lay on the stonework by the front tire. Her sunglasses crushed at her side and a scrape marked her right cheek, but no blood. No obvious wounds. Her eyes opened, but took a minute to focus. When they did, emotions clicked through like a hyperactive slideshow. Confusion, fear, anger. She rolled to her feet and headed into the house.

They were in the blast zone before he reached her. He grabbed her wrist and yanked her back to keep her from heading into the house. "What do you think you're doing?"

She wrenched her hand free. "It was a warning. If they wanted to kill me, I'd be dead. It had a ten second delay."

"How do you know that?"

The fog in her eyes lifted. "If you want to live, Mr. Stone, you'll walk away."

The smell of burnt pine and sulfur sharpened his other senses. This was no longer a morning diversion. "Are you threatening me?"

"Am I menacing? Because if I am, I'd like to know why I'm the on this side of the blast." She glared at him. "I'm warning you that the people who did this won't hesitate to kill you if they figure out who you are. Walk away."

She turned and walked into the house.

Logan raced to catch up; wishing he had a weapon and a clue as to what the hell just happened.

She snapped around when he inched through the blast. Her eyes sparked and her body braced for combat. "I thought I told you to go?"

"It was a nice line, lady, but I'm involved."

She clamped her mouth closed. "Enter at your own risk."

Splintered wood and acrid smoke filled the entry. Flash burns marked the earth-toned paint a good ten feet into the house, but the damage looked superficial.

Like she said, a warning shot.

Twenty feet ahead, the cherry floors gave way to a central staircase that belonged in a Southern mansion. Sofia climbed to the second floor, her rubber-soled shoes squeaking on the hardwood. Logan took a quick tour of the lower level and cleared the rooms one by one. The living room, dining room and kitchen were open, making the job easier. A small home office sat off the living room, but it was as empty as the rest. Not a soul in sight, and, outside of the blast zone at the front door, no sign of another incendiary device.

The place was as beautiful and sterile as a model home. There was no television, no computer, and no home phone that he could see. It felt like a mausoleum. Logan opened the refrigerator and was relieved to see it packed with food, because it was evidence that she really lived there and it wasn't just a stage for some elaborate game. He closed the fridge and followed Sofia up the central staircase.

Four doors lined a central hall. The first door led to a child's room, complete with bunk beds and a menagerie of stuffed animals. Logan knew about her son, four-year-old Eli Calvetti, who according to intelligence was scheduled for a visitation with his father starting today. Sofia's "mandatory" six-week vacation. Logan wondered if the boy's father was behind the vandalism to her car and the bombing, but it was too early to speculate.

He checked the room across the hall. It was a bedroom as impersonal as the public rooms below. The next door was a bathroom, but there was more personality in that little room than in the rest of the house combined. Hidden behind a shower curtain of yellow rubber ducks was a bathtub lined with rubber toys and bubble bath. Discarded pajamas dotted the floor and a tube of children's toothpaste stood open on the counter. The room had a different vibe then the rest of the house and Logan almost didn't want to leave it, but there was one more room to clear.

The door to the last room was open and showed a room as immaculate as the downstairs. It looked like an untouched photo from a magazine right down to the teacup and newspaper on the nightstand. In the center of the room, under a chandelier, stood a cherry four-poster bed with multiple rows of decorative pillows. Sofia stood at the foot of the bed and pushed against the solid frame.

"Help me," she grunted.

He glanced down the hall to make sure they were still alone before standing next to her and pushing the bed sideways. It weighed as much as two recliners, but gave under his weight. It slid noiselessly from the wall. After moving it four feet, Sofia stopped pushing and dropped to the ground. Her fingers brush the narrow spaces between the floorboards. He heard a faint *click* as the boards popped up to reveal a hidden compartment. The space was designed to fit the large duffel she pulled from the dark interior.

"You have weapons in there?"

"No," she hissed. She gazed up at him with eyes as hard as any field agent's. "Never carry a weapon someone can take from you."

"No one takes my weapon," he assured her.

Her jaw tightened. In Sofia's experience, men loved their guns, but it was even truer in Colorado where owning guns was a sport. "Spoken like a true man."

"Guilty as charged."

She rolled her eyes as she brushed past him. She opened a closet the size of his office and yanked several articles of clothing from their hangars. She wrapped them into a large wad and shoved them into the duffel before she disappeared into the back of the closet. The sounds of drawers opening and banging closed drifted into the bedroom.

"I have to call this in," he said loudly.

She peered around the corner as she shoved a DVD into the bag. "I'm sure my neighbors took care of that." She disappeared again. "We need to be out of here in two minutes."

It occurred to him that her uncertainty from this morning had disappeared. She was calm, too calm for a woman who'd just avoided a bomb, and self-assured, something else she had lacked two hours ago. "Why do you say that?"

"Because the Aspen Springs police are slow, but not that slow." She stepped from the closet wearing jeans and a slender green shirt with a logo across the front. "Look, Mr. Jones," she said, intentionally using the wrong name. "I appreciate the ride, but it's time for you to take your truck and ride on out of here."

"What the—"

She pressed a frigid finger to his lips and shushed him. It was effective because the feel of her skin against his lips turned his brain to oatmeal.

"It was nice to meet you," she said, and walked out of the room.

Adrenaline knocked through his body like a kick boxer. The zip of her touch only amped it up. His ears were still ringing from the explosion, but he didn't need his full hearing to know she'd just told him to kiss off. He wasn't in the mood. Pent-up frustration had him striding into the hall after her, itching for a fight.

She exited the room next door as he reached the hall. She stuffed a gray and fuzzy plush toy into her duffel and kept walking. She glared at him when he followed but kept moving until they hit the driveway.

Logan didn't let her get the first volley. "What the hell? Lady, you need to explain what just happened."

Her eyes sparked with the same energy that jammed up his system. "Should I speak slowly?"

"Skip slow." He gritted his teeth and fought the urge to yell. "Why don't you start with the truth?"

"You want the truth?" She paced to the edge of the driveway and back, stepping over fragments of the siding and what was once the front door. "The truth? Fine. Whoever took the time to set that bomb would very much like to know who is with me and where I'm headed. You can thank me for using a fake name and making it harder to identify you."

That stopped him short. "You think your house is bugged?"

"I live with that assumption every day of my life, Mr. Stone."

It had never occurred to him. He'd never given a thought to her isolated life. "That's a hell of a way to live."

She shrugged, but couldn't pull off a convincing level of nonchalance. Her hands shook as she dug through the duffel bag. She pulled out a new pair of sunglasses as sirens sounded from a few miles away.

"Time to go," she said.

"I can't leave. I'm law enforcement."

Her head snapped back as if he'd struck her, and for a moment her eyes seemed to water, then she blinked and settled a disinterested mask on her features. She put on her sunglasses and just like that, she was the Ice Queen again. "Of course you are, because my day isn't bad enough." She slung the duffel strap crisscross over her shoulder. "Feel free to stay."

She glanced toward the front gates before jogging the opposite direction and disappearing around the corner.

Logan felt raw inside from the look of betrayal she had leveled on him. Who was he to demand honesty when every aspect of his presence in her life, even on the periphery, was a lie? He vacillated between staying put, which he damn well should do, or following the crazy woman. The crazy woman who just survived a bomb and grabbed a go-bag from a hidden compartment in her bugged house.

How stupid can you get, Stone?

Logan jumped into the car and rammed it into gear. He sped around the corner before the local cops made it through the controlled access gates. He found her up the street, jogging toward the back of the neighborhood.

Her face betrayed no emotion when he pulled up beside her and rolled down the window.

"Want to explain to me why you left a crime scene?"

She kept jogging. "Want to explain to me why you joined my gym?"

"I like the Body Combat class," he answered quickly.

"Right." The glare she sent him would have withered a lesser man. "What's the name of your favorite instructor?"

"Why would I know that?"

"Why don't you start with the truth," she said, mimicking his comment from earlier.

If she knew the truth, she'd disappear, and for reasons he couldn't explain, he didn't want that to happen. Instead, he gestured to the house they were passing. "We're attracting attention."

She glanced through the upscale neighborhood. No one was outside, but an occasional curtain fluttered as the sirens drew closer. Uniform patrol officers would canvas the neighborhood and someone would remember seeing Sofia running next to his car. "Shit," he muttered. "My day isn't going that great either."

Sofia stopped and stared through his open window. "Do you think I set a bomb in my own house?"

"No. That doesn't explain leaving the scene."

At a crossroads, she spun on her heel and cut behind the car to an adjacent road.

Logan backed up, turned around and followed her down the cross street.

Irritation flickered on her face. "Are you arresting me?"

Direct again, and right on target. She hadn't done anything wrong. "No, but that doesn't answer my question. Why are you avoiding the police?"

Her breathing was edging toward rough as she continued to jog. She cast a swift glance toward the sirens that wailed two blocks away. "They're a complication. A delay I can't afford."

"Get in," he ordered.

"Are you arresting me, Officer?" she asked, and the way she moved felt like she was running from him as much as the police cars approaching her house.

"No," he said, and he had no clue why he wasn't at least taking her in for questioning. "Get in the car, Sofia."

The pace of her jogging didn't slow. "It wouldn't be smart for either one of us, Mr. Stone."

"Do it anyway."

She stopped in the middle of the road. Logan pressed on the brake to stop at her side.

"This little disappearing trick of yours might get you out of the neighborhood before the police catch up with you," he assured her. "But you're getting nowhere fast without a vehicle."

She yanked the duffel off her shoulder and looked like she wanted to throw it at him.

He smiled and reached across the seat to open the door. "Where to?" he asked.

She got in and slammed the door closed. "There's a maintenance gate at the east end of the neighborhood. I have a key to the gate."

"I'm sure you do." He couldn't keep the sarcasm from his voice. Not that his stupidity was her fault. Or maybe it was, he couldn't decide. He knew that until he'd had coffee with Sofia, he'd been a rule follower. He liked his job and was damn good at it. His last girlfriend said he loved his job more than he loved her. They'd broken up over it because she'd been right. He did love his job above anything or anyone, but he wasn't acting like it now.

He drove past a small dog park that was fenced off from a playground designed to look like an Old West fort and a soccer field of pristine grass that looked as untouched as all the yards on display throughout the neighborhood. He pulled around to the parking lot on the southeast side. There, behind a large, brown garbage Dumpster was an eight-foot gate with an industrial lock. "You have a key to this?"

She held the key just out of his grasp. "Do you have a phone?" Sofia asked.

Everything with her was a trade-off. He pulled his smart phone from his jeans pocket.

"Is it clean?" she asked.

"Yes," he growled. Like she had reason to distrust him. It was the other way around.

"Are you sure?"

"It hasn't left my possession since I met you, if that's what you mean."

They traded the key for his phone. He heard her dialing while he unlocked the maintenance gate.

"Meet me in twenty minutes at our place," she said into the phone. She clicked off without waiting for a reply.

Sofia knew what she had to do and it sent chills through to her very soul. Even knowing what she had to do, she didn't rush into it. She needed information. She was persona non grata with the old crowd, but there was one person who would give her the information she needed. Thanks to Logan's by the book driving, she arrived five minutes late to the campus coffee shop where she'd arranged the meeting, but as her friend was chronically late, Sofia figured she had a few minutes. She directed Logan to the parking lot in the back and opened her door the moment he pulled into a parking spot. "Thanks for the ride."

"You're welcome."

Sofia swung her legs out the door, but his next words immobilized her.

"We're not saying good-bye just yet. I'm going with you."

"What? No." Sofia tried to be firm, but her brain was still stuck on the fact he wasn't letting her go. "Why?"

He turned off the engine. "Call it curiosity."

"No." She swung her legs back into the car and slammed

the door closed. "Curiosity is not a good thing. Curiosity killed the cat."

"I'm a big boy. I can take care of myself."

"No." She said again. He had no idea who he was dealing with, and even if he did, Vicki would kill her for bringing this man to their meeting. "That's not enough to get you a buddy pass to this party."

He turned in his seat to face her and blessed her with a smile that was part flirtation and part threat, and her body reacted to both. Her pulse skyrocketed as she waited for the bomb to drop.

"How about a trade-off?" he suggested. "I go with you."

"A trade implies you have something to offer," she reminded him, but she already felt on the losing end of this exchange.

"Or I spend that time calling the uniforms and letting them know where to pick up a witness to this morning's bombing."

The threat of exposure made her hands shake. She grabbed her duffel and slid her hands up and down the strap. If he called the uniforms, they'd put Eli at risk, and she'd be buried so deep in bureaucracy that it would take weeks before she had the freedom to search for him on her own. She knew in her heart she didn't have that much time.

"That's not a trade, Mr. Stone. Where I come from, that's blackmail."

"I'm offering my silence in exchange for going with you."

She bit her tongue to hold back the sarcastic response. Why hadn't she directed him to someplace nearby rather than the back door of her safe place? She wasn't thinking clearly, that was certain, but she wasn't going in without a few concessions on his part. "I don't even know for a fact that you are a police officer," she said. "Where's your badge?"

"In my captain's office."

"Convenient."

His eyes narrowed. "Not for me."

"So you say. What did you do to lose your badge? Trample someone's civil rights? Use excessive force?"

Logan gave his head a sad shake. "You don't like law enforcement, do you?"

"They're a complication," she said, repeating her answer from earlier. In truth, the only police she had ever met were on her ex-husband's payroll, and no, she didn't like them. "You didn't answer my question."

"I'm on five days administrative leave for shooting a suspect," he grudgingly admitted.

She smiled sweetly. "Excessive force?"

"Self-defense."

She rolled her eyes. "I'm sure your boss will see it your way."

"But you don't see it that way?" he asked.

No, she did not see it that way. She saw everything through one lens: protecting Eli. Both the police and her ex-husband's people were a threat. She shrugged, mostly to herself, and accepted that she would cave to Logan's demand. She couldn't risk getting the local police involved.

Logan reached across the console and gently touched her chin, turning her to face him. She didn't want to look at him. She felt in a position of weakness and it didn't sit well with her. His fingers were insistent, and the pressure didn't ease until she met his gaze.

"I don't want to interfere," he said, but in his eyes, it looked like a promise. "Someone vandalized your car and bombed your house. I just want to make sure you're safe."

A lump formed in her throat. It had been so long since anyone cared about her safety. "After you know it's safe, you'll go away? Let me go my own way?"

He nodded. "As long as you're safe."

Sofia pulled back, away from his mesmerizing touch. "I need you to promise that you won't interfere at this meeting."

"Why would I?"

Because they were about to meet with her former sister-in-law, and Vicki Calvetti had been under surveillance from both the FBI and the mob for most of her life…and she didn't take kindly to strangers.

Chapter Three

Thursday, 11:15 a.m.

The smell of coffee and stale pastries hit her with a combination of memory and possibility. She ordered two cappuccinos and Logan's black coffee, paid cash, and headed up the stairs. A wall of windows opened up the once-cramped space. The coffee house took up two stories of an old building that originally housed a small shop and the shopkeeper's family. It had been converted so that the first two floors housed the coffee shop while apartments took up the third and forth floors. They rented for an obscene amount, considering the age and condition of the building. She and Vicki had lived upstairs the last two years of college, and that same coffee-pastry combination had scented their tiny apartment.

It's why the memory was so potent. College had been a time of youthful optimism. Now the place just seemed overpriced.

The coffee space was hip in a college-grunge way. An array of old sofas and chairs were arranged haphazardly around the open room. Sofia knew that students moved things around as they pleased and the owners left it that way. By the windows, four chairs upholstered in different patterns surrounded a chess table with two college kids battling away. Sofia chose a love seat in the back corner near Vicki's favorite ratty chair. There was a stairwell behind them, on the other side of the restrooms, if they needed an exit. Most people didn't know they existed, but it was through the back that Vicki arrived.

Vicki's wild, curly hair was down today, frizzy after yesterday's rain. Her skin was tanned a deep bronze despite the early season. Still in a bohemian phase, she dressed in a flowing skirt and a tight knit top. Bangles jingled on her arms.

The second Sofia saw her, a swell of emotion surged in her chest. She grabbed Vicki in a fierce hug and felt the tears gather, so close she tasted the salt. She let some of the stress ebb into the folds of her friend's arms, but not too much. Relaxing came at a price. Weakness. She forced herself to break away.

She cleared her throat. "I got you a cappuccino."

"You're an angel," Vicki said as she sank into her favorite chair and eyed Logan. "Who do we have here?"

Sofia didn't have a clue how to answer her former sister-in-law.

Logan took it out of her hands as they sat in the love seat near Vicki's chair. "I'm Logan."

"Vicki," she said with a stiff nod. "So you're not Sofia's friend Logan, or her bodyguard Logan, or her—"

"Just Logan," he finished.

Vicki slanted a gaze at Sofia. "No last name Logan. Can you trust him?"

Sofia gestured with her hands. "I don't know," she answered honestly.

Vicki nodded. "What's this about?"

Sofia considered how best to answer. Logan had promised to leave her alone after the meeting, but speaking openly in front of him might cause more complications. She started with a vague question. "Have you spoken to Nicky today?"

"No. Should I?"

Sofia weighed her answer. "Maybe. Have you talked to him in the last few weeks?"

"A little. Sofia, what's going on?"

The only way to answer without alerting Logan was to revert to the coded language they often used to counter listening devices, which had the added benefit of emotional distance. If she had to say the words outright—Eli had been kidnapped—she might lose it. As it was, her voice wavered. "A shipment was misdelivered this morning. It's missing."

Vicki bolted forward in her seat, all pretense of bored indifference vanishing. "Define missing?"

Sofia took a fortifying drink of coffee and set the cup on the table with shaky fingers. Coffee sloshed over the sides. She told Vicki the essential details, leaving out the part about Logan being law enforcement. His presence was hard enough to justify, even to herself. She knew better than trusting anyone, especially law enforcement, yet here she sat, next to him.

When she finished relating the morning's events, she released a pent-up breath. "I think it's Nicky."

Vicki pursed her lips. "I don't think so."

"You don't know what he's capable of."

"I know he likes to pull your chain. I think it's one of his greatest pleasures, actually, but I don't think he'd do it like this."

Sofia latched on to Vicki's phrasing. She didn't deny that Nick would kidnap his own son, just that it didn't seem fit his M.O. "You said you don't think he would do it like this. So you think he would do it?"

"Not at all," Vicki insisted. "I know what my brother is, Sofia. I have no illusions about what he does, but I don't think this is him."

"But you can't be sure, can you?" Sofia pushed.

Vicki unconsciously pulled at the nubs of string on the chair. "Let me see what I can find out." She set her cup down on a game-laden table and walked back toward the bathrooms.

"Who or what went missing?" Logan asked.

Sofia started. So far, she'd avoided his questions. As promised, he'd been quiet during the entire exchange, but he wasn't the type to stay in the background.

How much could she tell him? She turned and looked at him squarely. Obviously, her choice in men was all wrong, and, obviously, her judgment was impaired or she never would have married Nick, but still, she didn't believe Logan was a bad guy.

"Eli. My son."

"I thought he was with his father."

"So did I, but Nicky denies it."

The lines on Logan's face whitened, then flexed. "That changes things."

"I think my ex just revoked my parental rights." Her voice cracked like ice under pressure. She turned her gaze from Logan.

"He can't do that," Logan assured her.

The mountains in the distance drew her attention. Since she'd returned to Colorado, the mountains had been her sanctuary. She looked to them for strength, but today they didn't soothe her. Nothing could. She knew more than anyone the depths of her ex-husband's cruelty. "He thinks he can do anything."

"He can't," Logan said, his voice hard.

It made Sofia laugh, a sad, pathetic sound. It sounded like Logan didn't know who her ex was, because Nick Calvetti did anything he damn well pleased.

Sofia looked at Logan—really looked at him—for the first time. The shear stupidity of what she was planning earlier had prevented that. He had dark brown hair, cut short, dark eyes, and lips that ran a little thin. The stubble on his face indicated he hadn't shaved that morning. There were crinkles around his eyes that softened his hard demeanor. Her body warmed as she observed him and the physical reaction surprised her.

She wasn't made of stone—or ice, as she'd occasionally overheard—and it had been too damned long since she'd enjoyed a man's company, but Logan wasn't her type. The slight resemblance to Nick aside, she wasn't sure any man was her type anymore, but Logan had his attributes and she wasn't so far gone that she hadn't noticed. He wasn't like the nameless and faceless at the gym. That's why she never would have chosen him. The man stood out like a predator on the open plains. He was a fine physical specimen that stood several inches taller than her and had shoulders so broad they could engulf her in one swipe of his beefy arms. The black T-shirt he wore was just the right amount of tight to showcase his strength. A girl would have to be blind not to notice his nicely defined biceps, and—

Damn.

Sofia turned away to deny the urge that washed through her. She childishly wished that she could lean into Logan's strong shoulders. A man of innate strength, his solid bearing promised physical security, among other things, and there had been a time when she had prayed for that kind of deliverance, but that would be trading one cage for another. Her focus had to stay on Eli. Sofia took a deep breath and grabbed her coffee cup with strong and steady fingers.

When Vicki stepped back from the hallway, Sofia had her head—and her hormones—screwed on straight.

"He says he doesn't have him," Vicki announced. "He thinks this is your play to disappear with Eli."

Sofia shook her head. She'd forgotten to tell Vicki about the video. "I can prove what I'm saying. Is Nick here in Colorado?"

"Going to him is a seriously bad idea, Sof. He thinks you took Eli. He's ready to—" She glanced at Logan. "*Deal* with you in his usual way."

"I'll take my chances." Sofia grabbed the two-ton duffel and stood. "I know his tells; when he's lying and when he's bluffing. Face-to-face is the only way I'll know if he's telling the truth."

"I hope you know what you're doing," she told Sofia. She looked at the man at Sofia's side. "Good luck, Logan No-Name. You'll need it."

Logan didn't acknowledge Vicki as he followed Sofia down the back hall and onto the fire stairs in the back. She banged and clanged her way to the alley and parking lot beyond.

"Where we headed?" Logan asked.

Wouldn't it be handy to have someone like Logan at her side? "There is no 'we,'" she said, her words a sharp denial of her own need. In the alley, the smell of stale beer and burnt coffee had her turning toward the street, away from the alley where he'd parked his car. Her shoes stuck to the gooey asphalt, slowing her down, until the weight of her words stopped her completely.

There was no "we" to help her through this. She was isolated in a no-man's land between the real world and the world she had escaped. No one from her former life would dare help her without Nick's permission. No one in law enforcement would see past Eli's last name. All they cared about was Nick, not his son, and they wouldn't help. Unprotected and vulnerable, Sofia had no one to trust and no one to turn to for help. She wouldn't ask Logan for what he couldn't give. She wasn't sure why she wanted to, but that dangerous want had her backing away from him. "We both know you have to report this."

He matched her pace, easing forward as she stepped back.

"I do." It came out in the form of a question.

"You're required to," she reminded him.

"I am," he confirmed, but he wasn't reaching for his cell phone. He was reaching for her.

The back stepping stopped when she hit the wall of an adjacent building. The pressure of it, of him, though he didn't touch her, had her panicking inside with her stomach doing strange flip-flops. If he expected her to admit she needed help, he didn't know who he was dealing with. She didn't need anyone. She soaked up the warmth from the sun-baked bricks and let it bolster her courage.

"I know you have to report this," she repeated.

He acknowledged her statement with a barely perceptible nod, his brown eyes unreadable.

She placed a hand on his arm. It was solid and warm beneath her stiff fingers. It calmed the quivering that weakened her body. "Do me a favor," she asked. "Don't mention Eli. Not yet. Give me twenty-four hours."

"Twenty-four hours gives the kidnappers too much time."

"Please." She gripped his arm now, willing him to understand. "They'll kill my son."

• • •

The touch was a pipeline of energy feeding an insatiable beast. He'd been attracted to Sofia from the beginning, so maybe today and all the wrong turns had been wish fulfillment.

Not now.

The coil of rage that swirled in his gut only wound itself deeper at the thought of the missing boy. He could report it and get a team together, it's what he did, but he was on administrative leave. Five days mandatory after firing his weapon at a lowlife drug dealer who'd be out of jail in two weeks' time. So they'd pat him on the head and send him home. No one else would give a flying fuck about Calvetti's kid. No one deserved to lose a child. "It's usually about money."

"It's about power," she said definitively. "I know the kind of people I'm dealing with." Her eyes implored him, glistening with unintended honesty. The flutter of her thick lashes undid him.

He cursed under his breath. If she'd asked him to help, he would have said no. *You know I can't do that*, he would have said. The woman thought she had to do it alone, and that self-imposed isolation made him want to help despite the risks. "We both know I'm not letting you go alone."

"I don't know that." She shook her head and her watery eyes avoided his gaze. "I don't know you."

"I'm telling you. You can't do this alone."

"You said you'd leave me alone after the meeting." She yanked her hand off his arm and peered over his shoulder as if she wanted to run. "You promised."

"I said if you were safe. You are most definitely *not* safe."

She glared at him. "What about your job?" she taunted.

That was the million-dollar question. He'd had coffee with a mob-wife, then with the sister. Maybe he could lunch with the big man himself and completely compromise his integrity. "I don't have to be in until Monday. I'll report it then."

Because he was angry with himself, he grabbed her more forcefully than intended and led her to the car. She resisted, pulling away even as he pulled her with him. He was bigger and stronger. She didn't have much choice. He opened the passenger door, waited for her to get inside, and then slammed it behind her. He took a deep breath as he rounded the car and relaxed the tension building in his jaw. Getting angry would cost the boy.

"Where to?" he asked as he climbed behind the wheel.

"Wal-Mart."

He chuckled as he started the car. "I didn't figure you for a bargain shopper."

"I wasn't always…" She gestured at herself. "This." Whatever this was. "There are certain things you can only get at Wal-Mart."

The things she needed turned out to be two burner phones and a small backpack. The scent of fresh bread from the bakery at the front made his stomach growl and he realized it was past lunchtime. "When was the last time you ate?"

She shrugged, but didn't slow. He grabbed two deli sandwiches on the fly, a large bag of potato chips, and two bottles of water before following her to the self-check aisle. She looked up at him with a questioning expression as he scanned the items.

"Contrary to popular belief," he said, "You cannot live on coffee alone."

A slow smile lit her face before she ran her credit card through the register.

"You sure you want to do that? Credit card purchases are easy to track."

"I'm counting on it. It will give them something to do. A distraction, but it won't tell them anything."

Them? Who did she think *they* were? "Where are we going? Emphasis on *we*."

Her smile turned into a grim frown. "All in good time."

She directed him to a nearby park, but the afternoon storms had rolled in so they ate dry sandwiches and greasy chips huddled in the front seat. Large splats of rain fell onto the windshield, washing the bomb debris off the windshield. A gray haze enveloped the car and turned it into a cave that emphasized the sweet smell of her perfume. The rumble of thunder covered his uncomfortable response to the woman he shouldn't want. It was a relief to swallow the last bite of sawdust sandwich. When they finished, she asked for his phone.

"Don't you have two?"

"One for me and one for you." She crumpled their wrappers into the plastic shopping bag and held it open for him. "Toss your smart phone in here."

"You want to throw out my phone?"

She glared at him. "Yes."

The *duh* he heard was implied.

"Do you have any idea how expensive this thing is?" The cell phone contract was longer than the one he'd signed when he entered law enforcement.

"Do you have any idea how easy it is to track?" she asked.

He knew. He shoved the plastic bag aside and started the engine. "I'll plug it in at home so it can't direct anyone to us. Satisfied?"

"We don't have time—"

"I have a go-bag of my own to get," he insisted. A weapon at the very least. "It's non-negotiable."

"Fine," she said, but her tone implied she was definitely not happy with the delay. She grabbed the GPS off his dashboard. "This goes, too. Any other electronics?"

"ONSTAR."

"I'll take care of that when the rain lets up. It's easy

enough to disconnect."

"I have a garage," he offered. "You can take care of it while I get my things."

"Even better."

"How do you know how to do that?" he asked as he merged into traffic. He'd used GPS to electronically track criminals, it was like Batman's Kryptonite, but he hadn't a clue how to dismantle it.

"It took me awhile to figure it out," she said. She busied herself clearing away the debris from their lunch. "My ex always knew where I was. Every second of every stinking day."

"So you disconnected your ONSTAR?"

"I started there." She ticked things off on her fingers. "I tossed out my phone. I don't wear a watch. I don't carry a purse. I only use the same backpack at the gym because he already knows I'm there. I don't have conversations anywhere he could bug, including my house."

A feral gleam lit her eyes. The list gave her a sense of pride, he could see it, but the thought of her living like that made his stomach burn. Maybe that was his guilt talking.

"What about your duffel?" he asked.

"What about it?"

What Logan really wanted to know was what she kept in the bag. What did a woman need when she was running from the mob? "Can anyone trace it?" he asked.

"No, it's clean. No one knows it exists."

No one, meaning her ex-husband. He'd like to go one-on-one with the bastard, but first, he had to find Eli. Then he had every intention of making Nick Calvetti pay for his crimes.

They made the quick trip to his town house in silence. His neighborhood was solidly middle class, with bikes and toys littering the square front yards. He pulled into the garage and led her down the narrow hall to his living room. "What it lacks in size it also lacks in grandeur."

She smiled when she glanced at his comic book posters. Lithographs, he corrected, framed and numbered lithographs.

"It's nice," she said.

"*Nice* is the kiss of death and you know it."

She smiled politely, neither confirming nor denying his assertion as she followed him through the house. Logan climbed the carpeted stairs and went to one of two identical rooms on the second floor. Both of them could have fit inside her much grander master bedroom. The walls of his house were contractor white and the carpets a dull beige. He wondered what it looked like from Sofia's viewpoint, and as quickly as he wondered, he knew it came up lacking. What did it matter? he thought. Work was where he spent his time and energy. The house was a just place to sleep and grab an occasional meal. He yanked a bag from the top shelf of his two-by-six closet.

"No hidden compartment." She made a tsking sound under her breath. "Mr. Stone, I am disappointed."

The mocking tone brought him down to reality. She wasn't judging him or his house. This was a stop on the road to getting her son back. He tapped a code into the safe in his closet wall and pulled out a backup gun.

Sofia crossed her arm over her chest. When she spoke, there was no more humor in her tone, but judgment came through loud and clear. "I'm not a fan of weapons."

"Neither am I, but I find that the people I arrest are well-armed. If it makes you feel any better, I am a licensed professional."

"It doesn't. First of all, you haven't even shown me your badge."

The censure in her voice was unmistakable. He turned to look at her.

She'd gone neutral again, all closed off and cold.

"Sofia, I'm not lying to you. I am a law enforcement officer, and in all likelihood, I'm going to need a gun before this thing is through. Whoever has your son isn't going to hand him over after a sternly worded lecture."

A grim set to her lips, she turned and stomped down the stairs. The woman could judge all she wanted, but he wasn't leaving without it. He grabbed a box of ammunition from the top shelf and stowed it in the bag along with a few days' worth of clothes.

It had been several years since he'd worked a kidnapping. His choice. His last one hadn't gone well for the kid. The memory of it iced his veins. No kid, even Calvetti's, deserved what had happened to his last vic. Logan sat on his unmade bed and took a deep breath. He pushed aside the anger and wallowed for a minute in the fear of what could happen to little Eli Calvetti. When he stood, both the fear and anger were packed away in a tidy compartment he planned to leave behind for the duration. He didn't know how long it would take, but he had every intention of seeing this scenario through.

When he made it back downstairs, the television was re-hashing the morning news about an explosion in an upscale neighborhood. Police were seeking the homeowner and an unidentified male for questioning in connection with the explosion. That unidentified male would be him.

So much for a peaceful morning off. "You made the headlines," he said.

"So did you." She flipped off the television and reached for her bag. It sat open on the coffee table, neatly packed with her clothes. She was in the process of loading a DVD, a wallet, and a few other items into the very small and feminine backpack that she'd bought at Wal-Mart.

He plugged his phone into the charger on his desk. Problem solved.

She handed him the burner phone. "My number is in the contacts under Aunt Bertha. If this leaves your possession at any time, toss it."

"Aunt Bertha? You don't look like my aunt Bertha."

She smiled, the light not reaching her expressive eyes. "You're Uncle Ernie."

"I hope I don't look like an Uncle Ernie."

The permafrost she wrapped around herself when she saw the gun had not thawed and she refused to answer. She grabbed the duffel and backpack and headed down the hall to the garage. She tapped a framed photo on the way. "Cute kid."

Reflexively, he averted his gaze from the photo. He didn't have to look at it to know who was there. A boy, Caucasian, perpetually ten, with blond hair, blue eyes and overlapping front teeth. He was a little skinny for his age and he didn't like sports, but he liked comics. Logan didn't need to see the picture to remember, but he kept it just the same. He ignored it today because the past was something he couldn't afford to relive.

He followed Sofia, took his mind off the picture by watching the way she walked, the way her tight jeans swayed. When this was over, he'd pay the price for going off the radar. Whatever it cost him, he was damn well going to enjoy the ride.

They put their duffels into the open trunk. "I disconnected your ONSTAR, by the way."

"And how do I put it back together when this is over?" he asked.

"If you live?" She slammed the trunk closed.

He opened her door for her. "That's a given."

She glanced sideways at him as she slid in and tucked her backpack on the floor. "It's under your spare tire. An internet search should help you reconnect it."

"Or you could do it when we're done." He closed the door and smiled as he walked around. The look on her face had been worth it. She wasn't sure if he was serious, but he was. He planned to live through this and he planned to see her again. They both pulled on their seat belts. "Where we headed?"

"My ex has a compound in the mountains that he uses when Eli visits. I'd like to get there before dark."

"Any particular reason for the timetable?"

"Aside from wanting my son?"

"Yes," he said. "I'd like to know what I'm up against."

"I'm not sure I can find my way through the minefield in the dark," she said sarcastically.

"You're kidding. Right?" He pushed the automatic garage door opener. It chugged overhead as the garage door lifted and flooded the car with light.

Sofia didn't answer the question because she wanted

Logan to worry about what was up in the mountains. The more wary he was, the better equipped he would be for whatever they faced. Nick didn't have a minefield. He had worse.

When Logan didn't put the car into reverse, Sofia glanced into the side mirror. A sleek black SUV blocked their exit. Her car door opened before she could react.

"Going somewhere, Sof?"

Sofia's heart convulsed. How the hell had Nick found her?

Chapter Four

Thursday, 2:47 p.m.

Nick's friend Eddie D was like a surrogate father to Sofia. He'd worked for the family since before Nick was born and he'd always been kind to her, even when Nick wasn't. Sofia had liked him and never held him responsible for following orders. At the moment, Eddie had her arm twisted behind her back so tight her fingers tingled from lack of blood flow. He didn't seem like the old man she knew him to be.

Eddie and a goon she didn't recognize hauled her and Logan back into the town house. Nick dumped the contents of her backpack onto the couch and riffled through it like it so much garbage. A fourth man went upstairs, gun drawn. Sofia heard footsteps, the crash of something breaking, before the man trotted back down the stairs. "It's clear."

Nick paced the long edge of the room under the glare of spotlights that focused on the comic posters. The forecast called for tension with a promise of violence. His men stood like good little soldiers awaiting orders while Nick paced back and forth.

The minutes ticked by in agony as Sofia waited for Nick's inevitable retribution. She knew this side of her ex, the angry, punitive man she'd once thought she'd loved. This was turning out to be an epically bad day.

It was the first time she'd seen Nick since the divorce. He hadn't changed. He stood well over six feet with the shoulders of a football player and the style of a man who could afford the best. Some called him handsome, but Sofia didn't see the attraction. All she saw was the slime that oozed from his pores. He wore a black suit, white shirt, red tie, and a hard look in his eyes that hadn't always been there. It buried her in an avalanche of bad memories.

He looked nothing like the captivating boy she'd met in college. Her best friend's brother, down for a visit, who seemed too good to be true, because the illusions he wove around him were more convincing than the truth. Nick Calvetti was no Prince Charming.

The things she knew about him now would have sent that younger version of herself screaming from the room. The Sofia she had become wouldn't give him the satisfaction. Not that she didn't feel it. Her heart raced. Her breathing went shallow, and inside, a panic attack threatened. She thought she'd outgrown them, but she couldn't deny it when her vision narrowed and her hearing dulled.

She focused on normalizing her breathing. It was a small victory when her pounding pulse slowed. It gave her a sense of her own strength to realize she could recover. No matter that he terrified her still, no matter that his capricious moods sent her into panic, she wouldn't tiptoe around him to avoid the explosion that was sure to come no matter what she did.

He clasped his hands in front of him in a pseudo-pious pose she had grown to hate. "Sofia, I'm disappointed in you. I thought we had an agreement."

His voice was ridiculously reasonable. Past experience taught her that reasonable preceded insanity. In was in this reasonable voice he'd promised that the torture would be long and painful. That it would cost her. That he'd use Eli, if he had to, to prove his point.

No one left Nick Calvetti. Except by way of a body bag.

Eventually, with Vicki's help, she'd managed to escape him, but it had taken a year of hell before he'd relented. The agreement he so pompously lauded moments ago had come at the end of the year when he'd grown bored of cruelty. He had let her keep Eli, like Eli was a piece of property, so that she could "raise him up" …until such time as Nick decided Eli was ready to go into the family business. Anger surged, held in check by Eddie's unrelenting grasp.

Her mouth was not constrained. "What's wrong, Nicky? Are you so afraid of a woman you have to have her trussed up like a Thanksgiving turkey?"

"I see you found your voice," Nick said as he shifted his head, like a backward nod. Eddie let her go.

Sofia shook her arms to get the blood flowing and to shake loose the trembling that still threatened her calm façade. It had taken years of freedom and untold self-defense classes in order to get the courage to face him. Even now, Eli was the only thing that gave her the strength to defy him. "How did you find me?" It's what she always wanted to know.

He turned on the television and popped in a DVD. It was the surveillance video from Wal-Mart showing her with Logan. "This one." He jabbed at Logan. "He was easy to ID. You really aren't smart who you associate with, Sof."

"You're right. I married you."

His eyes narrowed and he stepped closer. Sofia raised her chin. "He's not the reason Eli is missing."

Nick towered over her a moment before pacing back to the TV. "You've got balls, Sofia, I'll give you that. Standing in front of me, you're denying what I know. Especially considering the company you keep." He gestured at Logan. "You're trying to disappear with my son. I told you what I'd do if you tried. No one, not even the Feds, will protect you from my justice."

"I'm not stupid enough to trust the government. Or you." She grabbed for her backpack, but Eddie caught her arm.

She slanted a sardonic gaze at Nick. "You know how I feel about weapons."

He nodded and Eddie let her go. She rifled through the things that Nick had dumped on the sofa. She pulled out the DVD from the gym surveillance and pushed it into Logan's player. Nick stood, watching the tape like the judge and jury he thought he was. His jaw flexed when Vince picked up Eli.

"You expect me to believe Vince isn't working for you?" she taunted.

He kicked the TV. It crashed off the stand and into the wall, crumbling like pieces of Legos. "I don't give a fuck what you believe."

The crash sent Sofia skittering back into Eddie. He held her up, but there was no comfort in his embrace. Her muscles tensed, ready to run, but Eddie stood like a boulder in her path. She wouldn't make it out of the front door.

Nick tossed a phone to Eddie. "Call my sister. Find out where her boyfriend took my son. Vince is not working alone."

"Her boyfriend?" Sofia asked.

"Keep up, sweetheart." Nick used the endearment as an insult before gracing her with a smarmy grin. "They've been hooking up for a year."

A year? Sofia's legs wobbled and wanted to collapse, but she refused to face Nick in a position of weakness. It was bad enough that he had found them; she wouldn't compound that by letting him see how badly that last bit of news hurt her. Hurt? No, *hurt* was too soft a word. She was devastated by the lack of trust Vicki had in her. In all that time, Vicki had never mentioned her relationship with Vince. Wouldn't a best friend share that kind of thing? Unless there was a reason *not* to tell.

Sofia paced, but every few feet ran into a wall of muscle. Nick and his goons weren't giving her enough room to think.

Good Lord, how much did Vicki know? The coffee in Sofia's stomach agitated like a washing machine. Why hadn't Vicki said anything when they'd met at the coffee place? Sofia thought about the minutes they had been together. Vicki had seemed characteristically bored. She'd pulled absently at the loose fabric on the arms of the chair while she'd half-listened to Sofia's story. Bored or nervous? Sofia wondered. Considering everything that had happened, she should have been more alert to the signs.

Nick snapped his fingers in her face. Sofia's eyes refocused on the man standing in front of her. "I'm not finished with you, sweetheart, so pay attention."

She saw the half-mad look in his eyes and knew an explosion was eminent. Sofia stepped past him, slowly as if her heart wasn't pounding at his proximity. She tried to think of a witty comeback to show how little he mattered, but her mind went blank.

Nick followed her. "My son disappeared on your watch."

"Taken by your bodyguard," she added. "A man you forced into our lives."

"The problem isn't Vince," Nick said. "It's you. Trying to live in the middle of the country without a care in the world. You can't keep Eli safe."

"I didn't think I had to protect him from his bodyguard," Sofia said accusingly.

She saw Nick's eyes narrow and knew she'd pushed too far.

He prowled toward her until she had to snap her head back to see his face. "You're the problem, Sof. You always have been. When this is over, I'm revoking your parental rights. You can't keep him safe."

Sofia's stomach churned, the coffee turning to acid in her gut. If they found Eli... She closed her eyes, forced herself to rephrase. *When* they found Eli, Nick would change his mind. It didn't matter that her plan had failed or that she'd never be free of him. All that mattered was that Eli lived.

Nick turned his attention to Logan. "The only reason you're walking out of here alive is because I can't have the heat of a dead Fed while I'm looking for my son."

Sofia whipped around to stare at Logan and it was like seeing him for the first time. He was taller than the man who had his arms pinned, and despite the situation, he looked relaxed as he stared down at Nick. He didn't look like a local cop. He looked like a man who already knew her ex was Nick Calvetti, mob boss.

"You're a Fed?" Sofia asked in a low voice.

Logan didn't look at her.

"You didn't know." Nick laughed. "Same old Sofia. Trusting to the end. He's been your babysitter from the moment you walked into that fancy gym of yours."

Logan frowned at Nick. Sofia's stomach lurched. She thought Logan was local law enforcement. How could she still be so stupid? Everything about the man screamed Fed.

Trust no one.

Nick stepped closer to Logan until they stood nose-to-nose. Physically, they were evenly matched. Similar height, weight, and build, although Logan was taller and Nick broader. Similar hair and eyes. They'd be evenly matched in a fight. Except for one thing. Under Nick's skin was evil incarnate.

Sofia's gnashed her teeth together in frustration. Nick might be evil, but he was an evil she understood. Logan? Under Logan's skin was a freaking government paid stalker. That's why alarm bells went off around him. She just hadn't listened.

Still nose-to-nose, Nick rammed a beefy fist into Logan's midsection. Logan doubled over against the unprovoked attack.

"She's untouchable," Nick yelled, his face turning an unholy red. "Get it? She's my wife—"

"Ex-wife," Sofia corrected. The sound of Nick's screaming sent her heart spinning into a painful rhythm.

"What's mine is mine, you know that. If this pampered

white boy with a pretty badge thinks he can touch what's mine"—Nick turned, caressed his hand over the scrape on her cheek before giving it a stinging smack—"even if it is old and dried up. He can't. It's still mine."

The feel of Nick's hand on her cheek made everything inside her shrink, but she didn't let him see it. Instead, she let him see the hatred in her eyes. "I'll never be yours again."

He slammed the back of his hand across her cheek and sent her stumbling back a pace. Blood oozed from the earlier scrape and the sting burned, but she refused to react. Her reaction was the only thing she could control.

"That's not the point," Nick said. He might have been speaking to a two-year old. His voice low, reasonable again. "I'm finished with you, but no one digs through my garbage."

His words gave her that familiar sense of worthlessness; ashamed that she'd ever been his to use and that she'd put up with his abuse. The trail of blood oozed down her cheek, a visual reminder of her sins. She glared at him, but held her tongue.

"And you." He nodded to Logan. "Your boss just got an anonymous tip and a copy of that video of you with Sofia. Fraternizing with the enemy."

Nick and crew were out the door before Sofia had time to digest everything he'd told her. He didn't have Eli. He'd been furious, because he didn't know who did. That thought terrified her, because as much as she hated Nick, she knew he wouldn't hurt his son. Someone else might.

Who had Eli? How many angles was Vince working? Who was he working for?

Logan hauled in a solid breath before unwinding from the blow he'd taken. He flipped the curtain aside and watched the SUV drive away. "They're gone."

Sofia started to shake. The thoughts, the worries, the information, were too much. Above it all, the thing that bothered her most was that Logan, the guy who had been there when she'd needed someone, was a Fed.

"You look ready to collapse." Logan put a gentle hand on her arm. "Have a seat."

Sofia yanked her hand from his grasp. "Don't touch me. Don't ever touch me." She tasted coffee and stomach acid climbing her throat and ran to the nearest bathroom.

• • •

Logan heard retching in the other room. He'd seen it before, the panic when a mother realized she might never see her child again. He knew the stages, had studied them before he'd experienced them firsthand. He wanted things to be different for Sofia, but knowing the players, the odds were against her.

Logan paced the room to walk off the spasms in his gut where Calvetti had jabbed him. The man didn't pull his punches, but Logan had more to worry about than the man who had just left. Somehow, Logan had completely screwed up his life in less than twelve hours. What had started as a bad decision to have coffee with a beautiful woman had ended up a complete cluster-fuck. He should have said no. Now he had problems on top of problems.

First, they had a little boy gone, and they'd wasted the first seven hours chasing the wrong suspect. Seven hours gave the kidnapper time to disappear. Anyone stupid enough to kidnap a mobster's kid would have a solid plan to vanish and that made finding Eli monumentally harder.

Logan knew Vince was the kid's bodyguard, but had had no idea that the man was involved with the sister. That added all kinds of questions, none of them good. No way in hell Vicki was as clueless as she'd pretended, but what worried him more was Vince. The man had to be bat-shit crazy to double-cross his boss, unless he was suicidal. They needed to find Vince before the bodyguard turned his special brand of crazy on the kid.

The second problem was lack of resources. Calvetti's "anonymous source" with the footage of Logan and Sofia together effectively blocked Logan's access to FBI information. If he went in, he'd spend the foreseeable future on the wrong side of the interrogation table. Before the day was done, his boss would question everything he knew about Logan.

Would his boss think he was in collusion with Sofia and maybe the mob? Logan wanted to say no. Hell, he liked his boss, but he knew FBI procedure. The delay would be catastrophic to Eli. No way in hell he could go in to brief his boss. He'd lose too much time, time for Vince to go underground, and his boss would yank him off the case and put him on the desk for the rest of his natural born life. If he didn't go in, though, he'd look like he was on the run. He'd gone so far off the radar there was no turning back.

The trickle of water on porcelain in the next room reminded him of problem number three. Sofia wouldn't trust him after finding out he was a Fed, but neither one of them would find the kid alone.

When she stepped out, the fresh blood had been washed from her pale and neutral face. It pissed him off a little that she used that mask on him. She yanked her belongings off the couch and shoved them into her backpack. She walked to the front door without a word.

"You need me to find your son," he said firmly.

She paused with her hand on the doorknob. "The fact that you're a Fed could get him killed."

"You don't have a clue what to do next. The first forty-eight hours of a kidnapping are the most important—"

"Don't tell me what I already know," she snapped. Her eyes flashed. "I don't trust you."

"I know that," he said evenly. "But I have access to resources you don't."

That wasn't exactly true. Now that Calvetti had slammed the door on Logan's career, he didn't have access to FBI resources, but there was no way he was leaving a kid hanging. "You need me to run down Vince before time runs out."

She let the doorknob go as she walked to stand in front of him. Her eyes shimmered with pain so deep it hurt to look at her. "If you involve other Feds, if you double-cross me to get to Nicky, or if you get my son killed, I'll serve you up to Nicky on a silver platter."

Given a choice between an altercation with Calvetti and the rage in Sofia's eyes, Logan would choose round two with the big guy. "Fair enough."

Neither one of them had been honest from the get-go, but like it or not, they needed each other. Logan headed down the hall to the garage. He avoided the picture of the little boy he couldn't save. Today was about the little boy he still had a chance to save.

Sofia followed in stony silence. They got into his car and backed out of the garage.

"From here on out, we play by my rules." Logan's toned brooked no argument, because he was through following Sofia like a lost puppy. It was time to find Eli.

Where was he and who had him? Was he still alive? Those questions would haunt him until he finished the hunt. They'd haunt him for eternity if he failed.

Determination flowed through him. He would do anything in his power to avoid failure. But what if that wasn't enough?

Chapter Five

Logan's rules meant the FBI playbook. First step, Vince's financials and known associates. It led straight to Vince's apartment, as she knew it would, even if she wasn't speaking to Logan. The FBI was nothing if not predictable. They had approached her when she'd moved back to Colorado and asked her to testify against her ex-husband. As if it were that easy. They hadn't made it through the front door. Today, Sofia wasn't going through the front door either. Her house was a crime scene and she couldn't go home, not now, maybe not ever.

While her house might have been off-limits, they still needed to get into Vince's apartment, which was located above her garage. The location made it next to impossible to avoid the police car parked out front. Logan drove around the block and parked near the house that shared a back fence with hers.

The clean streets and manicured lawns were empty, no sign of surveillance, but they sat in Logan's gray car for several long minutes, soaking up afternoon heat. Sofia squinted in the sunlight as she glanced around her neighbor's yard. There was at least fifty-feet between the street and the privacy fence that blocked off the back yard, but if they followed the line of the adjacent garage, no one was likely to see them.

"How are you at climbing fences?" Logan asked.

"There's a gate." Sofia pointed to the gate next to the garage. They could make it to the neighbor's yard without getting caught, but once through the gate, all bets were off. There was no way to tell if the family was in the backyard. The only things visible were the tops of trees that seemed to follow the fence-line.

"Not there," Logan said. His eyes were hidden behind what looked like government-issue sunglasses that concealed his expression. "Once we get through, we'll have to jump the back fence that stands between your yard and this one."

Sofia shook her head. "The fence won't be a problem." Logan still didn't understand the people he was dealing with. Like his boss, Vince didn't leave anything to chance. After moving into the garage apartment, he'd created a secondary exit. He'd built a concealed gate into the fence behind her garage, in case he'd needed a way out in a pinch. Or that's what he'd told Sofia. Now she suspected he'd been using it to sneak out at night to meet her former best friend. Sofia exited the sedan and slammed the door closed. They were both grade-A jerks.

Sofia looped the duffel's strap across her chest as she

had when she'd run out of the neighborhood earlier. Logan checked his backup piece and tucked it into a leg holster before following her through the neighbor's yard. They used the neighbor's garage for cover to the fence, and then entered the yard from the side gate. The yard was empty so they didn't have to deal with the neighbors. They were able to use the line of trees for cover to get to the adjoining fence between her property and this one. The hidden gate Vince had built was camouflaged and would have been near impossible to find in the cover of dark.

Once through the gate, Sofia felt like a thief, breaking into a house in broad daylight. A part of her wanted to skulk from the fence to the back door of her garage, but that was overdramatic. Besides, it was her yard. She'd be damned if she'd act like a thief. While Logan kept watch, she punched a code into the keypad next to the back door of the detached garage. It clicked opened. They slipped inside and closed the door behind them. Sofia went straight to the windows overlooking the front yard to look at the scene.

Logan pulled at her elbow. "Stay out of sight."

She shrugged from his touch. "Privacy glass. We can see out but they can't see in." She stopped at the window closest to the front. Yellow tape cordoned off the yard, and another set of yellow bands closed off the entryway. Raw yellow plywood with ASPD stamped on it blocked the front entry. An Aspen Springs police cruiser sat out front with two uniformed officers inside. The sight of them outside her home illustrated how little it took to bring Nick's world crashing into hers.

Behind the police lines was the place where she had gathered herself after Nick. It was built on a solid foundation of family and it hurt to see it a crime scene. "It's not Nicky's," she said without thinking.

"What?"

Sofia didn't know why she'd fractured the silence. She had nothing to say to a Fed, yet she wanted him to know. What? That Nick couldn't buy her. That she hadn't sold herself for money and pretty place to live. "The house. It's not Nicky's. My grandfather built it. He wanted me safe."

Logan looked at her blankly.

Explaining herself went against the grain, but she couldn't stop the words. "After the divorce, my grandfather wanted me to feel safe."

"And this house helped?"

Sofia rolled her eyes. Shook her head. Logan still didn't get it. "It made my grandfather feel better, but I knew it wouldn't solve anything. I won't be safe as long as Nick is alive." Nothing could protect her from Nick's world. Still, she had thought that when she did leave, it would be on her own terms.

She had been wrong.

About everything. Her bad choices had led to Eli's disappearance. Fear for him remained a constant clutch in her chest. Every second away from him placed the boy in more danger. She knew it, gut deep. They didn't have much time. Sofia took one more look at the two-story stucco home before turning to the stairwell that led to Vince's apartment.

The apartment was locked, but lack of a key had never stopped Sofia. She pulled a slim case from the front pocket of her duffel and used her sense of touch, more than sight, to do the job. The slim tools slid into place and the lock clicked open. A little zip of joy shot through her. The act of being good at something bad gave her a boost.

"Where did you learn that little trick?" Logan asked. His tone might have been intrigued, but it felt more like a law-and-order moment and she was on the wrong side of the law.

Sofia lifted her chin defiantly. "Survival's a funny thing. You'll do anything, work with anyone, to survive."

"The fact that you're working with me —"

"Proves my point," she answered.

They door swung open to a room that looked like something out of *Hoarders*. Chaos. Every drawer and cabinet was torn open, the contents tossed on the floor. Silverware, plastic, a phone book, and kitchen gadgets she'd never seen Vince use. "He doesn't live like this."

"Calvetti's been here," Logan said.

Sofia nodded. Chaos followed the man. Given the short time since Nick sped away from Logan's town house, the man and his entourage had just recently left. "The real question is what did they find?"

"And did they miss anything?" Logan slid on a pair of latex gloves before wading into the debris.

She wanted to hate him for the act of self-protection, but couldn't because self-protection was her prime objective. Yet today, all that mattered was finding Eli. She followed Logan into the dining room and skidded on a loose Scrabble tile on the floor. Nick had certainly been thorough.

Logan righted a small table Vince used as a desk and booted up the computer.

Sofia kicked loose Scrabble tiles around the floor and waited. "If there was anything to find, don't you think Nicky would have taken the computer?"

Logan didn't look at her as he brought up Internet Explorer. "Taking the computer past the police out front would have attracted attention and slowed them down. They probably copied the hard drive and sent it to their computer guy."

Sofia continued her seemingly random search through the debris. The computer Logan toyed with meant nothing to her. She had more personal considerations. She waited for Logan to immerse himself in the computer files before slipping quietly into the back bedroom.

The bed was tossed and the mattress slit as if someone had been looking for something hidden in the foam. Nick had been right to think Vince had something to hide, but Nick clearly hadn't known where to look. Sofia did. She glanced through the doorway to see Logan still preoccupied with the computer, giving her the freedom to search the closet. The closet door closed silently behind her. The darkness sucked the breath from her lungs.

"It's okay," she muttered, and forced herself to take a deep breath. Her pulse sprinted as her body wanted to run. She focused her thoughts onto Eli, on the feel of his soft little arms around her neck. "Just a minute. You can do it for a minute."

The panic released its unrelenting grip as she focused on Eli. The small closet was still pitch black, but Sofia was able to function, knowing she was doing it for Eli. She worked without light. A latch was recessed into the floorboards, but her knowing fingers found the catch and the lid flipped open to reveal a small cubby. The bag that matched her duffel was missing, as she had suspected, but three passports remained. She used the light from the burner cell phone to read the passports. There was one for Vince, which she tossed back into the hole, but the other two belonged to herself and Eli. In the passport photo, Eli was wearing an Elmo T-shirt. Sofia closed her eyes and tried not to think of the worst possible scenario.

What did it mean that Vince left these behind? She slid the two passports into her duffel as the closet door opened. The light washed over her, easing some of the tension in her shoulders. Still, the space was small and Logan stood between her and the door.

She leaned back on her heels and stared into the gaping hole in the floor. She pulled out Vince's bogus passport and tossed it to Logan. A Post-It note fell back into the compartment.

"How did you know this was here?" Logan asked as he thumbed through the passport.

Sofia stood and slid past Logan into the bedroom. She couldn't stand another moment in the tight space. Once in the open space, she took a fortifying breath and answered Logan with a phrase she had learned from Nick. "Keep your friends close and your enemies closer."

Logan turned on the closet light and peered into the compartment, pulled out a few pieces of paper until the space was empty. "Meaning?"

"This apartment was part of my deal with Nicky. I had to keep a bodyguard for Eli. Unlike Nicky, my grandfather really was in construction. He built the house and a friend built this. When Vince asked for a compartment, my friend built it, but he told me about it first."

"Don't you think Vince knew that you knew?"

Vince was well aware that she knew of his hidden compartment, but that made what he'd left behind even more confusing. "What did you find?" she asked.

"Looks like an airline reservation number. I can look it up on the computer." He handed her the passport and papers. The passport Logan handed her was a picture of Vince under an assumed name. She was familiar with it.

Was it a clue or misdirection? Sofia looked at the six random letters written on the Post-It note. KQX753. "If Vince knew, then why did he leave anything behind?"

Logan walked back to the dining room. He pulled up the internet and visited multiple websites until he netted a reservation under the name on the passport. "Does Calvetti know about that hidey-hole?"

Sofia dropped her duffel on the floor as she looked over Logan's shoulder at the computer. "I doubt it. He wouldn't have left it for us to find."

"Then he doesn't know where Vince is headed. Score one for the good guys."

Sofia didn't feel like they'd won any great prize. Her heart hurt, sickened by a combination of guilt and fear. "Where is Vince headed?"

"He had a reservation for a flight out of Denver at nine this morning. One adult and one child."

The timing of Vince's departure knocked her on her ass. Her legs went limp and she dropped like a punching bag to the hard floor. Vince had waited until she'd left for yoga before pulling Eli from the daycare. She rested her head on her knees and turned her head from Logan so he wouldn't see the tears. Vince had made a reservation, which had given him enough time to get to the airport in Denver with a few minutes to spare, but— "If I hadn't had coffee with you," she said, her voice weak, "I might have caught up with him."

"Stop," Logan ordered in a voice so uncharacteristically hard, it made her turn. "You can't play the what-if game. We need to work from where we are. No backtracking."

Sofia nodded, but the self-recrimination twisted her up inside. Logan didn't know the whole story or he'd be wondering the same thing. How did Vince plan all those details down to the minute, but *accidentally* leave the clues behind where only she could find them? Was this her fault? Had she started something that Vince had manipulated for his own benefit? "Where was the plane headed?"

"New York." He glanced at his watch. "They've already landed."

Again she wondered if this was a clue or misdirection? "Was there an international connection?" she asked.

"Not on this reservation. Who does he know in New York?"

Sofia half laughed, half sobbed. "There is a folder of known associates back at your office. Eli will be dead before we go through all of them."

"Don't," Logan ordered. "Don't think the worst. We'll start at the top of the list and work our way down. We *will* find Eli."

Sofia was startled by his determination. She lifted her head to stare at him. "Why do you care so much about what happens to Eli?"

Logan turned off the computer, a delay tactic Sofia recognized. "I—"

The door behind Logan squeaked and he spun to confront the intruder. The big guy who had been with Nick that morning aimed a gun at her center, but his gaze was on Logan. "Back off, asshole," the man ordered.

Logan settled into a ready stance, not visibly subdued by the sight of a gun.

Sofia rose slowly to her feet, trying to keep the man's attention on her. "Eli's my son."

"This is family business, and you're not family."

Sofia's lifted a hand to her throbbing head. She had never wanted to be a part of a family like the Calvetti's, but being on the outside kept her from the resources she needed to find Eli. If it were Eddie or Sammy C holding a gun on her, she would know what to do. This man was a stranger. She didn't know which buttons to push.

Beside her, Logan rearranged his position to reach the gun in his holster.

"He's my son," she said again to keep the gunman's focus. "I have a right. You could tell—"

The man swerved his aim to Logan. "Don't even think about it. I have orders not to kill her, but you're a different story. I have no problem doing a Fed."

Sofia didn't stop to analyze. If the man had orders not to kill her, he wouldn't. No one disobeyed the boss's orders. She stepped forward like a boxer entering the ring, slow and itching for a fight. She stopped just outside of the gunman's reach, dividing his attention between her and Logan.

He glanced between them and pulled the hammer back. "I'll kill him."

"I don't care," she said. The adrenaline made her sound calmer than she felt.

He turned the gun on her. "But I bet your friend here cares if I shoot you."

The gun stopped her. "Break Nicky's order and you'll be dead before the evening news."

The man grinned humorlessly. "He didn't say I couldn't rough you up."

To her left, Logan shook his head no, but she didn't take orders from him.

"That's a chance I'll have to take." She took a stance from her self-defense class and lunged forward, kicking the big guy in the kneecap.

He bent forward and cursed at her. "You'll pay for that, bitch." He swung a beefy hand. It connected to her right shoulder and spun her two feet back. She landed on her tailbone with a jolt that made the jab seem painless. Sofia sucked wind. Her eyes watered, dimmed momentarily while Logan charged into the melee. He landed a solid right hook that sent the already faltering man to the ground. The clatter of metal against hardwood gave her a moment to blink away the pain. She took a deep breath and rolled toward the fallen gun.

Grabbing the gun, she pointed it at the wounded man's face. "Who has my son?"

He glared at her from his prone position.

"Do you doubt for a second that I'll kill you?" She gritted the question through clenched teeth. "Who has my son?"

The man stared at her, his face as blank as a corpse.

The hammer pulled back as if by magic. She didn't think; she reacted. This is why she had trained, why she had learned to shoot, why she took self-defense classes. All she had to do was squeeze the trigger. One less animal to do Nick's bidding.

The gun training had been horrifying, over and over and over until she had learned to load a gun by rote and could shoot without thought. In her heart, she knew she could do it. So many nights she had imagined it. A chance for vengeance. Her hands shook. She'd feel safer, she promised herself, with one less member of the Calvetti family on the planet.

Stiff fingers wouldn't obey her brain. Tears tracked down her cheeks and her palm convulsed on the butt of the gun. "I can't do it," she whispered. "I want to, but I can't."

"Do what?" Logan asked. He turned the man onto his stomach like a flopping fish.

"Kill him." *Obviously.*

He didn't try to talk her out of it. Instead, Logan reached over and pried the gun away with warm fingers that burned her skin. "Get something to tie him up."

She stumbled back, turned her face from what she'd almost done, something a part of her still wanted to do. The salty tears stung the scrape on her cheek. She swiped at it and ignored the pain. She stepped farther from the grunting man who'd knocked her over and made her angry enough to kill. Almost.

A wave of nausea hit like a tsunami in her gut. She doubled over, expecting to empty her stomach, but she didn't have anything left. She felt used up. The energy that had jammed through her when she'd faced the attacker drained so fast, all she could do was put her head between her knees and breathe.

In minutes that aged like years, she centered herself. She forced herself to focus on the surroundings, because there was nothing left inside to use as a focus.

First, she focused on the solid pine her grandfather had used on the flooring. And didn't that pine smell just like Granddad's home? Sofia continued to focus on the room and soon her senses were in overdrive. The room smelled like garlic and onions and herbs. Vince liked to cook. God, she'd never thought of Vince as one of Nick's associates. He'd seemed so normal. The house seemed normal and once again, she'd placed her trust in the wrong person.

Sofia inhaled, used the surroundings and what she knew of Vince to find something to tie the guy up. Surely Vince had rope or something they could use as a restraint. She straightened and headed for the kitchen. While she rummaged through the debris that littered the kitchen floor, Logan wiped her prints from the gun. She saw him from the corner of her eye, but couldn't meet his gaze. She grabbed a roll of duck tape from a drawer on the floor.

Logan had turned the man onto his belly and knelt with his knee on the man's back. "Tape his hands," he told her.

"With pleasure." Sofia wound the tape tight, letting it dig into the flesh and pull at the long arm hair. "Lesson one, scumbag, never carry a weapon you're not willing to use. Too easy to take it from you," she said.

"You weren't willing to use it," he taunted.

"I didn't bring it to the party," she said coldly. His words stung, because as much as she hated what the man stood for, she hadn't been able to pull the trigger. She pulled a strip of tape and covered his mouth. "Keep talking and you just might change my mind."

Sofia stepped away from the man she had so desperately wanted to kill. Logan followed her into the kitchen. "Nice moves," he said. "The Body Combat instructor whose name I can't remember would be impressed."

Sofia shook her head. She was none too impressed with her own performance. She had taken steps, solid steps, to learn how to defend herself, and in the end, she was just as helpless as she had been the first night Nicky had taken a gun from her. "How much do you think he heard?"

"Hard to say." Logan scrolled through the man's cell phone while he spoke. "He must have been hiding in the garage below, waiting to see who would show up. He didn't follow us up right away. I would have heard him when I was on the computer, but he could easily have made it up the stairs while you were searching the closet. Given all that, he probably heard us talking about where Vince is headed."

Angry with herself and the man, Sofia kicked at the debris on the floor. "Did he text anyone what he heard? Did he make any phone calls?"

"Not in his phone history, but that would be easy to clear."

Sofia turned her attention back towards the man. The room around him looked violated and no longer a part of the safe haven her grandfather had built her. The man was already struggling with his restraints while they spoke. "That tape isn't exactly a straitjacket. It won't hold him long."

Logan pocketed the man's phone. "I know what will."

She took another look around the room, but didn't see anything that would keep a man that size locked down. She glanced at Logan.

"The local PD," he answered.

Sofia didn't like it, but she liked it better than letting this man work his way free to report to Nick. She needed to find Eli first.

"How fast can you run?" Logan asked.

"You've been stalking me." She poked at him verbally because it was the only defense she had left. "You tell me.

How fast?"

He aimed at Vince's computer and pulled the trigger. It shattered the case and echoed like an explosion. The sound shocked Sofia into stillness, but Logan grabbed her. She grabbed her duffel as they clambered down the stairs and into the backyard. Sofia found the hidden gate to her neighbor's yard and pushed through it. They had barely closed it when they heard the uniforms race through the door to her garage. They paused for a moment to catch their breath before finishing the trek through the neighbor's yard. It was a blur of green as they sped through to the street where Logan had parked his car.

"They'll call backup," Logan said as he led the way.

Sofia didn't waste her breath on a reply. She made it to his car at the same time he unlocked the doors. They were on their way to the maintenance gate, past the park, when a police cruiser blocked their exit. Logan cursed as he circled around the block.

"They figured out how you got out last time," he said.

"Obviously." She sucked in a lungful of air. "Any idea how to get past?"

Logan tapped the steering wheel. "I have one, but you're not going to like it."

"Turning me in isn't an option."

Logan pulled the car onto a side road. "Get in the trunk."

Her throat constricted. "What?" Her voice squeaked an octave higher than normal.

"The seat is a split back. You can feel the latch on the left side. Slide into the back while I get through the roadblock."

"What makes you think you can get through security without me?" She was not getting in the trunk unless he had a solid plan and a full bottle of anti-anxiety medication.

He yanked off the latex gloves and pulled his ID from his wallet.

"So you do have a badge?"

He parked the car in front of a vacant house.

"You just didn't want me to know you were a Fed," she accused.

Logan turned his gaze to her. "You're picking a fight to avoid my suggestion. Yes, I avoided the truth when you asked, but you know now. We need a way through the local roadblock and this is it."

The bottom of her stomach lurched like she was in a freefall, dropping quickly through the sky without a parachute. Sofia hugged the duffel to her chest. "I am not avoiding the subject. I happen to think it's a bad idea. I might not like the fact that you work for the FBI and I might not like that you lied about it, but—"

"When I said it was in my captain's office, I was speaking metaphorically. I am on administrative leave," he said in a soothing tone one might use on a crying child.

"A lie is a lie, but we're past that." She'd already made the choice to work with him. "As angry as I might be at the way you misrepresented yourself, I'm not as ready to burn you as you are to burn yourself. You can't use your badge to get us through a roadblock. You'll end up on the wanted list right next to me."

Logan nodded in agreement. He could see the panic in her eyes and the dread that bunched her shoulders. She didn't want to go in the trunk, but she still had a valid point. If he did this, there would be no going back. He could stop and explain and it would take twenty-four hours or more while they involved half the agency to find Nick Calvetti. And Eli Calvetti would pay the price. He hitched a thumb toward the back. "Just do it."

Lines tightened around her eyes. The air around her trembled as she fought to keep her face passive. She inched over the seat, opened the split back, and crawled into the trunk. She pulled the duffel in after her and it slithered into the black hole. Moments later, the seat closed but didn't latch into the locked position.

Close enough, Logan thought. He'd pushed as far as he could. He shifted into drive and pulled back around to the park and the roadblock at the back entrance. Two junior officers sat inside a marked car. Their lights flashed blue and red in the late-afternoon sun, but the siren was quiet. The passenger stepped out, hitched up his belt, and motioned Logan to stop.

Logan hit the button that eased his window down and took charge. "We have a single male suspect leaving the scene. Five foot eight, 200 pounds, thinning gray hair." Logan described one of the men that had been in his town house that morning. Anything to keep Calvetti's men off their back for a few hours. "He matches the description of Eddie D, a known associate of Nick Calvetti. Have you seen anyone matching that description pass through this gate?"

"Who are you?"

"FBI." Logan flashed his badge, fast enough to make his name unreadable, slow enough to make an impact. While he did, he noted the officer's name and rank from the everyday blue uniform. "How long have you been at this location?"

"Three minutes."

"Then he's already passed through." Logan put the car

into drive.

"Sir, you can't leave without—"

"You're impeding my investigation, Officer Lamb. If you interfere further, I'll have your badge."

The man flushed, waved Logan through.

He drove a few miles before parking in a residential neighborhood. "Sofia, it's clear."

The seat kicked forward. White shoes first, then jeans, Sofia dragged her duffel behind her. The haunted expression on her pale face was nothing compared to the deep frown that lined her forehead. But when she spoke, it wasn't of herself. "You'll never make it through airport security now," she said.

He nodded. "You think Vince is really in New York?"

"I think he wanted me to know he was in New York." She started to say more but clamped her mouth closed.

"Do you think your sister-in-law is with him?"

"*Former* sister-in-law," she clarified mulishly as she snapped her seat belt into place. "And no, I don't think she's with him. She was having coffee with us when he was thirty-thousand feet in the air."

"It's no accident that she's dating Vince."

"I know, I know." She rolled her eyes to the ceiling as if to will the emotions away. "Did you know? Did the FBI know they were involved?" The tone of her voice was an accusation.

"Not that I'm aware of, but we didn't have anyone on her full-time. We kept tabs, of course, but not too close. You would have had better access to her personal life."

"You'd think," she complained. The stark contrast between the woman who had kneecapped a known mob associate to the one who came out of his trunk was drastic. Now, an air of defeat wafted around her. Her shoulders were stooped and her eyes vacant. "Vicki doesn't talk about herself much, ever really, even when we were in college. That's how I didn't know about her family. I was trying to remember the last time she mentioned a man and I had to go back to sophomore year in college."

The next question made Logan want to wince inside, but he had to ask. "And Vince?"

She turned to him, her eyes watery and pained. "Never. Not once did he mention that he was dating someone. I didn't even realize he knew Vicki."

"I'm sorry, were you—"

"No," she grimaced. "Ugh. No. But I thought…" Sofia dug through one of her bags until she found her sunglasses. She pulled them on like body armor. "I thought we were friends. If not friends, I certainly never considered him the enemy."

In that world, the line between friend and enemy was tenuous. "We need to talk to Vicki. She knows more than she let on."

Sofia shook her head. "I need to get to New York."

"She might have information we need. Are you willing to risk—"

"I know what's at risk," she snapped. Her lips narrowed to a thin frown. "The question is whether you're willing to risk the trip."

Once again, she didn't ask. She couldn't admit she needed help. The woman was defiantly independent with an undercurrent of fragility that she hid behind an icy exterior. The combination made him unnaturally protective. Which was ironic since less than twenty-four hours ago, she was on his watch list. He rubbed his hands down the front of his jeans as if to wipe away the doubts in his mind. "I'm in."

The smile that softened her lips was slight, but real. "I know where we can get new IDs. We can use Vince's passport to speed things up, but it's going to take time. And money."

"Where to?" Logan asked. Somehow, Sofia always ended up leading the way, but she was the one who knew how and where to get a fake ID. As much as it galled him to use their illicit services, he needed to save Eli, and that meant New York. If they didn't get arrested first.

Logan drove to the counterfeiter knowing he was committing a third degree felony and fraud, and that was just the start of what a federal prosecutor would charge him with if he got arrested. So they wouldn't get caught, he determined. They couldn't afford to get busted before they found Eli.

Chapter Six

Thursday, 6:32 p.m.

Back-door deals with people on the other side of the law always gave Sofia a sense of euphoria. She liked playing outside the law just as much as she enjoyed working outside Nick's underground network. It felt good to be bad. It felt even better to be one step closer to following Eli to New York.

Another band of thunderstorms blew in with high gusts and raindrops the size of quarters. Sofia watched the rain through the glass door of an internet café. The counterfeiter could remake the passport for Logan, but even money and a longstanding friendship couldn't get the job done before morning. Logan waited outside in the storm while she made airline reservations in their assumed names with a credit card that she kept in her duffel bag for an emergency. The other option was a last-minute, one-way ticket paid for with cash. It would raise too many flags.

The rain didn't ease up, so Sofia dashed through it to Logan's car. She handed the boarding passes to him while she buckled into her seat.

He flipped on the interior light to look at them. "You have a thing for Aunt Bertha," he teased. His eyes had smile lines that made her think that once upon a time, he'd liked to smile. The implied intimacy and the softness of his smile made her like him more than she should. He was trouble with a badge. She wanted to put up a wall, build some distance between them, but the crinkle lines around his eyes made her smile in return. It was the charm of his almost-smile that helped her forgive him. Fed or not, he was a good man.

"What? Bertha doesn't sound like an international woman of intrigue?" she asked in a teasing voice.

"Not in the least."

She pulled the second boarding pass to the front and pointed to the name. "How about Ernie?"

He shook his head and gave her a wry smile. "Not so much."

"Then they're the perfect names to get us out of town."

He tapped the itineraries. "Did you pick the seats or let the computer?"

"I did," she answered, and knew immediately what he had noticed on the printouts.

"You don't want to sit next to me?"

Sadly, she did, which was enough reason to stay separated. She folded her hands on her lap. "It's better for you if we aren't seen traveling together. I'm… I…" How did you tell a man that in the not too distant past you considered him the enemy? "I'm still not sure I trust you—"

"Sofia—"

She put a hand on his arm to stop him, but the arc of energy that charged between them paralyzed them both. Her gaze shot to his and she saw awareness and heat. The depth of it stripped down her barriers and she stared at him with the same honest gaze that had seared him in the gym café.

He broke contact by turning his attention to the itineraries and folding them neatly into their separate envelopes. Sofia took a deep breath before she resumed where she'd left off. "I know what you're risking to help me, Agent Stone. I won't turn down the extra help, but I should. If I had any morals left, if it were anything but my son at risk, I'd step out of this car and walk away."

"I'd follow," he countered. "You can't find Eli without me."

"I have resources," she said. A network of people with a grudge against Nick Calvetti.

"And you're not afraid to break the law," Logan added with a raised eyebrow.

"I'm not ashamed of that," she said defiantly, but she was, in a way, sad that life had turned out that way, that lying, and she'd done her share of it, was as easy as breathing. It wasn't the way she had been raised. It wasn't anything her grandparents, God rest their souls, would sanction, but lying and breaking the law were justified. Anything was justified to save Eli, but the way Logan had said it, as if it were something to be ashamed of, put her on the defensive. "I didn't ask you to come along."

"No, but I won't let you go alone. I need to find Eli."

He'd said *I*, not *we*, and that one minor slip told her

more than any other words that had passed between them. She thought back to all the times he had helped her, and none of them made sense in light of what he did for a living.

"Why?" she asked. "Why do you need to find my son?"

Logan turned off the inside light and handed her the itineraries.

With a hand on his arm, sitting in the rain and the dark, he was physically close, but emotionally distant, and still his touch warmed her frigid soul.

"Why does it matter to you?" she repeated.

He started the engine, flipped on the headlights, and pulled into the early evening traffic. He kept his eyes on the road, his focus so strong she knew he wouldn't answer. Sofia pulled her hand to her lap. Whatever pushed him was none of her business. She certainly hadn't told him everything about herself. The man was entitled to his privacy, but she still wondered what drove a man like Logan Stone.

He pulled into a drive-thru restaurant. The voice on the intercom was a disembodied connection to the outside world, proof that life went on without her. Logan asked what she wanted, but she refused. She couldn't eat. It would stick in her throat like the dread that gathered in her gut. They wound their way through the line of cars until a girl in base-ball cap handed Logan a bag and a large soda. He wolfed down a sandwich while he drove through the city.

Sofia stared through the *swish-swish* of the windshield wipers and tried not to fill the silence with anxious thoughts. The lights of oncoming cars invaded the cabin of the car with an erratic rhythm that unsettled her.

"I lost a boy once," Logan said.

So wrapped in her own thoughts, Sofia jumped at the

sound of his voice. Her heart convulsed, then settled down in the wake of his renewed silence. They hadn't spoken in several minutes, but she knew he was answering her question. Why did it matter to him? "Not your own child," she asked, although she knew the answer. He was not a grieving father, but in many ways, whatever had happened had altered him as much as if he had been. She saw it in the determination that drove Logan and the tight wrinkles that now lined his eyes.

"I was new to the Bureau." He rubbed a hand over his mouth and down his bewhiskered jaw as he remembered. "It was my third case, hotshot new kid on the block with something to prove. We did everything right, did everything by the book."

The evil that existed in the world didn't follow the rules. Maybe Logan hadn't learned that yet. She hated to ask, but felt compelled. "And the boy?"

"He was ten, the kind of kid that still held his mother's hand in public and said 'I love you' to her in front of his friends. He wasn't a jock or a brain, he was just an ordinary kid who collected comic books and played video games."

Sofia pictured the framed comic book posters on Logan's wall and started to understand the man behind the badge. Whatever happened with this boy, it made an impact on Logan, enough to put those posters on the wall, but more, to change the way Logan saw the world. "What did he look like, this boy?" she asked.

"Blond hair, blue eyes." Logan's tone was flat and emotionless, but he didn't need to say anymore.

Sofia knew exactly what the boy looked like. "The picture in the hallway of your town house."

Logan gritted his teeth and stared at the oncoming traffic like it was the enemy. He nodded in answer to her question. "Someone had contacted him online about a rare comic. We didn't know until after."

A teardrop slid down her cheek and the shock of it hit her with a suddenness that left her incapable of hiding her emotions. She turned to stare out at the gray and muddy night. She had known depravation of character, the depths of human cruelty at Nick's hands, but even in that world, no one harmed a child. She mourned for this unknown boy, and for the man next to her who felt wholly responsible for this child's death.

Logan cleared his throat. "We try to create emotional distance, but there isn't enough distance in the world when you see a family fall apart. When you find a body too small to fit inside a body bag."

The image of a little boy in a body bag was a blow that sent her reeling. The thought of a tiny body on a long, cold slab in the morgue finished her off. Sofia gasped, drew a breath, and tried to ward off the panic, but it was too late. She was seconds away from hyperventilating, but she couldn't stop it. The breathing became sobs and the lone tear became a stream of them. Sofia bit down on her lips and forced the waterworks to stop. She needed to focus on her son, not this lost boy, and she knew that Logan's story was a cautionary tale.

She hated to do it, but she had to know. "Was it your fault?"

The squeak of wipers against the windshield was the only sound for several minutes. His voice was hard and detached when he answered. "I ask myself that every day."

A part of her wanted to tell Logan that it wasn't his fault. Evil existed in the world and death was the fault of the men who pulled the trigger, but even if that were true, it would have been little comfort to the family of the blond boy she'd seen in the picture. The man who had lured that little boy was a killer, but Logan was the man who had failed to bring that boy home. Sofia swiped at her wet cheeks with unsteady hands.

What would she do if Logan failed? What if the man she depended on failed to find her son?

At a stoplight, he called her name. Sofia turned to face him without covering the tears and the terror that his words stirred. The dashboard lights gave an eerie glow to his eyes. "I can't leave this alone, Sofia. I should. I haven't spent the last seven years building a career to go this far off the grid, but I won't lose another kid."

It was a promise she couldn't even exact from Eli's father. Sofia glanced back out the window. Rain slid down the glass like tears. A piece of Logan had been irrevocably altered by the death of that boy, and losing another might well destroy him. Sofia swallowed the knot that clogged her throat. They were bound together, she and Logan, until they found Eli.

The light turned green and the car edged forward before she dared a glance in his direction. In the twilight with only the interior lights casting a glow, he was all hard, from his strong nose and cheekbones to the unbending line of his forehead. Despite the hard angles and harsh light, he didn't intimidate her the way he had that morning.

"I realize you're risking your career. I'd like to insulate you as much as possible. I think if we limit how much we're seen together, it will help you when this is over. If it looks like you were tailing me through the airport and on the plane, and even in New York — "

"I'm not lying on my incident report," he said with finality.

"You should." Sofia took a deep breath to clear away the tension. "Like you said, you'd follow me. That's all you're really doing now, except we're sharing the same car."

"That's bending the truth."

Sofia laughed cynically. "Bend it, break it, shove it in a box. You do what you need to survive."

Logan shook his head. "I'll stick with the truth."

The simplicity of the statement reminded her of her grandfather, maybe of herself when she was young and stupid. "It's still better that we keep our distance in public. They're looking for me with a man. Traveling alone offers a modicum of anonymity."

He didn't respond, just kept the car headed down the road. Where to was anyone's guess. They couldn't pick up the passports until morning. Until this moment, she'd blocked all thought of spending the night with Logan. She had thought she could just keep moving until she found her son, but they'd have to stop and spend the night somewhere. Heat flashed across her skin and an ache of unmet need fisted in her stomach. The intense chemistry between them terrified her because she needed to keep her focus on Eli. Sofia turned down the temperature on her side of the car.

This morning, she'd been willing to go on vacation with Logan, had every intention of seducing him, if she were capable of such a thing, but right now, she couldn't even consider sharing a hotel room with him. Couldn't give in to the buzz of physical attraction that zapped through her system at his touch.

It wasn't about anonymous needs anymore. The man knew too much. He knew who she really was and what she was capable of and whom she had married. If he didn't, maybe then she could give in to the sizzle that made every space they shared electric. Maybe then, she would risk some physical release. Sofia lifted her thick hair off her neck. Compartmentalize, she ordered herself. It was something she was good at, sectioning pieces of herself away to deal with later. Right now, she had to concentrate on Eli.

"I realized something when I was in the trunk," she said to distract herself from his nearness.

"That you don't like enclosed spaces?"

That was an understatement. "No, I am well aware of that piece of my emotional make-up, thank you very much."

"Then what?"

"Sammy C wasn't with Nicky today." Sam Capadonna was Nick's number two man. "The one thing I'm sure of is that Nick will send his best man to chase the most reliable lead."

"So if we find Capadonna—"

"We find Eli. Maybe," she hedged. "If he can find Eli."

"It's logical," Logan said. He reached over to squeeze her hand. He said something else, but it was lost on her. The jolt that zapped between them steamed the interior of the car.

Sofia pulled her hand away, wondering if he felt the electricity as well. "Where are we headed?" she asked. Her voice rose, squeaked a little.

Eyes forward, he tapped the steering wheel with too

much nonchalance. "As long as we're in town until the morning, we have a few more leads to follow."

Sofia knew in her gut that Eli was in New York, so she was mystified by Logan's response. "Where?"

"Vince's known associates."

The bodyguard didn't have many friends in Colorado. Sofia thought of the uber-masculine man who lifted weights with Vince at the gym. Creepy, yes, but worth a stop, no. She was too tired to guess. "Who are we going to see?"

"I don't trust your former sister-in-law."

Oh, hell, Sofia thought. They were headed through Old Colorado City, past medical marijuana shops and tattoo parlors, on the way to Manitou Springs. In short, they were on the road to Vicki's house. An ache pounded at the base of her skull. She didn't want to think about it. The minute Nick had mentioned that Vince and Vicki were an item, Sofia knew that she would have to confront her friend, but she hadn't wanted to dwell on it. Vicki had been the only person in the world Sofia had trusted, the only safe harbor she'd had during the divorce and the drama that led up to it. Vicki had convinced Nick to let Sofia go. She was probably the reason Sofia was even alive. How could Vicki be involved in Eli's kidnapping?

The how didn't matter. "I don't trust her either, but won't the FBI have her under surveillance?"

"She's not under constant observation, and since no one has reported Eli missing, there's no reason to think they would increase security now. Just in case, I'll drive around to check for a surveillance team before we go in."

Sofia nodded. In a dark part of her soul, she hoped the FBI was watching, because she wasn't emotionally ready to confront Vicki. Her hopes were dashed when Logan announced the area clear and pulled into a parking space a few houses down from Vicki's.

"How do you want to play this?" Logan asked. "Good-cop, bad-cop?"

"That won't work on her," Sofia said sharply. "You can't play her." The way she said it made her sound like a petulant child, which was how she felt. In truth, she was insecure and whiny inside, resisting the direction Logan was pushing her. She couldn't keep her nerves contained, and the more she tried, the more her hands shook. The anxiety over facing Vicki was worse than facing Nick, because Nick would only kill her. Vicki's treachery would tarnish what remained of Sofia's trust. The shaking in her hands spread to her limbs, exposing her for the coward she was.

Logan grabbed her hand and squeezed. He didn't offer words of sympathy that would have made her feel weak, nor did he condescend to remind her why they were doing this. He just offered his support and waited with compassion. The man understood her too well. She averted her gaze lest he see the emotions shimmering in her eyes. She turned her face to the black night and composed her features while she hardened her resolve. She didn't let go of his warm hand until she felt fully restored.

She moderated her tone before continuing. "Vicki was a psych major and the daughter of a mob boss. You can't play her."

He nodded, in sympathy or support she couldn't tell. "Then how do we play it?"

Sofia massaged her fingers over her temples and willed the throbbing in her head to subside. "I'm too tired to play.

I'll just ask and gauge her response."

"Your own personal lie detector?" Logan asked with a skeptical edge to his voice.

Sofia's emotions were all over the charts, but there was one thing she was certain of. She knew Vicki better than Vicki knew herself. "I may not be as reliable as a polygraph, but I can promise you that if she's involved, I'll know it."

"I hope you're right," Logan said, "Because it looks like the suspect is home."

$\cdots$

If Logan hoped to gather Intel on the Calvetti family while Sofia and Vicki talked, he failed miserably. How two women could talk so long and say so little was a great mystery. They'd developed a style of communicating that eliminated all names, recognizable events or anything that might be used against them in a court of law. It was as impressive as it was irritating, but Logan wasn't ready to give up.

After Vicki refilled her coffee cup from a pot in the kitchen, Logan grabbed an empty cup and filled it from the same pot. He made sure the prima donna Vicki drank hers before he trusted the coffee enough to drink it. It had been sitting on the warmer long enough to burn his tongue and it tasted stale, but he wasn't drinking it for the flavor. It was shaping up to be a long night.

The kitchen was a show of wealth, with granite counters and maple cabinets. It was large for the neighborhood, looking like it had been added onto the house recently, with a back door that probably led to a million-dollar view of the mountains. It rubbed him raw, knowing where the woman got her wealth. She had no shame. Logan walked back into the living room, which was a strange contradiction. It was old-fashioned, designed around the age of the house, but still managed to be homey rather than Victorian-ugly.

The front door was a solid wood piece that probably dated to the late 1800s, as was most of the ornate trim around the door and the oversized front window. The carpeting was modern, something expensive no doubt, but the floor beneath creaked as he stepped from the kitchen into the older part of the house. He leaned against the wall separating the kitchen and the living room and watched the two women.

Sofia wedged herself deep into the red cushions of the sofa as far from Vicki as she could get, bracing her feet against the floor and actively pushing back as though to put distance between herself and her former sister-in-law. As the conversation continued in calm, civilized tones, Sofia's eyes darkened with anger and distrust. She fisted her hands at her sides. From his vantage point, Logan saw her flex and relax her fists in the same way she had gripped the butt of the gun when she tried to shoot the goon in Vince's apartment. If she had a weapon, he was fairly certain Vicki would be the first target, but Sofia didn't act on the anger.

Logan didn't know the kind of restraint it took to sit and play nice with a woman like Vicki Calvetti, but Sofia managed for a half hour before the conversation ebbed. Sofia maintained her damnable mask like a pro, never once betraying her feelings. She was stronger than he gave her credit for, and he gave her credit for superhero strength. He took another sip of the bitter coffee and watched exhaustion finally overcome Sofia and her eyes began the long blinks that preceded an unwanted decent into sleep. She tucked her feet under her and settled into the cushions.

Logan poured himself another cup of coffee. He had every intention of having his own conversation with Vicki, and it wouldn't be polite, but he'd wait until Sofia fell fully into unconsciousness so she wouldn't interfere.

Vicki turned down the lamp, but kept her eyes on Sofia with a look of realistic concern. Logan didn't buy the charade. He took a seat at the end of the sofa near Sofia's feet, opposite Vicki's chair. The two sat like boxers waiting for the ding of the bell to announce the next round. In a few minutes, Sofia's lips parted and her breathing evened out. She seemed guileless in sleep. The tight lines around her mouth relaxed and her features opened up in trusting innocence, so at odds with the face she showed the world.

The smell of her perfume was anything but innocent. Like the woman, her scent was strong and earthy and sexy as hell. She was a contradiction he wanted to solve. The gray stuffed elephant in her arms exposed another aspect of her character as she pulled it into her chest like a shield.

"It's Eli's," Vicki said softly.

Caught in Sofia's orbit, Logan was startled to realize he'd forgotten Vicki, which was a mistake. The mob princess was a viper, sitting pretty in her snake pit, and it was unwise to forget the danger she presented, but Logan found his focus split whenever he was around Sofia. It was as if he and Sofia had been trapped in a bubble ever since the bomb exploded at her house. Everyone else ceased to exist. Vicki most certainly did not belong in their tense little world. She spread disinformation, amplifying Sofia's pain with every lie she told. Sofia deserved more from someone she trusted, even someone as morally bankrupt as Vicki Calvetti.

Vicki gestured toward Sofia with such a loving look on her face, it was almost believable. "She will barely wear the same outfit twice for fear of electronic devices, but she makes sure her son has his Ellie every night to sleep. She's a good mom."

He glowered at the other woman. "You don't have to tell me that," he said. Sofia was a fierce mom. He'd never met a parent who wanted so desperately to pursue and exact revenge, nor one who seemed quite so capable of doing just that.

Vicki refilled their coffee cups, the bangles on her arms jangling. "I assume you trust me as far as you can throw me and you'll be up all night keeping watch?"

"That about covers it," Logan answered.

"Ditto." She turned out the kitchen light and turned off the overhead living room light. A woman prone to drama, she stretched out the tension as she prepared the house for the night, not at all affected by the fact that he studied her every movement. When she finished, Vicki curled her bare feet under her on the overstuffed chair she sat in like a throne, looking like a self-satisfied cat. "I can live with the fact that you're a Fed, and that you wormed your way into the situation, but I can't live with the fact that you somehow convinced Sofia to trust you."

Logan leaned forward to rest his arms on his knees. He stared straight at the woman he couldn't make himself like. She was pretty, maybe even beautiful, with her olive skin and witchy eyes, but beauty alone did not impress Logan Stone. Something about Victoria Calvetti was all wrong. He didn't like the easy way she wore her brother's wealth. "You don't know your former sister-in-law very well if you think she trusts anyone anymore. Even you."

Vicki glanced at Sofia; then returned her attention to Logan. "I hope you're wrong about that."

"I'm not." Logan rose in agitation, pulled a blanket from the back of the sofa and wrapped it around Sofia's sleeping frame. As the blanket settled, her perfume floated in the air like a musky cloud. Strong and earthy, he thought again as the scent captivated him. Logan closed his eyes, compartmentalized it, before returning to his seat. He stared across at the woman who was neck-deep in the kidnapping of Eli Calvetti. "She has no reason to trust you. You're dating the man who walked away with her son and you won't give us a single lead."

Vicki shrugged. "I don't know anything and—"

"Bullshit."

The curse cut through her innocent air and she glared at him through narrowed eyes. "I already told Sofia, all I know is that Nick took a flight to New York shortly after he left your place."

If she'd said that, then the women's secret language was even more incomprehensible than he'd realized. He needed clarification. "Is that from something you told him or—"

"My brother does not seek my counsel." She said the words with a wounded pride, as if she resented it.

"Because you're a woman?" Despite Sofia's warning that he couldn't play Vicki, Logan knew that Calvetti's chauvinistic ways had to gnaw at a woman like Vicki. She would want to change it, get in her brother's good graces, or gather her own power around her. "How far would you go to prove yourself to your brother?"

A glimmer of some unknown emotion flicked through

her eyes. Anger? Fear? A thought occurred to Logan that hadn't occurred before. Maybe Vicki was as trapped as Sofia had been. "How far would you go to free yourself from him?" he asked.

Vicki set her coffee cup on the end table and straightened her shoulders. The bitter glare in her eyes was the only thing that showed she'd understood what he was insinuating. "Did Sofia tell you about my brother?"

Yeah, he got to her, Logan though with a surge of satisfaction. Who said he couldn't force a reaction from Vicki? He shrugged in answer to her question.

"I don't imagine she did," Vicki said. "At least not the truth."

"And what is the truth?" he sneered.

"He's a psychopath."

That much was true. He'd seen enough of Calvetti's file to have a fair profile. "Is that a professional opinion?"

"Personal," she answered. "But he has been diagnosed as a narcissist. Not the run-of-the-mill selfish prick I seem to date," she admitted, "but a rather frightening portrait of an all-American-kill-or-be-killed psychopath."

"Most criminals are narcissists," Logan said. He knew the statistics, had studied it extensively at the Bureau, but he didn't need to prove himself to Vicki. He merely wanted to keep her talking and give her enough rope to hang herself. "They believe they deserve whatever it is they steal, kill or maim to get, and they think they're too smart to get caught."

Vicki raised an eyebrow in question. "You ever busted my brother and made it stick?"

It grated on Logan to answer. "No."

"Then maybe he is too smart."

"Not likely." Logan knew that mentality. The *I'm too smart to get caught* mentality would bury Calvetti one day. He had an ego that wouldn't quit. The sister would suffer the same fate. Logan leaned back and let Vicki fill the silence.

"He's not normal smart," she continued with a rueful shake of her head. "As kids, I could best him at any test, surpass him in IQ without blinking, so I used to think I was much smarter than he."

On the surface, Vicki's revelation seemed spur-of-the-moment, but they lacked an emotional honesty, so they came across as rehearsed. "But you're not smarter?" Logan added a skeptical tone to his voice. "Is that why you studied psychology?"

"Are you trying to profile me?" Vicki asked.

"Does it matter?"

She shrugged her petite shoulders with practiced indifference. "Despite what you think, I'm not involved in my brother's business activities."

"I never thought you were," Logan said. He narrowed his eyes as if to see her better. The woman was trying to change the subject, to lead him down some preordained path, but he was having none of that. "So maybe your brother is smarter than you give him credit for."

Her eyes flashed with anger. "I don't doubt his intellect, I just understand the source of his power," she snapped, her cool demeanor melting with the heat of her response.

"Which is?"

"He's evil smart. He's fifteen steps ahead of you right now and you'll never know what he has planned because your mind doesn't work that way."

"And is he fifteen steps ahead of the kidnapper?" Logan

asked. "Vince doesn't strike me as particularly cerebral."

Vicki's eyes narrowed. "If you think Vince is the mastermind, you're farther behind the power curve than I thought."

"So tell me, then, who is the mastermind? You?"

Vicki leaned back in her chair and took a satisfied sip from her coffee cup. "Flattery will get you nowhere, Logan No-Name."

"Aren't you the least bit concerned for your nephew?"

Light flared in her eyes like something from the pit of hell. "Don't you dare doubt my love for Eli." She gestured to the pictures on the side table and the mantel. The boy was on the small side, with dark curly hair and eyes like his mother. His smile was like a fallen angel and probably got him out of trouble more times than not.

This angelic boy with eyes like dark pools was not one he wanted haunting his dreams, and that thought angered him nearly as much as Vicki. "Why are you protecting his kidnapper?" he barked.

For a moment, she stared at him as if trying to decipher the why and how of his need to find Eli. After a moment, she heaved a light shrug. "Vince isn't behind this," she assured him. "You want to know who is, figure out who benefits. Who has the power to make it happen?"

"You're the one on the inside," Logan said, fighting hard not to raise his voice and wake Sofia. "You tell me who has the power."

"That's what you have to figure out, isn't it?"

"Figure out? This isn't a game," Logan said, the anger in his voice unmistakable.

"You're right, it isn't a game, and there's far more at risk than you know." Vicki stood and walked toward the back of the house, turning out lights as she went. "I expect you'll be gone before I wake up. Lock the door when you leave."

What was at risk? What was she insinuating? Vicki was off her rocker if she thought money and power were more important than Eli's life.

• • •

Sleep blanketed Sofia and wrapped her in the dark. Dreams beckoned, memories of Eli, promises of better tomorrows. The temptation to drift pulled her deeper. A metallic *click* woke her like a nightmare. The sound warned of imminent danger. She'd heard it before, the mechanical sound as someone pulled back the hammer of a handgun. Someone was armed, ready, and close.

Sofia jerked upright. In a vulnerable position, she refused to give up without a fight. She had a chance in the darkness *if* the gunman were far enough away and *if* he didn't see her. Adrenaline shot to her muscles. Legs tangled in the blanket, Sofia thudded off the couch like a dead body. She kicked and batted at the blanket to no avail.

How much time did she have? How close? She fought a silent battle with the blanket, a sob trapped in her throat.

Someone put a hand over her mouth and Sofia froze.

Chapter Seven

Friday, 1:52 a.m.

A scream lodged in her throat and instinct made her shrink back, but the man's grip was unyielding. She thrashed against the calloused hand.

"Shh," Logan whispered. "In the kitchen."

Thank God. Sofia sagged in relief. It was Logan's hand cautioning her to keep quiet. Someone was in the kitchen, and gauging by Logan's reaction, it wasn't good. She nodded that she understood. Logan released her and evaporated into the shadows. The panic threatened as he left, turning every house noise into an invisible threat. Her lungs screamed for air, huffing like she'd just finished a run. Too loud, she thought.

She tried to pull a calming breath but it hitched in her throat. She was too exposed on the floor, so she worked to free herself. Her numb fingers fumbled with the blanket.

Where was Logan? She felt safer knowing he had her back. Sofia lay between the sofa and the coffee table and tried to will the blanket from her body. Footsteps tread lightly on the kitchen tile. It sounded loud to her, like the creak of a door in a scary movie, but in truth, it was stealthy. She would have slept through it if the sound of the gun hadn't woken her. Ironic that the heinous experience from her past had saved her.

Sofia softly exhaled. Like a slack rope, the blanket fell away from her relaxed muscles.

Freed, she crawled behind the couch and the minimal protection it afforded. The footsteps stopped as they reached the carpet at the edge of the room. The moment of silence—filled with horrific anticipation—ended with the whine of a bullet through a silencer. It would not have been loud enough to wake her. It would have traveled through her body on the way to the couch where it now lodged. She would have died in her sleep, most people's highest hope and her second-worst nightmare.

Immobile, Sofia huddled against the couch. Every nerve in her body trembled at what had almost happened. She wanted to run, faster and farther than ever before, but movement might draw another bullet, and besides, the attempt might land her flat on her back if her legs gave out. A spasm shot through her quads to give credence to her worries. No part of her was exempt from the fear.

The lights clicked on. Sofia cowered, even knowing her hiding spot wouldn't survive the light.

"Drop it," Logan ordered. The bite in his voice was harder than she imagined possible.

Sofia peeked around the edge of the couch. A man stood

a few steps into the room with Logan at the wall behind him, as if he'd been lying in wait. The shooter was an unknown. As tall as Logan, but broader through the chest, he wore all black, including a ski mask. Logan stood a pace behind with a gun at the stranger's back.

The gunman released his weapon. It fell to the carpet with a thud.

"Hands behind your back."

"You won't shoot an unarmed man," the stranger taunted. "It goes against your training."

In one swift move, the stranger slammed back into Logan, using his arm and shoulder to ram Logan into the wall with enough force to shake the house. A loud *snap* cracked the air while the gunman ran for the door. He made it three steps, then staggered back.

The moment slowed as if time itself was stunned. The man fell, landing on his back and sending another quake through the house. The sound of gunfire followed like a surreal echo that should have preceded the spray of shattering glass peppering the room. An eerie hush followed.

"Sniper," Logan yelled. "Stay down." He held a hand to his ribs and the other grasped the gun as he headed out the front door. What kind of crazy person chased a sniper in the dark? *Stay down*? What else was she going to do? Paint a target on her forehead??

Sofia hunched into an even lower squat behind the couch. She was still numb with the realization he'd left her, and not just her, but the injured man the sniper had shot.

Minutes ticked away and spasms shot up her legs as she maintained the uncomfortable squat. Sofia dropped forward onto her hands and crawled away from the windows. She peeked through the legs of a side table to see into the bright room beyond. To the right, the kitchen remained a black hole where the boogeyman hid. To the left, the front door stood wide open. The curtains at the window's edge blew in a light breeze. Shattered glass littered the floor like sparkling jewels. No place felt safe.

Gurgling like the sound of someone breathing water emanated from the space between the kitchen and front door. Between those fluttering curtains and the darkness lay the man who had tried to kill her. He sprawled near Vicki's chair, deformed like a child playing Twister. His left leg twitched. Sofia darted back. The gurgling grew thicker, drawing her out of hiding.

The man turned his face toward her. Behind the mask, his hazy gaze met hers. Panic and pain mixed with the silent scream in his eyes. Sofia averted her gaze. A mass of thick goo wet his shirt, spreading with each beat of his heart. As she watched, the harsh gurgling stopped and his chest stilled. Blood oozed onto the beige carpet.

Sofia sat back on her heels and took a deep breath, but it didn't stop the shakes. This was a first, watching a man die. She could have gone to the grave without the experience. The horror of watching the life drain from his eyes was beyond imagination. Her thoughts returned to the man in Vince's apartment, the one she'd wanted to kill. For the first time, she was glad she didn't shoot. Watching this one die was enough. It weighed on her soul. She couldn't conceive of being the person responsible for his death, even if he did deserve it.

There had been a time when she hadn't realized what Nick did for a living. She knew now, but there was a difference between knowledge and experience. The body in front of her was the reality of what her ex-husband did. Whether Nick or someone else sent the shooter, they were all the same.

The absence of sound was a force in the room. What hid in the silence, in the gloom outside the room, turned fear to panic, the anticipation as thick as her breathing. One thing she knew for certain. Today was not a good day to die. Eli needed her. She crawled to the gun the dead man had tried to shoot her with. Sofia lifted it with numb fingers and held it like a talisman to her chest. The weight of it gave her false security that fled the instant the kitchen door squeaked open. She snapped the gun toward the sound. Eddie walked through the kitchen door.

He wore black Dockers and a long-sleeved black turtleneck that disguised the paunch drooping over his waistband. Black gloves covered his empty hands and a black ski mask was pulled over his graying hair. He looked like an assassin grandpa, on his way to the golf course. His presence shouldn't have surprised her. If he didn't have a key, and he likely did, he could have picked the lock. He was the one who had taught her how. Now he was facing her like an executioner all in black.

Her heart fell. She didn't want to believe Eddie would kill her. She didn't want to believe anything that had happened was real.

Eddie kept his gloved hands out. "You're not going to shoot me. Put the gun down."

"To make me an easier target? I don't think so."

"I wouldn't kill you, Miss Sofia. Nick asked me to keep an eye on Vicki. Protect her."

"And I just happened to be at the right place at the wrong time?"

"I know what you think of us. Me. But I would never kill you, Miss Sofia. Even if Nick ordered it."

Tears watered her eyes. How many times had he called her that?

Everything's okay, Miss Sofia.

He got delayed at the club, Miss Sofia.

I'll take care of that for you, Miss Sofia.

The shaking in her arms turned to full-on tremors. Eddie was right. If she couldn't shoot the goon in Vince's apartment, then there was no way she could kill Eddie. She lowered the gun. It was just as well. The stinging in her eyes prevented her from seeing clearly. She wanted to scream at him, to blame him for everything that had happened, but it was all she could do to whisper the question that mattered most. "Who has my son?"

"I don't know, Miss Sofia."

Sofia snorted. It was an inelegant sound, but it was the best she could muster.

"It's the God's honest truth. Someone is nosing in on Calvetti territory. Someone gave Nick until midnight Sunday to cede territory. Or else."

The "or else" was her son. "Why are you telling me?" She was certain Nick didn't want her to know.

Eddie frowned. "Nick won't cede a single square inch."

"He'll let Eli die," Sofia whispered.

"You didn't hear nothing from me." Eddie pulled on a black face mask as he backed out of the room. A moment later the back door *swished* closed, echoing through the empty house.

Only her and the dead body remained as the front screen opened. Sofia swung the gun at the intruder.

Logan closed the door behind him. "The shooter is clear."

Sofia lowered the gun to her lap. She took a deep breath. Cleared her vision. Forced tense muscles to relax. "I can guess who killed him."

"Who?"

"Eddie. He was just here."

"So Calvetti is behind this."

She hated Nick with a passion reserved for spiders, snakes, and creepy-crawlies. Blaming the shooting on him would add more fuel to that hatred. Sofia took a deep breath. It also didn't make sense. "I don't think so. He had no idea I was here."

"Eddie or Calvetti?"

"Neither. Eddie was here to protect Vicki."

"Or follow her," Logan said.

"Follow her? Where?"

Logan pulled a handkerchief from his pocket. "Her relationship to Vince has to make Calvetti wonder."

Sofia nodded. Doubt is what had brought her to her best friend's door. Nick would have been equally suspicious of his own sister. Maybe more than suspicious. Would he kill his own sister?

Logan used a handkerchief to lift the gun from her lap and wipe it down.

She looked up at him. The earlier violence left a swirling pattern of bad energy in the room, but Logan soothed it, soothed her. Just his presence calmed her nerves. Settled her thoughts.

"Eddie gave me a warning."

Logan kept working as if he hadn't heard. He tossed the gun next to the body and pulled back the mask in one swift movement. Sofia didn't have time to avert her gaze.

Logan watched her reaction. "Recognize him?"

Death was ugly. It had a broad face with unholy color and round soulless eyes. Now she had a face to go with the dead body. A face to match others that tormented her dreams.

She expected to know this man, to recognize the face of someone who wanted her dead. Sofia shook her head. No. She didn't know him.

"We have to get out of here," Logan said.

"How long has it been?" she asked. The time she spent watching the dead man had seemed interminably long.

"Five minutes, maybe, seven tops, but the local PD will be here quickly considering everything else that has happened today," Logan said. He reached out a hand to help her up.

The numbness in her fingers thawed at the touch of his warm, strong fingers. The man was the antidote to her cold soul. Sofia allowed herself a moment to breathe in and absorb his strength before rising to unsteady feet.

If she looked up from the dead body, the room had an eerie normalcy to it. A white coffee mug sat on the table near Vicki's chair and another cup rested on the end table where Logan had been when she'd fallen asleep.

How had she fallen asleep with all the turmoil? She'd felt herself drifting, had pulled Eli's elephant to her chest. It smelled of baby shampoo and innocence. It was like holding Eli and she'd drifted into a hopeful dream. The throw from Vicki's chair had covered her. Such a Vicki thing to do, to look after her, even in her sleep.

"Vicki!" Sofia gasped. In the chaos, she'd forgotten her friend. Sofia snatched Eli's elephant from the tangle of blankets on the floor before heading down the hall to Vicki's room.

Logan grabbed her, tried to hold her back. "Don't."

"Why?" Sofia glanced back, but couldn't read Logan's expression.

"No one knew we were here," Logan explained.

Sofia's eyes flew wide. "You mean she was the target?"

"Possibly."

"I have to make sure she's okay." Sofia yanked her arm from Logan's grasp. "Good God, what if they got to her first?"

She burst through the door without knocking. A velvet comforter covered the bed like a jewel box. An empty jewel box.

"Almost like she knew it was coming," Logan said, and he didn't sound surprised.

The little hole in her heart blew wide open. Sofia gave voice to her suspicions. "There are two possibilities. Either Vicki was the target or she gave us up."

"One way or another, your sister-in-law is neck deep in this mess."

Sofia pulled Ellie to her, wishing foolishly for Logan's embrace. She'd never felt so alone. Even when she'd left Nick, she'd had her best friend.

Not anymore.

While they drove through the darkness to get the passports, Sofia told Logan all that Eddie had said and done. She told him everything, which was a first for her, and when she got to the end, when Eddie had left through the kitchen, she couldn't help adding, "He saved my life."

"I had it under control," Logan insisted, his tone tense. "I disarmed the shooter and you were unharmed."

"Yes, but he eliminated the threat."

"Sofia, ask yourself the point in killing the shooter after I'd disarmed him? What Eddie did was kill a suspect before I could question him. We needed information and Eddie got in the way."

"Well, pardon me for living," she muttered. "If it comes down to it, and it did, I'd rather be alive than dead. Eddie saw to it."

The bite in Logan's tone matched the hard set of his clenched jaw. "Protecting you is my job."

"It was his job once." Sofia had a strong urge to roll her eyes. Men and their pride were no small matter. In her former life, pride mattered more than life. "You're not exactly on the clock right now."

"I still think like an agent." The low growl in his throat was part anger. The other part was harder to define. "I still think like a man," he added so low it was nearly inaudible.

The quiet lengthened as flashes of light from oncoming cars revealed his tight expression. Maybe she'd misunderstood, although there was no misunderstanding the barely constrained tension. The air in the car was as electric as the dark sky after a storm. If it were Nick, Sofia would wonder what she had done and then she'd worry about how he would punish her for the infraction. Logan's seething silence unsettled her already taut nerves. "Why are you angry?"

They drove to the next stoplight before Logan answered. "We walked into a trap, Sofia. No one knew we were there and I didn't see it coming."

"You're not infallible," she answered.

Logan waited for the light to turn green before crossing the intersection and pulling into a convenience store. Sofia's heart pounded with anxiety that refused to settle. This side of Logan worried her. "Are you angry?" she whispered.

"Not angry. Furious," Logan answered.

God, she hated the powerlessness she felt. She straightened in her seat and prepared for the worst.

After parking on the side of the building, Logan unbuckled and turned to face her. A reflection of the neon sign glittered in his dark eyes. Sofia shivered. Logan always seemed unflappable, even when he met Nick face-to-face, but strong emotion burned in him now. It filled the car with waves of frantic energy. Her pulse skyrocketed.

He grabbed her shoulders, turning her to face him. Energy zipped through her like it had when she'd awoken in the pitch dark at Vicki's.

"I screwed up," he said.

"Oh." That wasn't at all what she expected him to say. The stress that had accumulated in her body converted to a different kind of tension, something she hadn't felt in years. Sofia's instinctual urge to run failed her. She didn't want to fight the sizzle of awareness that coursed through her at his touch. She tried to take a deep breath, but it caught in her throat.

He leaned forward, his fingers firm on her shoulders. "This isn't pride talking, Sofia. I could have gotten you killed by going there."

So that's what bothered him. Even off the grid, he was still on the job. Tears bit at the back of her throat and she didn't want to admit why that bothered her, but the answer was there in her plummeting mood. She didn't want to be a job to Logan, but what more did she expect? No way would he see her as a woman. Not after the day they'd had. She cleared her throat. "There were three of us there. None of us saw it coming."

"I wouldn't say that," Logan answered. "Vicki saw it coming. I should have." He stared at the ceiling while his hands slid from her shoulders to her biceps. Anger continued to pump off him in waves.

When the anger faded and his grip turned to a caress, Sofia responded to his touch. It made her feel like a woman, not an assignment. The softness of it made her want to cry. Why was it so easy to stay strong when faced with anger and danger than it was to stay strong in the face of kindness? Ripples of desire spiraling through her body, centered where his strong hands held her. If she was an Ice Queen, she was melting at his touch.

She'd been attracted to him from the first time he walked into the gym. She'd kept her distance. And one touch made her want…

Everything a woman wanted from a man. It's why she'd chosen Mr. Mediocre at the gym for her misguided plans. She wouldn't have had to worry about tricky emotions and dangerous desires. It wasn't easy to avoid those things with Logan, because she did want him.

When he turned to her, there was anguish in his gaze. "It's the way I think, Sofia," he said, his voice as rough as the whiskers on his chin. "My mind is always making connections, planning contingencies, but around you…"

The grip he had on her arms softened until he was making small circles with his thumbs against her bare skin. Her breath hitched. Yes, that's exactly what she wanted, Logan's touch on her bare skin.

Instinctively she leaned closer, hovering over the center console. The energy in the car flashed hot and melted her resistance. She swallowed, her mouth suddenly too dry. Logan's gaze followed her movement, watched as she licked her lips. Her heart pounded in her chest. Sofia watched his fingers move against her skin, mesmerized by his controlled strength.

He followed her gaze. The second he realized that his touch had turned erotic, he yanked his hands back as if they were on fire, but the passion in his eyes only added to the flames. The desire that flushed her skin didn't abate when he stopped touching her. If anything, the distance seemed to fuel a need to push for a reaction to the obvious chemistry between them. He leaned away, his chest rising with unsteady breath and the rough sound of it was like an aphrodisiac. No way was he immune to whatever just transpired between them.

"I can't put you at risk. I need to think straight." And the husky tone of his voice said he was having a hard time doing that.

Good. It helped that he felt the attraction too. The tension building within her eased.

Logan felt it, even if he wanted to deny it. His pupils were dilated and he stared at her like she was chocolate and tomorrow was the first day of Lent. Sure, she might be forbidden, but no one could withstand temptation forever. Not when it was so close.

The car roared to life as Logan started it back onto the road.

So he thought to ignore the attraction? Good luck. He might be a rule follower, but she wasn't. He didn't stand a chance in hell.

They drove several miles with a dozen unspoken words between them. When he spoke again, the huskiness was gone from his voice and she missed it. "Among other things, I want to know why Eddie saved you."

That question took a bite out of her pride, but she tried to bury it. Logan was just looking for answers. Connections, he had said. "Eddie's always been protective of me," Sofia offered.

"But if Calvetti ordered it," he clarified, "would Eddie kill you?"

A chill seeped into Sofia's bones, a memory of a time she wanted to forget. "Eddie asked me once— No," Sofia clarified, "he begged me not to provoke Nicky."

"Meaning?"

The memory was a nightmare that never faded. She knew it had hurt Eddie to see the pain Nick had inflicted on her, but Eddie was a company man. "He told me that he would never kill me, even if Nicky ordered it, but I think Eddie would do anything the boss ordered, including killing me. That's why he asked me not to provoke Nicky. He doesn't want to be in that position."

"So we can assume Calvetti didn't order your execution."

Not yet, Sofia thought, but she was not relieved. That contingency could still happen. "Eddie probably told the truth when he said he was there to keep an eye on Vicki, but the question is why."

Logan glanced at her. "Would Calvetti put protection on her without her knowledge?"

"Unlikely," Sofia answered. "This far from the city, why would anyone bother to hurt her unless—"

"Unless she's involved."

"And Nicky doesn't trust her," she added. Given recent events, Nick had to be suspicious of Vicki and her relationship to Vince. "Eddie wasn't protecting Vicki, he was following her."

"Most likely. Would she work for the competition?"

Sofia didn't know the answer, but she wanted it to be no. "Vicki has always worked her own agenda. Most days, she's several steps ahead of everyone."

"It sounds like the mob princess would do anything in her own interests."

"Kidnapping Eli is not in her interest," Sofia insisted, but inside, the doubts intensified. Vicki had been elusive when they'd spoken last night. Something had been hiding in the little tells, the way her fingers had nervously worked the fabric of her clothes and the constantly averted gaze. She hadn't made eye contact, which meant she had something to hide. What she was hiding was anyone's guess, but Sofia desperately wanted it to be guilt over Vince rather than guilt for her own behavior. "Vicki's out-of-the-box thinking is what helped me escape Nicky. That had nothing to do with what was best for Vicki."

"But it didn't really cost her anything?"

"Oh yes it did. Vicki came out here to go to college. That's how we met, but she had no intention of living in

Colorado. Not that her father would have let her."

"Then why is she here now?"

"That was her punishment for helping me. Her move to Colorado was more exile than choice."

Logan thought about that for a minute. "I know this is going to piss you off, but have you thought that maybe she wants to go back to the city bad enough to get involved with the wrong people?"

"Without knowing the players, I can't speculate on her involvement."

"Spoken like a lawyer," Logan complained. "So let me be more direct. Do you think she's involved?"

It seemed disloyal to think it. Sofia leaned forward, tension charging her overtired body. Rather than fight it, though, Sofia took a deep breath and eased back against the seat. Sometimes, the truth was overrated. "Yes. I do think she is involved." And it killed her. "Have you heard of any territory disputes with the Calvetti family?"

"No, but New York isn't my area of responsibility. Not even close."

She was his area of responsibility. That knowledge twisted her up inside. Just as quickly as it surfaced, she ruthlessly locked that thought away. She'd made the choice to work with Logan after she knew he was a Fed. It did no good to keep harping on it. Instead, she wondered who would challenge Nick so directly? Sofia had never paid attention to his business dealings—she'd wanted nothing to do with that life—but now it was something she regretted. Maybe if she'd paid more attention, she'd know who Nick's competitors were.

Who had the brass balls to take Nick Calvetti's son?

The new passport and ID for Logan passed Sofia's brutal inspection. She handed over a small fortune from her get-out-of-town money. It hurt to give up the security that the money provided, but Sofia reminded herself it was for Eli. She was one step closer to Eli.

She went back to the waiting car shrouded in darkness. The car drove through the night, the headlights revealing just enough asphalt to keep them on the right path, which was a fair analogy for where she was at the moment. She had enough information to stay on the path, but not enough to know her destination.

Right now, it was too early to head for the airport. They couldn't arrive so early that they would sit in the open for too long. Even factoring in potential delays and city traffic, it was too early to leave, which was good, because Sofia had a final stop to make. She directed Logan down a road that bordered rough apartments on the west and a commercial area on the east. They passed a bowling alley and a weed-filled lot before turning into a storage facility. She told him the combination to the gate as he pulled in.

"This isn't the best time to dig through storage."

"We need money," she said. "This is where I can get it. Besides, I can't go through the airport looking like myself. I have a disguise waiting here."

Logan grudgingly agreed and entered the code before driving through the narrow alleys between the garage-like storage units. For the second time in twenty-four hours, she was thankful Logan wasn't much of a talker. He left her to her thoughts, which were a jumbled, chaotic, un-caffeinated mess.

Every moment she spent away from Eli cost her.

The tight control she maintained was degrading. She was shaky and her stomach churned. None of that was good for her son. He needed her whole and thinking clearly.

"They won't hurt him," Logan said as he pulled up to her storage unit. "They need Eli for the Sunday meeting with Calvetti."

Sofia's chin wobbled with the tears and fears she wouldn't express, because she couldn't let negativity win. She yanked her emotions back under control. "Then we have to find him first."

"We will," he said with finality. His tone challenged her to disagree.

She wanted to believe Logan. She wanted to trust him, but what if they were already too late?

Chapter Eight

Friday, 4:37 a.m.

Logan knew better than promising the impossible, but he couldn't watch her agony any longer. In the past twenty-four hours, she'd lost her son, endured a bombing, been chased and shot at and threatened. She'd watched a man die. She did all that with only a few hours' sleep and very little food. He didn't see how she'd make it much longer.

She stepped out of his car and unlocked the unit.

"What's so important we had to stop?"

She shoved open the door to reveal a car parked inside.

Even in the dim, pre-dawn light, he could tell it wasn't just any car. Logan stepped from his vehicle for a closer inspection. He whistled at the sexy car. "You have a classic Thunderbird parked in a storage facility in a dumpy neighborhood."

"I do," she said with a saucy grin.

"Why?"

"Who would expect it?"

Who indeed? No one would leave such a valuable car in this place. Nothing about Sofia was ordinary, but this was beyond extraordinary. The T-Bird was in factory condition with paint and interior that glowed in the weak light. A major road was less than fifty feet away and the sounds of early morning commuter traffic roared past, their headlights casting long shadows in the tight space.

Sofia tossed the duffel bag in the passenger seat of the car, then reached into her backpack and pulled out Eli's elephant. She put it into the duffel. "Anything you want to leave here?"

Logan was torn. In the end, he left his extra ammunition, his gun and the extra clip. He wouldn't make it through security with it. "Can you get me a gun in New York?"

She frowned. "You know how I feel about—"

"A gun beats fists and knives." He was asking her to break the law, to break a personal code against weapons. He was asking her to do it for her son.

The downward cast of her eyes didn't hide her displeasure. "I'll make a few calls."

With his gun tucked into the glove box of the old car, Logan stuffed his clothes back in his duffel.

"You might want to change." She gestured at his T-shirt.

He glanced down to see blood spray across his chest. He'd been closer to the dead man than he'd thought. He and Sofia would have to deal with that, the emotion of watching a man die, but for now, he compartmentalized it. There were practical things to consider.

He glanced around the small storage facility for a place

to change. Unless he wanted to climb into the passenger seat of the hot rod, he didn't have many options.

"Why don't you change on one side of the car while I change on the other?" she said.

Logan nodded and pulled the garage door closed, but he winced at the stab of pain that ran across his midsection. He had hit the wall hard when the gunman rammed him and he felt bruised front and back. He shook off the pain because he didn't have time to coddle it.

As the door clanged to the cement floor, the enclosed space became a black hole, shadowy and silent. The absence of traffic noise exaggerated every sound. The single overhead bulb cast everything in shadow. Logan blessed and cursed the low light as he thought about the woman on the other side of the room. He really didn't need to see Sofia change.

Sofia stepped behind the car. "No peeking," she teased.

Correction. He wanted to see her change, but he knew better. He tried to give her privacy. He averted his gaze, turned his back, and distanced himself from the smell of her perfume, but he couldn't close his ears. The sound of her unzipping her jeans followed by the sound of her hands gliding the heavy fabric down her thighs until it flopped quietly to the ground was as loud as a bomb in his head.

Logan unzipped his jeans to try and camouflage the sound of her, but he still heard the whisper of her shirt being pulled over her head.

"I can't believe you have a T-bird." His voice was unnaturally loud.

"It's just a car," she said, her voice not covering the intimate sounds of clothes falling to the ground.

"I have to disagree with you on this," he answered. With

efficient movements he changed into clean jeans and a T-shirt, but his imagination combined the memory of her perfume with the sound of soft fabric gliding over skin. He tried to block the image from his mind, the wonder of what she looked like naked. The softness of her skin. The smell. *Hell.*

Logan took a deep breath, hard with the sound of her. "That is not your average car. Why do you have a hot rod?"

"It was my grandfather's."

"A man of good taste."

"I don't know about good taste. Simple. All he needed was my grandmother, this car, and some old comic books."

He heard another zipper, a covering up of bare skin, and the rustle of soft fabric. "Now you're being cruel." He swallowed. Took a deep breath. "What comics? How old?"

She laughed and the sound trickled over his skin.

Logan leaned against the car.

"I don't know. The box is on the floor to your left."

Logan kneeled down and his ribs throbbed at the movement. Still, he was glad of an excuse to bend over and cool off near the cement floor. The light was faint in his corner of the storage, but he could see enough as he opened the cardboard box. The dates on the first few copies were enough to know there was a small fortune sitting in that box. "Leaving them out here should be a crime. Do you know what the cold and damp can do?"

"It's Colorado. We're dry enough."

"The cold?"

She laughed again. It wasn't a girlish giggle. It was soft and controlled and it washed over him like warm rain on a hot afternoon.

The trunk opened, then slammed shut. There was more

rustling of fabric. "Tell you what," she said. "When this is over I'll let you figure out how to store them."

He folded the cardboard cover back into place. "I'll hold you to that."

He recognized the smattering of noises that filtered across the small space. Hair and makeup. It was oddly intimate in the confined space.

"That's awfully optimistic of us, assuming we'll be here to do something so mundane."

"Sofia—"

"Don't," she said. "I appreciate your attempt to reassure me—"

"Is that what I was going to do?"

"Yes, but I'm better off dealing with reality. Everything won't be all right. Most likely. It's okay with me if it goes to hell. I don't care what happens, as long as Eli lives."

He didn't know how to answer that, so he stood and leaned against the car. His job made him cynical at times. He could calculate percentages and risk factors and probabilities, but these weren't things you told the victim or their families. Add to that he had an unnatural urge to protect Sofia from what he knew were difficult truths.

He didn't know why. She was strong. She had to be. He didn't know a single person who could walk away from the mob the way she had. True, she hadn't been part of the operation, but she was a part of the family, and you didn't leave on a whim. On top of that, she'd lived the last two years in a fishbowl, every action and every conversation under a microscope for observation.

She'd been watched by Calvetti, who had the resources to pay others to do the watching, but that didn't make him any better than a psychotic stalker, and she'd been followed by the Feds. By Logan. He felt a twinge of guilt for his part in that, for putting her in a no-man's land between a crime family and the government where neither side trusted her, or left her alone, though she'd broken no laws.

"Nicky doesn't know about it."

"It?" He was having a hard time keeping up with the conversation. "The car, the storage, or the comics?"

"None of it. No one does. I keep the car running and well stocked."

"Stocked?" He'd seen her pull a set of lock picks from her duffel, along with cash, a stuffed animal, passports and Lord knew what else. He wouldn't be surprised if she had a Slim-Jim to break into cars and everything she needed to hotwire it. She was resourceful, he had to admit, and her little bag of tricks came in handy. The one thing he was certain she didn't carry was a gun, and that suited him fine. The thought of this particular woman being armed was incredibly dangerous.

"You can turn around now," she said.

Logan turned. The woman across from him no longer resembled the demure Sofia Capri Calvetti of his FBI file. She looked taller and lush. Fuller. It wasn't just her body that had changed. She was blond now, with long strands that curled around her pale face. She had a mirror propped on the shelves in the back of the storage and was applying makeup to cover the scrape on her cheek.

Fascinated, he stepped closer. What a skilled woman could do with a makeup brush was bewitching, and he'd always been drawn to magic. He was also drawn to the woman across from him in a way that was no less mystical. With a few flicks of a brush she turned her eyes smoky, then followed with a swipe of mascara that turned her lashes into something from a magazine ad.

When she turned to face him, the air stirred with the scent of recently applied perfume. He knew that smell in the dark, from sitting with her as she slept at Vicki's. He took a step back.

"What do you think?" she asked.

His mouth went dry. What he thought he couldn't say out loud. "You don't look like Aunt Bertha."

She spun to show off the transformation. The movement fanned her earthy scent across the small space, surrounding him in a musky scent that would tempt a monk. He wanted her. Until yesterday, she'd been a pretty woman he was paid to watch. Nice gig if you could get it, and while he'd always thought her sexy in touch-me-not shades, the woman behind the shades was far more alluring.

"Do I look like me?" she insisted.

She looked like sin in a dress. A blond Mata Hari in stilettos. Drawn by the sound of soft fabric and silky skin and a temptation he no longer tried to deny, Logan stepped around the car. If the sound of her undressing had him hard, the smell of her had him ready to do disreputable things to her in the backseat of her grandfather's car.

He made himself stay a step away or he'd give in to the need to touch her. "Where did you get the wig?"

She tapped the trunk. This close, her eyes shimmered a newly acquired dark blue. Despite the illusions she wove around her through a myriad of small changes, he'd know her anywhere. That, he realized, wasn't a failure of the disguise but a testament to years of watching her. After today, she would never be able to hide from him. "You'll pass security."

"What about you?"

He swallowed, wet his tongue, and tried to think beyond

single syllables. "My name will be on a watch list, but they won't spare agents to watch the airport." Not yet, he hoped. "With the new passport, I'll be fine."

"You don't have to do this." Sofia stepped forward and laid a hand on his arm. "If I were a better person, I'd find a way to leave you here, lock you in here if I had to. I'd wish you wouldn't go."

"But I will," he said. "For Eli."

Sofia's eyes watered, an anomaly she blinked away through sheer force of will. "Thank you." There was so much emotion in the words, so much she didn't say. Then she stepped forward and planted a soft kiss on his cheek.

The brush of her full lips on his bare flesh dropped Logan's IQ like he'd been shot with a Taser. All he could do was respond to the electrical impulses that short-wired his circuits. This time, he initiated, and it was not a sweet kiss of gratitude. He scooped his arms around this lush, unencumbered Sofia and slid his lips across hers in a fierce kiss that had been two years in the making. He kissed her in a way he had no right to, but had hungered to from day one. Hard and fast, he tasted and she moaned as she slid closer.

She leaned into him, trailed her hand up his arm and around his neck. Every inch of skin she touched burned. Logan's hand slid down her backside and wandered the curves he liked to watch. Her backside was firm and round, and he thanked God for every mile she logged on the treadmill. He pulled her closer until her heat pressed against his groin. He wanted to take her right there, would have when she slid a hand down his chest and whispered what sounded like an invitation, but she used her hand to push him back.

The stale air of the storage room slid between them.

"We have a flight to catch."

Logan stepped back, sucked in a lungful of air. His intoxicated senses swelled with the essence of her. It took several minutes and painful distance to unwind from the spell. He opened the door to the noise of morning traffic and let the early morning chill finish the job. They didn't speak as the moments bled into long minutes. She stepped from the storage shed first, and when Logan followed, she closed and double locked the unit. They wordlessly climbed into his car.

Neither broke the silence as Logan drove on autopilot toward the airport. When the sun rose half an hour later, Logan turned his gaze to the woman who was — and wasn't — a mobster's wife. He had no right to ask, but he needed to know in the same way he had needed to kiss her. "Do you still love him?"

"I never loved him." A fracture broke the perfect disguise and her full lips shattered into a bottomless scowl. "I was nineteen when I met Nicky. He was a handsome, worldly man, and I'd never left the great state of Colorado. I lived with my grandparents for God's sake. I didn't know a thing about how the world worked.

"Nicky wooed me from a distance. He sent funny texts and little gifts. Nothing too ostentatious that would raise suspicions, just little things that drew me to him. I found out later that Eddie bought them on Nicky's orders. By graduation, I was convinced that I was ready to take the New York art world by storm with Nicky at my side. He fed the illusion."

Logan knew how manipulation worked, how psychopaths like Calvetti drew victims, but he couldn't understand how Sofia, the strongest woman he knew, could fall for it. "If you didn't love him, why did you marry him?"

She laughed, a hollow and cold sound like the fake neutrality she affected. "I loved who he pretended to be."

Logan released a breath, knowing how the story would end. "When he stopped pretending?"

Her eyes narrowed, squinting against the morning sun. "It got scary," she whispered.

They drove the rest of the way in silence.

Sofia breezed through DIA security as planned. Logan had dropped her at the curb. He would follow after parking the car. With any luck, no one would connect them. She rode the tram to her concourse and stopped for coffee with the ease of a woman on vacation, at least on the outside. Inside, she considered all the things that could go wrong. Logan didn't have a disguise. He was traveling under an assumed name, but if the Feds were watching the airport, they *would* recognize him. On top of that, Nick could try to prevent her from interfering in New York, not that he would recognize her. She'd been careful, but she didn't want to bet her life on it. She certainly didn't want to bet Eli's.

She avoided the long, moving walkways in favor of a quick stroll to the end of the concourse, then back to her gate, keeping an eye out for anyone she recognized. As far as she could tell, no one was waiting for them. She sent a quick text to Uncle Ernie before selecting a seat in the waiting area. She chose with her standard paranoia: facing the crowd with her back to a wall. She had a full view of the waiting area and concourse beyond. She plastered a blank look onto her face and pulled out a book she had no intention of reading.

The disguise was intended for the final stage of her plan, the original plan. That one started with a vacation, the one she'd invited Logan to join her on. That was meant to be phase one, reconnaissance. Now he joined her on a completely different mission, something far more vital. Recovery. In the past twenty-four hours, she'd lost hope for a positive outcome. She didn't feel anything except a random desperation she refused to voice.

She turned the page in the paperback and scanned the waiting area. No wise guys. No Feds. The coffee cooled untouched beside her.

She glanced down at her book. Regret was a wasted emotion — Nick had taught her that — but Sofia regretted her trust in Vince, and in Vicki for that matter. You'd think she'd have learned, but apparently it would take someone — like the man last night — to put a bullet in her brain for her to finally figure it out.

Trust no one. She and Eli were all each other had.

She turned a page. Scanned the gate area. Glanced back down.

Logan was in the gate area. His strong energy reached her before she saw him. He'd chosen a seat across the waiting area, with his back to the concourse and his front facing her. Several dozen passengers sat or stood in the area between them, yet she didn't need to look up from her wordless book to know he was there. It was as if his kiss had bound them together in some unfathomable way. His presence made her want to relax, but she fought the urge. Complacency could get Eli killed.

She turned a page. Scanned. Stared back at the book.

The gate agent called for boarding, but she waited until the first surge ebbed before picking up her bag and heading to the gate. Logan was behind her, with a businessman and his laptop standing between them.

And she'd be damned if she didn't feel better as she eased into her window seat, knowing Logan kept watch from two rows back.

• • •

Logan cast a disinterested gaze around the cabin, just as he'd watched everyone in the gate area, but he didn't recognize anyone from a mug shot. Or from the office, he thought wryly. He kept his vigilance until they pushed back from the gate and steered down the runway. Only then did he allow his gaze to linger on Sofia. Even as a blond, with too much makeup and a stiff spine, she was beautiful. The camouflage couldn't hide the aristocratic features like her high cheekbones and patrician nose. Her proud posture.

Not that the man next to her, or anyone else for that matter, bothered to look beyond the clothes that clung to her curves. The buttons that glided down her sides and their not-too-subtle curves assured it. She couldn't have chosen a better skirt to draw men's eyes away from her face. It's as if she'd planned to be noticed, but for all the wrong reasons. No one would remember her face because they weren't looking at it.

The man next to her turned, tried to engage her in conversation, but she smiled politely and peered into a book. Logan had seen that move, or something similar, at least a dozen times at the gym. It wasn't unkind, just an invisible do-not-disturb sign that men recognized. The passenger leaned back in his seat as the plane tilted up for take-off.

Logan let his attention linger on Sofia until the plane leveled off. Then he mimicked her companion and released his seat into a reclined position. Everyone on the plane had gone through security so no one had a weapon. No one knew they were on this flight. Logan had no idea what would hit them when they landed, but he had every intention of getting some rest before phase two of this hell broke loose.

. . .

The throb of the engines couldn't drown out the safe energy from Logan, two rows back, an energy that didn't fade as the plane made its interminably long flight to the coast. The man beside her slept, and Sofia willed herself to do the same, but the more she demanded her body to relax, the more tightly her muscles bunched. What would happen to Eli while she slept? Would she know, somehow, if he was hurt? Or dead? The unfamiliar contacts swirled with unshed tears. Crying wouldn't help a single bit, she scolded herself.

Sofia blocked the images from her thoughts and asked the stewardess for more black coffee. If sleep wouldn't come, then she'd put her mind to good use.

First, she reviewed what had happened the morning Eli had disappeared. He woke up grouchy. Vince had told him that while he was at his father's, he was going to horse camp, and Eli wanted to go that very minute. It was so like Nick to ruin her last day with her son. No matter what she promised, even Chuck E. Cheese, it wasn't enough to sway the little boy from thoughts of horses. It wasn't until they'd settled into the routine of the gym that he calmed. He galloped like a pony into the craft room. He hadn't turned to smile at her. He didn't say *I love you*.

Sofia squeezed her eyes shut and tried to picture her little boy as he had been that morning. That's the way she would find him, she vowed.

There was no undoing the past. She couldn't stop Vince from leaving early and taking her son. She could only find him and make him pay for what he had done. He would tell her who had planned this, because she had too many suspects and not enough time. What time she had, she would use to her advantage.

Living as a Calvetti had given her insight into the world in which they lived. It ran like a business, much like any other, except Nick was a despot, not a CEO. Still, it had a chain of command that started with Nick and ended with Sammy C. While Eddie acted as personal bodyguard for members of the family, Sam Capadonna acted as vice president. His command was obeyed as swiftly as one from the head of the family. Nick trusted him implicitly, which meant Sam would be at the heart of the problem.

It was possible that Sam was running the business side of things during the crisis, but Sofia thought it more likely he'd be put to use on their number one problem: the territory dispute. If anyone knew where Eli was, it would be Sammy C, but Sofia couldn't get within a block of the man. Not unless she wanted to end up in her own private hell again. No, there had to be talk, someone with access who had heard stories or had a theory. Someone had to know where the threat originated.

Sofia needed to know, even if the threat came from

Vicki. The Russian mob had had a female head of family for years. Was Vicki attempting a coup? It was possible. Vicki had manipulated Nick to secure Sofia's freedom. Her best friend was a practiced people-reader, skilled in the art of manipulation, and adept at coming out on top. It had never occurred to Sofia that Vicki might use her powers for evil, but was the idea such a stretch? It would take little effort for Vicki to bend Vince to her will. Stronger men than he had fallen into Vicki's web.

And then there was Eddie. Seeing him at Vicki's had startled Sofia, because his main job was Nick's protection. He had no business that far from his boss unless he was working his own agenda, and that thought was terrifying. The man had more knowledge than anyone of the inner workings and schedules of the Calvetti family. If someone outside the family needed information and access, Eddie would be the man for the job, assuming he could be bought.

After living with the Calvettis, Sofia was convinced everyone had a price. She forced herself to relax against the seat as she released her thoughts and fears about Eli into the subconscious realm. Somehow, without her constant interference, her brain would make the connections and find the answers.

Instead, her mind focused on someone she was pretty sure couldn't be bought. Logan Stone. Her heart sped at the mere thought of him. Impossibly, this upright, by-the-book, strong man had kissed her. Not a shy kiss, or an angry kiss, but a full-on, I-want-you kiss that was so hot it had straightened the curls in her wig.

It had been too long since a man had wanted her. The kiss, along with the hard ridge pressed against her that showed the strength of his desire, was more than enough to increase her blood pressure. She wanted him, and no one could be more surprised than Sofia. Life had been about survival since long before she left Nick, and in the end, they hadn't even shared a bed. Since then, no man had interested her. No man was worth the risk, but with Logan... Desire heated her blood and tingled on her skin wherever he touched her. Right now, thinking about it, thinking about those toned biceps and a black T-shirt that covered a body she wanted to explore, a knot formed low in her gut.

How she could want a man so outside her sphere? A Fed no less. It was beyond reason. Her body had a mind of its own, because despite the risk, she wanted him with mindless abandon. Maybe because everything else seemed so hopeless. The attraction was something vital and primitive and life affirming at a time when she needed it. She wanted to lose herself in him, to hide in his strong embrace. She wanted to find herself in him.

The stewardess asked the passengers to pull their seats into the upright position and the cabin slowly stretched awake as Sofia lost herself in memories of one hot kiss.

The years with Nick had made Sofia paranoid. She knew that and tried to work around it. She tried not to worry about being followed and tried not to imagine a threat in every person that approached her. Her pulse rose as she left the gated area and the protection that the TSA checkpoint provided. Even here, in the mass of bodies disembarking the plane, she felt Logan's presence. He watched her and it added a different kind of excitement to the march through the airport. For once, she didn't fight the sense of being watched, she reveled in it. She added a little sway to her hips and a smile to her lips, wondering if Logan could see. More, she wondered if it got to him.

It was thrilling in an odd way, this cloak-and-dagger game she played with Logan as he kept pace behind her, to the right at the moment, behind a loud family with too many kids and not enough sense to keep them all together. Sofia had to slow down so she didn't lose him in the mass of bodies rolling toward baggage claim.

Over the years, Sofia had developed a knack for avoiding unwanted contact as she glided through a crowd, because contact could come in the form of a knife just as easily as someone trying to cop a feel. The crowd parted for her as the quick tap of her heels urged everyone out of her way. Logan kept dozens of people between them, even took an adjacent escalator to maintain the separation, but she still knew exactly where he walked. His energy was like a lucky charm she carried with her. She almost turned, just to see his face, but that would ruin the illusion of separation. Moments later, someone called his name.

"Hey, Stone, where's your girl?"

Sofia tripped on her heels. She double stepped to get her stride under control and looked around, trying not to panic. She always had an out, always found a loophole. She saw it ahead and to the right. A bathroom she knew had an exit on the other side. Ten steps and she'd be there, but she didn't know how much time she had before the man calling out to Logan recognized Sofia.

The stroll through the airport no longer felt like a game.

Chapter Nine

Friday, 5:13 p.m.

Jonathon Lowe was an eager lawyer turned agent that Logan had met at a conference last year. Even then the man had grated on his nerves, and it wasn't just his nasal tone. He was too caught up in his own hype. Today, his voice in the crowded airport was like the screech of a jet on the runway. Logan set his jaw and kept walking until the other man grabbed his arm. He turned as if he'd not heard Lowe calling him halfway through the airport.

"Lowe, what a surprise." His tone said it was anything but a pleasant one.

"Where is she?" Lowe repeated. He looked around the vicinity as if he half expected to see her here.

Logan's heart thundered. Where was Sofia, indeed? "Who?" he asked as though mystified.

"Sofia Capri. Isn't she why you're in town?"

Jesus, Logan hoped no one had seen her duck into the ladies' room. He didn't have to try to play stupid. "What are you talking about? I'm on administrative leave."

"Right." Lowe smirked.

"Really. I'm out of the loop."

"The golden boy on admin leave." His voice held an undercurrent of malice.

Logan had no idea what he'd done to offend the man and he didn't care. He just wanted information. "Drug bust gone bad," Logan insisted. He had no intention of explaining himself to the desk jockey. "Why would anyone call me in?"

"I heard you were a workaholic. I didn't think admin leave would keep you from getting your hands in this deal."

"What deal?" Logan's voice betrayed his impatience. It was like talking to a woman. He wasn't getting a single straight answer from Lowe.

"Sofia Capri."

Logan wanted to throttle the shorter man and get it over with. Either he was blown or he wasn't, and the more time he spent with an agent, the greater the risk. "What about her?"

"Her son was kidnapped."

"Calvetti's kid," Logan prompted.

"What, have you been living in a cave? It was all over the Bureau today."

Logan stepped out of the main line of traffic, away from the baggage claim, so he could chat one-on-one with Lowe and give Sofia time to escape. "I can't believe I'm missing it. Who's behind it?"

"Last I heard, your gal was behind it. Calvetti came in himself. Walked into the New York office and claimed his ex-wife kidnapped his son and what was the FBI gonna do about it."

Logan no longer worried about Lowe, but he had a strong urge to get his hands on Calvetti. The bastard. Setting her up for the kidnapping was a sure way to keep Sofia on the watch list. Calvetti had people on one side of the fence trying to kill her and the other half out to arrest her for kidnapping. Things had only gotten worse since last night's sniper. "Looks like I picked the wrong day to take time off."

For the first time, Lowe looked around the dwindling baggage area. "You going soft on us? Meeting a girl?"

Logan shrugged it off. "Family thing." It was true enough. It was a Calvetti family thing, and his aunt Bertha was waiting for him.

"I'll let you go, man," Lowe said. He clapped Logan on the back. "Stop in before you leave town. Catch some lunch."

"You got it." Logan bit back a groan as he headed to the taxi stand. Sitting still on the flight had made his ribs stiff and the bruises on his back from where he'd rammed the wall were tender as hell. Lowe's not so friendly slap on the back hit a few nerves. Logan wondered if the gunman last night hadn't cracked a rib or two, but Logan didn't have time for an X-ray. He needed to get underground. If Lowe made it back to the office tonight and mentioned seeing Logan, the Bureau and its none-to-shabby assets would descend on Manhattan. They'd pull the detail off Calvetti to look for his ex-wife, endangering Eli in the process. All of which freed Calvetti to shore up his territory in peace.

None of which took into consideration that Logan's own career would be over. Logan slid into the first available cab and sent the cabbie to an address near his destination as he worked damage control in his head. He hoped to hell Lowe took the weekend off like a good bureaucrat. Logan needed the weekend to finish this. They could work it out. By Monday morning, Eli would be with his mama and Logan would debrief his boss, assuming they were still alive.

• • •

Uncle Ernie hadn't sent the all-clear text yet. Sofia pulled on Jackie O shades and stared out the taxi window at the place she once called home. It left her flat. The buildings, the traffic, the bridge, they were nothing like the mountains and prairies of Colorado. These buildings and the anonymity they provided were a prison. As the taxi neared Manhattan, she felt the glass buildings close around her and her breathing went shallow.

She could do this alone, she promised herself. She had to. She had come to depend on Logan, on the thought of having backup, but she could get the job done with or without him.

It was possible he had been taken into custody. She regretted that. More, she felt a twinge of guilt. He should never have gotten involved. Still, she knew he wouldn't do anything to risk Eli. It's not that he'd promised. Any man could break a promise. He wouldn't because he wouldn't risk a child's safety. She trusted that. She trusted him.

And wasn't that a fine mess to trust someone?

A man. A man whose resemblance to Nick faded with each moment, with each truth that he told her. When he sent the all-clear text a few minutes later, it did little to ease her fear. The sound of someone calling his name in the airport was branded into her brain. *Where's your girl?* someone had asked. Had they meant Sofia? Or someone else? The last thought was almost as disconcerting as the first. She wanted answers, but had to wait. There were some things you couldn't ask in a text. Not unless you were absolutely certain who was on the other end.

The taxi pulled up to an entrance of the subway. The need to avoid a tail was so ingrained that Sofia didn't give her convoluted path a second thought. If someone were following her, she would know before she reached the relative safety of her hotel. This kind of paranoid backtracking was as normal to her as drinking coffee in the morning.

Sofia took a moment to compose her expression before paying the cabbie and stepping into the smog-filled air that was Manhattan. It had taken months to get used to that when she'd moved here with Nick, but now it covered her like a familiar blanket in which she hid as she descended into the subway. She took the next train three stops. She waited until the doors were ready to close before jumping out. No one followed her last-minute dash from the train, so she waited for the next train and took it another stop. She climbed out at dusk and walked two blocks to the nearest hotel.

The sidewalks were choked with bodies moving in every direction. The noise of the traffic added another layer of protection as she moved anonymously through the streets. Yet every jostle worried her. Who might be looking for her? And what would they do when the found her?

She entered the lobby, checked for a tail, exited out the side door before entering another hotel through a staff entrance. With each step she took, she wondered if Eli were in the city. Was Nick here? A fission of fear coiled through her suspicious brain. Was someone following her? The anxiety was a hazard of her former life. She made her way through the littered back halls to a crowded hotel bar.

Friday night. A few hazy looks met her gaze, but no one in particular noticed her. No one followed. She exited the way most entered, past a hostess stand and through glass doors into a lobby that belonged in New York. Glass walls, marble floors, and floral arrangements larger than her entire entry hall. It was the kind of thing that had seduced her when Nick first brought her to the city. The sense now wasn't one of awe. It was one of fear at being in the open. When she saw a familiar form, her heart convulsed.

Not Nick. Not the FBI.

Logan stood at the registration desk wearing his off-duty uniform of jeans and a T-shirt. From this angle, she saw that his hair was longer in the back, grazing the collar of his shirt, and she wondered, briefly, what it would feel like running through her fingers. Her wandering mind took in the play of his muscles even in relative stillness, and couldn't help but appreciate his strength. Her heart skipped another beat before racing ahead. Why was she so affected by him?

She was just glad to see him after the incident in the airport, Sofia rationalized. She adjusted the strap of the duffel on her shoulder and took a deep breath before stepping to another clerk on the far side of the registration desk.

The heels of her shoes clicked against the tile, but even that didn't draw his attention. Logan finished checking in and strode to the elevator without so much as a sideways glance, just as they'd planned, but she admitted to herself that she was disappointed—a little—that she hadn't seen his face. The worry she'd felt on the taxi ride had faded. She no longer cared how he'd gotten away or who had seen him at the airport. Those weren't the questions on her mind as she took the same elevator to the twelfth floor, walked down the same hall to a different room.

The question in her mind was if he had a girl. *Where's your girl?* a voice had asked.

Her heart thumped like she'd run a marathon. Why did it matter? Her breathing went ragged and it had nothing to do with the walk down the hall. It had everything to do with a kiss that never should have happened and the man in the room next to her. She unlocked the door, her hands trembling.

It was just a room, she told herself as she released a breath of unrealized tension. A typical room with one bed, one desk, and one fabulous city view. This view of the city had always been her favorite. She could see all of it, or most of it, from this isolated corner as she stared out the window wall. Gone was the fear of being observed. Here, she was the watcher. Sofia dropped the duffel on the bed and stared at the door to the adjoining room.

An adjoining door. That was new to her. She didn't adjoin anyone, and hadn't in years, but at this very moment, Logan was in that adjacent room. Waiting. She took a deep breath. The room was muggy from disuse. She turned the air conditioner down to rid the room of the humidity that was the start of a New York summer. The air turned on with a slight hum and Sofia moved on to more important matters.

There were too many thoughts running around in her brain. Eli. Logan. Almost getting caught. Not enough sleep. She didn't know where one ended and the other began. She didn't know what to do next. She went back to the desk — let her fingers brush the adjoining door on the way — her emotions conflicted. Or not.

Eli came first.

She made a few necessary calls from her burner phone. The first went seamlessly as she ordered a gun over the phone like a pizza. They would deliver it as part of room service. *A gun.* Sofia wanted to throw up. She gave them Logan's room number because there was no way she was allowing a gun in her room. It went as quickly as ordering from a catalog, once she'd dropped the right names and security codes. Sofia didn't want to think about it. When she hung up, she took a moment to ease the tension roiling around in her gut. As much as she hated guns, she dreaded the next call even more. She was about to put herself and another innocent at risk.

The wife of a mob boss didn't have many friends. An ex-wife even less. The women in her sphere didn't like her because of the power Nick wielded over their men. So in her time in New York, they had endured her presence with polite smiles and petty jealousies. New York had been a friendless place for her in the beginning, but she'd found ways past barriers. She had wanted friends and she'd slowly earned them. It was one of those ladies she called now. She didn't dare call the home phone, but thought the work phone might be safe if she didn't identify herself or the situation. She just hoped Juliana was still at work.

"Dayspring Spa. How may I help you?"

Tears clogged her throat at the sound of a friendly voice. "Hey," she said, her voice husky.

"Oh, thank God," Juliana said. "I was so worried about you." She paused, then her words hurried onward. "When you missed your appointment, Mrs. DePhillipo, I thought maybe something had happened."

Sofia breathed a sigh of relief. Juliana knew it wasn't safe to talk on the phone. "Do you have anything open tonight?" she asked.

"I can't."

Sofia heard the regret in the other woman's voice, but it was nothing compared to the disappointment she felt. She wanted to beg Juliana, but before she could, Juliana spoke softly into the phone.

"My husband is waiting to drive me home."

"Of course." Sofia understood. There was no way Juliana's husband would ignore Sofia's presence, or even allow his wife to take an extra client this late in the day. "Tomorrow?"

"First thing," Juliana promised. "Nine o'clock."

"Thank you," she said, her voice strained with a combination of regret and gratitude. Juliana risked a lot to see her.

"Be safe," Juliana said as she hung up the phone.

Sofia set her phone on the desk and collapsed onto the bed. It gave under her weight, sagging like her soul. One more night without Eli. Too tired for anything, including sleep, she wanted…

What she wanted was Eli without the complications of his biological father. She wanted her grandfather. She wanted her grandmother to rub her back and coo empty promises. She wanted her best friend who wasn't her best friend anymore. Hell, she wanted what she couldn't have, Sofia admitted.

The problems of life were beyond her capacity to handle alone. She pulled off the blond wig and set it carefully on the desk for the next day. Pulling off the disguise was like peeling away layers of body armor. She removed the thick layers of makeup to reveal the scrape and bruise from the bomb blast, and with it came the knowledge of how easily she could be broken. Her insides trembled. The thoughts beginning to coalesce in her brain didn't help.

She wanted comfort. From Logan. He made her want to bury herself in his powerful arms and let the world disappear. More, to trust him with the whole truth, something as foreign to her as the streets of Manhattan the first time she'd walked them. It wasn't such a big step, she told herself. Logan knew most of her secrets.

Sofia plucked off the fake lashes and scrubbed away the glue residue. He knew that she was a mob wife—an untouchable—a prisoner in her own home. He wasn't afraid of her or her ex. She couldn't remember a man who wasn't afraid of Nick Calvetti. That alone sent dangerous desires coursing through her overtired system. What she wanted was far more treacherous than a volcanic kiss in the pre-dawn light.

The shaking spread to her legs. She dropped to the bed and yanked off her stilettos. At the heart of it, she didn't want to think. She didn't want to be alone. Sofia took a deep breath that didn't bring the corresponding relaxation. The key to her situation was Logan. No strings attached. He was a workaholic. The only reason he'd come this far was to retrieve a missing child. When it was all over, he would go back to his work and her secrets would stay hers.

God, she even had to justify it to herself. She was too tired to worry about boundaries and consequences. Fact, she was too keyed up to sleep, and even when she tried, like on the plane, a host of nagging fears kept her awake. Fact, she was useless to Eli unless she got some sleep, and her tired brain offered up a quick and easy solution, guaranteed to unhinge her tension.

Sex.

It was reckless. She knew that. What was the worst that could happen? Nick could find out. Kill Logan. Kill her. Raise Eli.

Bad question.

Sofia bounced off the bed to pace the narrow passage between the end of the bed and the adjoining door. She couldn't be fatalistic. Nick didn't know she was in town. There was no need for him to ever find out anything happened.

If Sofia *let* anything happen.

No. Sofia stopped midstride. She was acting like a crazy woman. She dropped to the gray carpet for twenty quick pushups and even then, the trembling in her arms didn't ease. They were both adults. It certainly wasn't a hardship. The one kiss had freed her from years of isolation. She wanted—no, *needed*—the release his touch would bring.

Like the sweep of a magical wand, the justification put an end to the debate. Her breathing normalized. The tremors stopped. Sofia pulled the pins from her hair and combed it out with her fingers.

No more excuses. Sofia grabbed the stilettos and slid them back on her feet. They made her feel like an Amazon. She'd done what she could for Eli tonight. It was time to deal with the man on the other side of the door.

She rolled her shoulders and pulled open the door to the adjacent room and met a familiar gaze. It wasn't his face she'd been looking for earlier, she realized, but his eyes. The feel of men's eyes on her—for all the wrong reasons—was common for Sofia. She was used to pretending she didn't know, but the constant surveillance wore her down like a bad set of tires.

Until Logan's eyes.

One look at him and the stress in her shoulders melted. One look in his eyes and she felt safe. The look in them was pure Logan. Intelligent, you could almost see his mind whirring, making connections and deciphering clues. He'd showered, his hair still damp, and he wore a clean T-shirt and jeans, although he was barefoot, which seemed so very personal. Here was the Logan who was done for the day, unbuttoned and ready to unwind.

The room was dim. He hadn't bothered to switch on the overheads, so the only light was filtered in through the window. The dark made what she was about to do easier. She took a step forward, then another. Keeping eye contact, she eased the door closed behind her.

Logan didn't move. He watched as she leaned against the door with her hands trapped behind her. "My friend can't meet me until morning."

"I'm sorry. I know you wanted…" He stuffed his hands in his pockets. "My resources are dried up. If I go in, they'll keep me in."

"Then I'm sorry, too," she said. And she meant it. "Maybe you should just go in—"

"No." He paced away from her. "I won't leave Eli in the wind. I have a buddy I can call tomorrow, but that's another night—"

"Stop," Sofia said, touched that his worries matched her own. "I have to believe that he's safe until Sunday."

Logan paced like one of his comic book heroes in a cage, strong, but restless. He wore a few days' growth on his jaw that made him look untamed as he wore a path in the freshly vacuumed carpet. His tether was short with the bed on one end and the mini-bar on the other. Next to the mini-bar was a whiskey he'd poured while he'd waited.

She'd never seen him unsettled, not even when Nick could easily have killed him. It sent a shock of fear through her. "Something's wrong. Logan, what aren't you telling me?"

He stopped by the mini-bar and took a swallow of whiskey. Ice clinked against the glass as he set it back on the counter. He rammed his fists into his pockets before turning to face her. His brown eyes flared, then narrowed. This wasn't about Eli.

The kiss they had shared sizzled between them. The chemistry was like a physical presence in the room, and it was that tension that had him prowling like a caged predator. He wasn't sure what happened next, and Logan Stone always had a plan.

His uncertainty gave her courage and a sense of her own power. She'd already made her decision, minutes ago on the other side of the adjoining door.

"About that kiss." Her heart tripped, skipped a beat; raced ahead.

He paused midstride, looked back at her. The look on his face was desire. And regret. "Sofia."

"If you say you're sorry, I'm leaving."

He stepped closer, his gaze searching hers in the dim light. "This is wrong."

"Says who?"

"According to every code of conduct in the book."

"You're not an agent right now, Mr. Stone."

He shook his head to deny her. "As a man, then. It would

be wrong to take advantage of you."

She was the one taking advantage. "It would be wrong to ignore me. I can't take being invisible anymore."

"Ignore you?" He shook his head, yanked his hands from his pockets in defeat. "I can't get you out of my head." He stalked forward, braced a hand on either side of her face. "I smell the scent of you with every breath. Two rows away on a plane and all I can smell is *you*."

The beat in her chest flexed at the raw desire in his words, the tethered control in his tone.

He leaned into her, brushed the stubble of his beard against the soft skin of her neck. "The smell of you. Mystery. Sex. Woman. It makes me hard every time I breathe it in."

The rough admission sent the pulse jumping against the soft brush of his lips. She didn't dare touch him. Didn't dare fracture the moment.

He leaned in. "I knew you would be soft," he whispered as if speaking to himself.

He brushed a hand through her hair; let it rest on the curve of her neck where his lips had been. "When I heard you undress in that storage shed, I wanted to slide my hands where your clothes had been, feel the heat and the soft." He closed his eyes. "The wet."

His words unsettled the calm she'd pulled around her on the other side of the door. Her mind jumped five steps ahead to where his control snapped, to where he didn't whisper and tease. She wanted that snap. That loss of control.

"None of that can compare." He groaned and let his thumb rub the length of her neck. "To the feel of you."

The sound of him, the touch, spiked her nerves. Need twisted through her and he had yet to touch her the way she wanted, to use his hands as he did his words. She swallowed; wet her lips. "Kiss me." It came out a whisper, rough with a want too deep for one night.

He rested a thumb on her pulse, felt it hitch and hike as he watched her with eyes as smooth as fine whiskey, but there was a fire beneath the smooth to match the lava flowing through her veins. She rose up, exhaled the breath she'd been holding, and knew he felt the brush of it on his lips. She waited. A heartbeat. Two, before he took what she offered.

His lips devoured, shattering the calm in the little room, melting the distance between them. She gave back, tasted and nipped and just sank in, dropped into the moment, into Logan, into the kiss that thawed and heated and gave, just gave, everything. It became a heated battle of lips and teeth and tongues. She tasted the whiskey on his breath, but it wasn't the whiskey that intoxicated her. It was Logan.

The kiss was rough with need and anger—his and hers—that was nearly as palpable as the energy that charged between them. She was angry at the world, at Nick, at the past five years and she gave it to the kiss, let it fuel the fire.

Logan gave as good as he got, but he held his anger close, let it seethe under his skin as he fed on her. It was a different kind of anger, personal, angry at himself, at the situation, at her. At caving to the desire that flared, because she knew—*knew*—by-the-book Logan didn't break the rules and he was breaking them for her. It pissed him off more than a little. She felt it in the hard bite of his kiss and the tension in his tight shoulders, but he held it in check. Ice to her fire.

His hands lied as they touched her, barely skimmed the surface as if hard, cold Sofia might break if he let that anger bleed through his shields, but Sofia had lived too many lies and she'd have none of them now. If they were going to have this one night, she wanted it true.

She wanted the heat, the hardness, the *need* of him with every touch. And she'd take the anger, too, because it was honest.

She eased back, her breath shallow. "I'm not fragile."

The pupils in his eyes enlarged. His chest rose and fell in a rapid cadence with hers. He let his forehead rest against hers, never taking his gaze from her.

"*Touch* me. Really touch me," she said.

"I am." He rubbed a gentle hand across her injured cheek as if to prove the point, but restraint tightened his jaw.

She bit his lip, angry now, baiting. "I need it. The anger, the heat," the desperation, she thought; it had to be desperation because that's how she felt, desperate to touch and be touched. Challenging now, she leaned into him and ran her hands from his waist, up his chest—God bless the bench press—to his shoulders in a long, raw seduction. It was something she had wanted to do since the gym, though she'd have denied it. The flex of his muscles sent a thrill through her. She loved the hard strength of him as he braced against her.

He closed his eyes.

She tilted her hips, rolled them against him.

He lifted his hands to her body. They hummed with restrained power.

Anticipation fed her blood.

What if he didn't hold back?

What if *she* didn't?

She slid her hands under his shirt and let her cold fingers caress the warmth of his skin before she yanked the shirt off and it fell to the floor, leaving his chest bare to her touch.

His muscles flexed against her touch and he drew a ragged breath into his lungs.

She needed.

He needed.

That was enough. She leaned forward to whisper in his ear, "Don't take it easy on me."

He caressed up her sides until he'd lifted her arms overhead, against the door. His eyes snapped open with wicked intent as he grabbed her wrists and locked them together.

When he pushed her against the door, he owned her. He took her in a kiss that unhinged everything she had locked away.

Chapter Ten

Friday, 7:19 p.m.

The point—sex and no romance, now not later—came through like an All Points Bulletin. It pushed into the realm of fantasy, the ones he had when he watched her in kickboxing or running flat out on the treadmill. And she'd just given him permission to turn that fantasy into reality. He wanted to savor, not take her like fast food eaten over the kitchen sink, but he was starved for her so he gulped her down before he'd even begun to unwrap her.

He trapped her hands over her head, against the door, and took what they both wanted. A long, hard kiss that vibrated with frustration. Lips met and challenged, tongues tangled as Logan let himself slide into the sweet taste of her mouth and drown in the musky scent of her perfume. She arched, pitting his hardness against her heat, and then she upped the tension by wrapping a leg around his, the heel of the stiletto digging into his calf. He'd thought of little else since he'd seen her in those fuck-me shoes.

The woman didn't want him to hold back? Fine by him. The thought sent his body from willing and able to right-here-right-now.

"Don't. Move. Your hands," he ordered as he released her to explore the woman he had wanted for far too long. If she touched him, he'd be undone, and before that happened, he wanted to map every curve, every angle, every dip of her soft skin. He wanted to kiss every nerve without the repercussions of touching an untouchable. He knew this act would cost them. It was forbidden, in her world and his, and he didn't care. All he wanted was to hear her moan.

He fumbled with the buttons that had teased him since the kiss in the storage unit. Made him want to know, to see, to touch what lay beneath. Buttons the size of silver dollars lined her curves from hem to chest like landing lights for jets.

"The buttons." She panted, her breath faltering. "They're not real. The zipper—"

"I know." The buttons were for show, but they tempted him. The way they traveled from the hem at her knees.

Up her thighs. Over her hips. In at her waist. Until the final curve at her chest.

Slowly, he followed the feel of the big, wooden buttons down the length of her. He bent to the hem, lifted it, his hands following the path the buttons had taken, raising the fabric one tantalizing inch at a time. He eased his hands up her bare thighs, let his lips trail where his hands had explored, rubbed his bewhiskered chin on her exposed flesh.

The heels tilted her forward and revealed the long

stretch of muscle on her outer thigh that flexed beneath his hands. He moved the dress higher, over her hips, and teased the fabric of her underwear with a light touch.

Black lace.

"You're trying to kill me," he whispered.

"Never," she answered. Her hands dropped to his shoulders. Her legs trembled.

He left his hands at her waist as he rose to her. Her eyes were closed against him, but her skin was flushed in the dim glow of the city lights. He turned to lead her to the bed.

"No." She grabbed his hand, pulled him back. "Here. Now."

The panic in her voice unmistakable, he knew the bed was off-limits in the same way guns and ammo were out. His erection flexed, the tension increasing with the knowledge she didn't want it easy. She wanted it raw and fast. The urge to take her was as strong as it had been in the storage unit, but he wouldn't settle for anonymous. Not with Sofia.

"Then look at me," he said.

She opened her eyes. They had been hidden from him today—by distance and sunglasses and time—and he'd missed them. Missed the expressiveness.

Desire glowed in the enlarged pupils. He felt his own need flex against his jeans. With a knowing smile, she slid her hands down to unbutton his jeans and pulled the zipper low until she touched the hard length of him. He closed his eyes to fight the urge to lose himself in her touch. She nipped his earlobe as her hands got creative, sending him into an agony of need, but he didn't want to lose himself so quickly and give so little.

He grabbed her hands roughly to fight the urge to take

what she offered against the door, but sex—good sex—wasn't about taking. Not until she was hot and ready for him. Not until she begged. "No hands."

Her eyes narrowed but stayed on his face as he eased his hands around her backside between the lacy panties and the silk of her skin. He eased them down to drop at her feet.

Her chest rose and fell when he found the hot, sleek folds at her core. He dipped a finger and used the moisture to ease the friction as he once again circled her wet core. Her head dropped back against the door. "Please."

He teased between the wet folds, taking her to the edge before he pulled back. She clutched at him and moaned. He nearly came undone at the sultry sound of her moan. "What?"

"I. Need. You." Her eyes glowed with a desire so strong it burned.

"You have me," he rasped.

"In. Me."

Another time, he'd take her to the edge, make her wait, stretch it out for them to savor, but her moaning directive sent him over the edge. He lifted her against the door and she wound her long legs around his waist so he felt her wet and her heat and her soft body. They wanted, needed, together. Logan braced, entered her as she arched against him, against the door that rattled with every move.

Vulnerable and pliant in his hands, Sofia was as open as she would ever be to him. Maybe more than she was open with anyone. He fought his own need as he moved to her rhythm; eyes locked as he took her to the edge and let her fall.

She never took her gaze from him. Even when her head

dropped back against the door and her fingers dug into his shoulders. She cried out in her own release, eyes on him.

Then, and only then, did he allow himself to drive to his own release.

Now he had her, all of her, and there was no hiding.

The knock on the door woke Sofia like the hammer of a gun being pulled back. She tried to roll out of bed, but found herself trapped beneath Logan. They'd collapsed on the bed, after. Exhaustion had claimed Sofia before she could consider the ramifications of sleeping with a man. Not the sex. Sex was easy, but sleeping? That required intimacy.

The knock sounded again. No one knew they were in town. Or did they? Her heart raced into full panic mode without passing Go.

"Get up," she whispered.

He opened his eyes, and the crinkles around them winked into a deep smile. He leaned in for a kiss.

Sofia pushed him off and jumped up. "Someone's at the door," she hissed. She tugged her skirt over her hips and smoothed it into place. "Are you sure no one followed you?"

"Relax." He stood, rearranged himself and zipped his jeans. "I ordered room service."

"When?"

"Right before you came over," he said.

"Oh, well." Her heartbeat leveled off. "Ask who it is?"

He did.

"Room service."

Sofia's brain was beginning to wake. She obviously

hadn't been asleep long, but she'd been in deep. Waking disoriented and confused her.

"Just a minute," Logan answered. In a softer voice he spoke to Sofia. "It's just dinner."

"I can't be seen here," she answered.

"Last I checked, we were two consenting *single* adults."

"Not like this." She tugged at her tousled hair. "Not as Sofia."

He led her to the adjoining door and planted a soft kiss to her lips. "Fine, Aunt Bertha. Go hide in your room. I'll call you when the coast is clear."

"Wait." Her brain finally engaged. "There might be a special delivery with dinner."

He lifted a brow. "You're just now telling me?"

"My lips were otherwise engaged." She slipped into the other room, but not before he saw the blush spread across her cheeks. It took just a few seconds, but she used that time to wipe the sleep and the sex from her mind. She adjusted her skirt, ordered her heart steady and her face composed. She returned with an envelope from her duffel. "If he offers you dessert on the house, give him this."

"What?" Understanding lit his eyes as he took the envelope of cash. "The gun."

She nodded and pushed him out the door, back to his own room. "Hurry."

"Wanting to get me all to yourself?"

She shoved the door in his face. Sofia was waking up, the anxiety taking over once more. She had hoped the sex would insulate her from the fear, even if only long enough to sleep. It had, for the few minutes they had slept. Now that she was awake, the panic bubbled through her veins. She was ready to get this gun business over with. It was one of the calls she had made earlier. She had discovered the seller through Juliana. What neither of them could have known was that it was a mistake at the time.

No one would sell to Nick Calvetti's wife. Not without letting the big man know. Lesson learned the hard way. This time was different, she told herself. Logan was buying the gun, as far as anyone was concerned, but that didn't stop the angst fluttering in her chest. If anyone figured out that Nick Calvetti's *ex*-wife was behind the transaction, there would be no avoiding a confrontation. No one running weapons in New York would let it go. When she heard the door next to her clatter closed, she peered thru the peephole in time to see the back of the deliveryman. At the same time, Logan propped open the adjoining door.

"All clear."

Sofia swung towards the sound of his voice and without conscious thought, moved to him and laid a hand on her chest. "Did he have the gun?"

Logan pulled it out, rammed a clip into place.

The sight of it sent a wave of nausea through her. She stepped back. "Put it away. Please. I don't want to see it."

"You okay?"

No. She was most definitely not okay. She wanted to throw up, but she could fake it until she was okay. She'd done it before. "I just need a few minutes to clean up."

"Hurry," he said. "Don't let your dinner get cold."

That stopped her short. "You ordered me dinner?"

"Of course." The tilt to his eyebrows told her he was mystified by the question. "You're running on two days of little sleep and no food. You didn't even eat the airline peanuts."

"You saw that?"

He nodded.

The feeling of being watched irritated her so her words came out sharper than they might have otherwise. "I had coffee."

"Coffee is not a food group."

She still felt ill at the thought of the gun he held, so food held no particular interest, but she was being petty and she knew it. "I'll just go clean up."

"Don't be too long." He left the room but kept the door ajar.

She didn't bother to close it as she slipped into the modest bathroom for some privacy and a shower. The hot water soothed the exhausted ache from her shoulders. She let it pour over her head and visualized stress slipping down the drain. For meditation, she'd had better, but it helped even out the raw edges.

She was more relaxed when she stepped from the shower. What to wear, what to wear? The dress was out. She'd never be able to wear it again without thinking of Logan taking her against the door. Her cheeks flamed at the memory, so she tossed the dress into a laundry bag. She wasn't sure that particular memory was a safe one to keep. It would do no good to want in real life, to remember what had been and hope for more. There would be no repeat performance.

She wrapped a towel around herself and went to inspect the meager contents of her duffel. Nothing appealed to her. What she really wanted was a pair of oversized pajamas to lose herself in, but she'd forgotten to pack any, maybe subconsciously hoping to be back home before she needed them. So much for positive thinking.

"You can just wear the towel," Logan suggested from the other room.

Not going to happen.

But Sofia smiled. It wouldn't do to remember, but it was nice to be appreciated. It had been a long time. She went back to the bathroom and slathered on lotion before pulling on the hotel robe. It was two sizes too big, covering her from neck to calf. It was comfortable, a definite plus after a miserable day. She yanked a comb through her hair before following the smell of marinara to the adjacent room. He'd had the waiter set up the table near the window.

New York glistened like a black diamond. Even damaged as she was by her time in the city, she appreciated Manhattan at night. Somewhere out there, her son was sleeping. Alone. No Ellie the Elephant, no Mommy, no one but Vince. She sent a prayer into the Universe that Eli was safe for the night

"He's fine," Logan said.

The man managed to pinpoint her private thoughts as if he had a direct line. It was disconcerting. She'd gotten used to her mask and everything that separated her from the outside world. It was hard to let anyone into her private hell.

Logan lifted the lids off the dinner plates to reveal her favorite Italian dish.

"You know my favorite restaurant in Manhattan?"

He nodded.

"Please tell me that's not in a file somewhere."

Logan squeezed her hand. "Just enjoy it."

The FBI had as much nerve as Nick, following her around like she was the criminal. She wanted to be angry. She couldn't imagine how long the FBI had tailed her to know the tiny details of her life, including her favorite restaurant. Sofia took a deep breath. Logan had been trying to think of her. Creepiness aside, his gesture was sweet.

She'd been ridiculously charmed when he'd bought her lunch at Wal-Mart. It was one of those things a woman missed, without realizing it, until she had a taste of it again. It was a relief to have someone taking care of her. It was relief to have Logan.

Her heart flip-flopped a little, going all soft and gooey for the man sitting across from her, against all better judgment. Always against that, because caring for him, losing herself in him, was dangerous. The best outcome she could hope for was a return to her normal life.

Normal did not include a man like Logan Stone.

They ate in silence as Sofia savored the flavors of Little Italy. The spices, the raw ingredients… She groaned in delight. No one cooked like this anymore. No one in Colorado cooked like this, anyway.

It was nice to find a good memory of her time in the city. It was nicer still to add dinner with Logan to the short list of things she liked about New York, but it was riskier than the sex, which, despite the intense pleasure, was as risky as thermonuclear war. What were the words to that old song? Hurt so good?

She was giving more and more of herself to him. She trusted him and trust scared her. She was accustomed to taking care of herself since no one else was around to do it for her.

Logan did, her conscience taunted.

She took another bite of the best Italian food in the country, and allowed herself to enjoy the sensual pleasure of the food and the man. He was a good man and a fine-looking specimen at that. Sofia leaned away from her half-finished plate. "What is it with you and food?"

He chewed his chicken Parmesan. "You may be able to survive on coffee and breath mints, but I need something more substantial. As long as I'm eating, I aim to eat well."

"Do you cook?" She couldn't picture it.

"No. But my mom did. Does. She makes biscuits and gravy good enough to cure your coffee addiction."

It was weird thinking of him with a family. He seemed so solitary. "Do you see her often?"

"Sunday dinner, every other week."

The jealousy was short-lived, but deep. It's what she could have had with her grandparents if she'd stayed in Colorado. What she should have had, but gave up for Nick Calvetti and a life in the big city. The thing she resented most about her time with him was the wedge he'd slammed between her and her family. It was subtle, at first, how he let them know they weren't welcome in her new life. They were all she had. Now they were gone. She'd let him steal precious time from the people she loved.

Sofia pushed her plate to Logan as he finished his meal.

"You should eat," he said.

"I did," Sofia said. "I'm used to sharing with Eli."

Logan frowned at her, thought about it, left it alone. He twirled her spaghetti around his fork. "What kinds of things do you do with him?"

"Everything." Sofia didn't have to think. Everything revolved around Eli. He was the one unspoiled thing in her life. "Actually, this is the most adult interaction I've had in years."

"You get out every day. At the gym," he reminded her.

She shrugged. "I don't talk to anyone. I don't know who is safe to talk to. I don't know who is working for whom."

Logan pushed both empty plates back. "Like me."

"Like you." It didn't hurt so much now, knowing that Logan had been sent to spy on her, not when she counted on him to watch her back. Maybe what they had shared, what she wanted to share with him, was a mistake, but Sofia pushed forward anyway. "Most days, after my workout, I go home and watch Bert and Ernie with Eli."

"Bert and Ernie?"

"As in *Sesame Street*," she explained.

He shook his head. "As in Aunt Bertha and Uncle Ernie."

She smiled. She couldn't help herself. "I told you. I don't get out much."

"I'm feeling a lot less confidence in a plan where we're named after puppets."

The skin on her cheeks heated. "They're adored by children everywhere."

"Including Eli?"

"Especially Eli."

Logan walked around the table and pulled her to her feet. "I will do everything in my power to bring Eli back to you."

"I know." Sofia backed away from the contact. It was natural to be repelled by the thing she wanted most. "I know it now, that you will help Eli, but when we first met, I didn't trust you. I didn't know you and then I found out you were a Fed."

"And trusted me even less."

"That pretty much sums it up." She stepped farther from him, feeling the need for distance, but afraid the separation would become permanent once she finished this. There was one more thing she had to do and she looked forward to it like a trip to the dentist. Logan had risked his career for her, maybe even his life. The least she could do was trust him.

"There's something I need to tell you," she said, her voice jittery.

"You're really a CIA agent in deep cover to break up an international drug ring?"

She wanted to laugh, which was the point of his ridiculous suggestion, but it came out a demented snort. What she was about to do was going to hurt. She was going to tell the truth.

"Nicky was right. I *was* planning to disappear with Eli."

Chapter Eleven

Friday, 9:47 p.m.

The chicken Parmesan curdled in his stomach. "What did you say?"

"I was going to take Eli and run."

"Jesus," Logan muttered under his breath. What had he tied his future to? "Is this"—he gestured to the two of them—"part of the plan?"

"No. And yes." She shook her head against his harsh tone. "It got out of hand. Mixed up. You've got to understand."

"No. I don't." Logan had a nearly overpowering urge to pack up, wipe his prints clean, and leave before any more damage could be done.

She reached out to him but he backed away from her touch. Too much peril there.

Her eyes glistened with unshed tears. "Please. I'm trying to be honest. Let me."

The pain in her eyes was real and almost more than he could endure. Isn't that what had brought him here. Sympathy? "You have two minutes."

"When I first left Nicky, it was all I could hope for to be away from him. For Eli and me to be free. Safe."

Sofia turned her back on him, feasting her eyes on the glittering city below. The silence stretched on, eating up the minutes he'd allotted her. She cleared her throat before continuing. "They call it PTSD. Post-traumatic stress disorder."

"I know what it is. Get on with it."

She continued as if he hadn't spoken. "They come out of the blue, your demons, and hunt you down no matter how safe you think you are. They're just figments of your hyperactive imagination, except not all of mine were imagined. For every average Joe at the gym who got too close, there were just as many who reported to Nicky. Or the FBI."

He couldn't see her eyes. Couldn't know the depths of her despair or the extent of her lies. He couldn't trust her when his own instinctive response was to comfort her. He resisted that urge, forced himself to be cruel. "You brought that on yourself."

"You're right, of course." She placed her palm flat against the plate glass as she stared out at the city.

"It was worse, in some ways, than living with him. I didn't know who to trust, so I trusted no one. But I still had my grandparents. They were alive at the time, although I guess you know that."

He did. It was part of her file. Part of the personality profile. Beyond that, he remembered the lethargic workouts after her grandparents died, within weeks of each other, and how she'd seemed so lost.

"You don't know what it's like to be so alone," she whispered.

Logan heard the tears in her voice and stiffened his spine. He'd already let this unhealthy attraction sway him more than he should. He ticked off the crimes against her.

He'd gone AWOL. He'd aided and abetted. He'd forged documents. He'd purchased an illegal handgun. Logan forced himself to give no mercy.

"That's when Vince took pity on me." Her voice quivered and he imagined tears to match the despondency.

No mercy, he ordered himself.

"And I was so lonely, I let Vince break the rules. It was selfish of me." Her hand reached up and swiped at the tears he couldn't see. "We assumed Nicky knew. It would be ridiculous to think he didn't, but we didn't see a problem with it. We weren't the least bit friendly otherwise. All we did was play Scrabble on Sunday nights, the nights I used to spend with my grandparents.

"Eventually, he started cooking dinner before I came over. It was perhaps the most normal time in Eli's little life."

Logan thought back to his own childhood with a stay-at-home mom. No weapons. No bodyguards. He tried not to sympathize.

He failed.

"It started one night, midwinter, after my grandparents had been gone for several months. I came for our usual Sunday dinner. He had it spelled out in Scrabble tiles. *Do you want out*?

"He'd never been unkind. Never seemed the usual type Nicky hired, other than his size. But I was terrified of a trap. I left without a word. A week went by and we didn't speak.

The next Sunday, same thing."

Sofia rested her head against the clear glass.

Logan saw her reflection. Tears streamed down her cheeks. He felt the impulse to go to her, comfort her, but he needed to know how the story ended. "Your time is up."

She watched the city below with glazed eyes. After a moment, she continued in the same emotionless voice. "You don't know what it's like to go weeks without speaking to another adult. I had no one to trust and I did want a way out. Over several weeks, then months, we discussed options. Vince wasn't one of Nicky's usual bodyguards. He was just some poor dumb kid; no different than I had been when I married Nicky. He'd gotten involved in something way over his head."

"No," Logan said. She'd pushed her credibility too far. "You don't *accidentally* get involved with the mob."

She turned on him then, her eyes angry and red. "I had no idea what I was getting into," she hissed.

"I'm talking about Vince."

"Same difference," she muttered. She turned back to the plate of glass and the careless city below. "We all needed a way out. He was in just as deep as I was. No one left *the family*. There was never anything between us. He was only a few years younger, but I felt so old."

She swiped at more errant tears. "It was like a game. We didn't expect to win, but we played anyway. We bought fake passports a few weeks ago. What a rush. I could almost feel the freedom." Her laughter was bitter. "We hid them in Vince's apartment."

So she had been hiding something from him when they'd searched Vince's apartment.

"Mind you, we never spoke aloud, never wrote anything down. All in Scrabble tiles. It was all set."

"Europe," he said. She had needed a patsy to be her accomplice, to travel with her so she wasn't a woman traveling alone with a child.

She nodded. "You weren't my first target, you know," she whispered.

"What poor schmuck had that dubious distinction?"

"He was nameless and faceless," she muttered. "Safe."

Not safe. If a civilian had been with her when this started— Logan didn't want to think of the consequences. More, he didn't want to think of her with anyone else, and that thought was about as stupid as every other decision he'd made in the last thirty-six hours.

She turned abruptly and went to his whiskey on the opposite side of the room. It was watered down, the ice long since melted, but she drank it in one quick swallow. Her face creased in displeasure. She reached in the fridge to grab one of the little bottles and drank it straight.

"Sofia—"

"Let me finish," she rasped, her voice hoarse with whiskey.

The urge to go to her was stronger than logic, stronger, even, than self-preservation. He went and wrapped his arms around her.

Tears streamed unchecked down her cheeks. "Let me finish," she whispered.

Wordlessly, he nodded. He led her to the bed and sat with her in his arms.

"When it happened yesterday…"

Her face contorted in agony. The terror in her eyes

burned like looking straight into hell.

"It's the way it was supposed to happen in our plan, but it's all wrong. I'm not behind it. Someone else took Eli away. They're using my plan against me. I can't help feeling this is my fault. If I hadn't plotted this. Hadn't wanted more…"

"It's not your fault."

"The hell it isn't," she spat violently. "I plotted against the devil. I knew better. I knew better than anyone the consequences of my actions, and I still took them."

Logan couldn't follow her logic. She'd devised a plan, yes, but she hadn't acted. He'd been on the receiving end of her attempt. Logan smiled at the memory of Sofia, flustered and uncertain, trying to convince him to go to Europe with her. As if her wanting it would somehow bring it to fruition. She had a plan, yes, but she hadn't the skill to implement it. "It's not your fault, love," he said.

"Don't call me that." Fresh tears streamed down her cheeks. "You're not nameless and faceless," she said. "You're not safe."

"Why would you want that?"

"Safe?" she said. "It's all I want, all I've ever wanted. I can't ignore you and I can't control you and I…"

She closed her eyes, but not before he saw the agony.

"I can't pretend you mean nothing to me," she whispered.

For the first time since she started her story, Logan's anger diminished. That one sentence was the only truth he needed. He meant something to her. What he couldn't think about was what he felt for her. It was risky territory. He needed to think about this rationally. "If this is true, the plan starting with you, I needed to know it earlier," he said. "It would have saved us time in Colorado if I knew."

"I couldn't tell you."

"You should have trusted me."

"Trusted the Fed assigned to watch me?" She spat it like a curse. "You would have judged me by who I married. You would have made different choices and left Eli to suffer for my mistakes."

"You don't know that," he said.

"I know men like you, just like I know Nicky. If I had told you after the kidnapping, after the bombing, you would have hauled me in like the law and order man you are. I couldn't risk my son."

"That's conjecture," he objected.

"It's the truth. Yesterday, all I knew was that you were a Fed sent to spy on me."

That stopped Logan. Yesterday was a lifetime of choices ago. Even he didn't know what he would have done. If he wasn't sure of himself, how could he expect her to be? His tone softened. "Who knew about your plan?"

She dropped her head to his chest with a defenseless thud. "No one. Just me and Vince and our Scrabble tiles, and even Vince didn't know when I planned to leave."

"And Vicki?" he added.

Her tears damped his shirt. "I can't believe she would hurt Eli."

Logan kept Vicki on his suspect list, silently, as he didn't want to add to Sofia's distress, but that didn't stop Logan's brain from working. Someone knew, and was using, Sofia's plan. Vicki was tied up in this, but there were more involved. He didn't know the motive, but he would. All they had to do was figure out which someone Vicki was working with.

He felt Sofia's surrender in his arms. She was numb, all

but empty in his arms as her eyes drooped into sleep. He let her go. They both needed all the rest they could get.

Logan reached for the warm body that no longer shared his bed. He shook off the fog of sleep and the disappointment that she hadn't stayed. Not that it surprised him. He didn't imagine Sofia's rigid life left her open to sharing a bed. But he had hoped.

As fast as it was, he was falling for her. Stupid, risking his life and his career, but regretting what already *was* was pointless. He cared for her. Her early morning absence left a hole, more than in the bed. He turned to see the time on the digital alarm and found himself staring into the barrel of a gun. Logan sat up, sleep and regret vanished.

Sofia sat in a chair facing the bed. How long she had been there was anyone's guess. She wore the blond wig and new clothes.

She was the Ice Queen again, her eyes hidden behind sunglasses she didn't need. "Never say no one can take your gun. That kind of arrogance will get you killed."

She ejected the clip like a pro, tossed them on the bed, and walked from the room.

The door *clicked* closed before Logan's body mobilized. In all the operations he'd worked, he'd never had a woman pull a gun on him. At least not one he knew. Doing it right after sex was a sure way to emasculate a man. And she knew it.

Logan jammed his legs into a pair of jeans, but by the time he made it to the hall, she was long gone. He didn't think. He didn't second-guess. He packed his duffel, wiped the room clean of prints, and shut the door just as quietly, and as firmly, as she had. He was done. Despite evidence to the contrary, he was a good agent. He liked his job and most days, he was good at it. At the moment, he had a humbling feeling he'd been played.

She'd taken his weakness, the memory of losing a kid, and used it to involve him in something that could cost him his career. All for a woman who had planned to kidnap her own son. She'd lied to him, manipulated him, and pulled a gun on him.

Damn. He was having one hell of a bad week.

As Logan waited for the elevator, wounded pride and anger aside, he realized that he didn't want to believe she was the mastermind behind the whole twisted plot. Sofia seemed genuinely worried about Eli. Even if he didn't want to believe it, her behavior didn't give him much choice. The woman was the opposite of too much information.

In most cases, he condensed an overload of information into a cohesive picture. From a wide range of sources, he gathered evidence, pieced together a timeline, and uncovered the truth. With Sofia, he never had enough information to make an informed decision. He didn't have evidence. The only reason he was 100 percent sure of the timeline was that he was there. He was no closer to the truth now than he had been forty-eight hours ago.

Intellectually, he applauded her actions. Her exit strategy in Colorado was worthy of a professional. Getting out of town and staying off the radar were handled with a precision he envied. The woman had skills. He understood her choices, even her evasiveness. It's not like she knew who to trust. He understood, except the gun. The gun made no sense.

The elevator opened. Logan rammed the button for the lobby. Sofia was an overfilled balloon, leaking information only when she'd reached max capacity and needed to decompress. Sooner or later, she would explode.

He knew her profile. She was a loner, but highly intelligent. It wasn't just about trust. Sofia wanted to control the information and the outcome. She didn't want to share.

Fine. As far as he was concerned, he was out. He needed more than she had given him. He didn't know which end was up in this case. He didn't have a clue which suspect in this cast of misfits had kidnapped Eli. Maybe it was Sofia, maybe not, but she hadn't given him room to maneuver.

As the elevator slowed upon reaching the lobby, Logan knew he was making excuses. He was connected with Sofia, and if it hadn't been for the wake-up call with the gun, he'd still be in deep. The only thing that had changed was the knowledge that if it came down to it, Sofia would let him twist in the wind. That's all he needed to know.

He'd been stupid enough for long enough. It was time to haul his ass in and let the fallout to his career begin. All this he decided before he hit the lobby with his duffel, a burner phone he didn't want to use, and a gun he hadn't obtained legally. He breezed through the lobby wearing sunglasses. The less evidence he left behind, the better.

Outside in the hot summer sun, he paused to get his bearings.

"What did she say to get rid of you?"

Vicki had followed him out of the lobby. The wannabe gypsy with her flowing skirts and costume jewelry sidled up beside him like a car double parked.

He didn't look down at the five-foot nothing con woman. "I don't know what you're talking about."

"But I do. Know what I'm talking about, that is." The slight woman rummaged through an oversized bag until she found a pair of sunglasses, which she put on against the harsh light. "I watched her leave half an hour ago. I know that look."

"If you saw her, why aren't you snapping at her ankles instead of mine?"

"I am not some annoying ankle-biter. Sofia is my best friend. I know her. She wasn't in the mood to talk." Vicki twisted a finger against her temple. "Woman thinks she has to do it alone."

"Nothing stopping her," Logan muttered.

"That's what I was afraid of. You and I have to talk."

"Lady, I don't trust you."

"That's a shame, because I'm starting to like you, Logan No-Name. Come on." She wrapped her arm through his, her bracelets clanging against his arm. "Let me buy you breakfast."

"I'm not hungry."

"I doubt that. I know Sofia. There's no way she slowed down to eat this morning, but a man like you needs sustenance."

"Woman needs to eat more," he admitted grudgingly. He let himself be led along, mostly to see where the mob sister was trying to mislead him.

"There, you see, we do have something in common. Concern for Sofia."

"Wrong," Logan intoned. "Right now, the earth could swallow her whole and I wouldn't lift a finger to stop it."

Vicki's laugh was like a clear bell. "Liar. It's why I like you, by the way. Because you *are* concerned for her."

"Not anymore."

"See, she did do something to frighten you away."

"I don't frighten," he said.

"I could have predicted this." She led him into a bagel shop and ordered for both of them when the server appeared. "I hope you're not offended. It's more expedient that way."

"It's your dime," he said. He leaned against the metal chair.

"I don't know what Sofia sees in you. You don't talk much, do you?"

"And your friend Vince does?"

She gave him a wicked smile. "Vince has other charms."

The server set down a basket of bagels, cream cheese, and two cups of coffee.

"Where is your friend Vince, by the way?"

"The blueberry is fantastic," she said, smearing cream cheese on half a bagel.

She didn't bother to answer his question, but she didn't deny it either. Vicki knew Vince's location.

Logan leaned back with his cup of coffee.

"Go on, eat. Sofia hasn't spoiled you on her caffeine-only diet, has she?"

"I'll eat when you stop playing and give me something I can work with."

"I'll bet I could, play you, that is." She winked as she bit into her bagel.

Logan shoved his seat back from the table. "Thanks for the coffee."

"Oh, fine." Vicki set her bagel back on her plate. "If

you're going to steal all the joy from it."

"Talk."

Vicki wiped bits of cream cheese from her mouth onto a napkin. "Sofia did *whatever* it is that she did to get rid of you because that's her nature. She didn't mind using you to get Eli when she didn't know you, but when she started to care for you…?"

"Woman's soul is too black to care about anyone but herself," Logan corrected.

"Wow, she must have done a number on your ego. Wouldn't care to dish, I suppose?"

Logan glared over the rim of his coffee cup. He didn't understand how Sofia and Vicki were friends. Two more different women he could not imagine.

"Fine," Vicki acquiesced. "Sofia had no choice but to get rid of you so you wouldn't get hurt in this whole fiasco."

Too late. "You're saying she did *whatever* this morning to protect me. Pardon me for raising the bullshit flag."

"It worked." She nodded to the duffel at his feet. "Your bags are packed, honey."

Hell, Logan thought, that sounded like Sofia. She'd certainly picked the most effective route to the job. His balls were still shriveled from having her pull a gun on him while he slept.

"What's more," Vicki continued, "that's why I know she would never have followed through on the plan to take Eli."

"You knew?"

"Obviously, but you already guessed that. The plan keeps her sane, it's what gives her hope, but Vince and I both knew Sofia would never do it. As long as Nick's alive, she's bound to him. No plan and no amount of self-defense classes are going to change the fact that she fears him more than death.

"What's more, she wouldn't have risked Vince that way. She might, and it's a big might, take the risk for herself, but she would never endanger another."

The sister-in-law was right. Logan slammed down his coffee and grabbed a bagel. He should have figured that one out for himself.

"How long have you been following Sofia?" she asked.

"Long enough."

"Long enough to know that what I'm telling you fits her profile?"

"What else?" he growled.

Vicki tore off a bite of bagel and chewed it thoughtfully. She swallowed a sip of coffee before continuing. "You know, it would be so much easier to have this conversation with Sofia."

"Then why aren't you?"

"Because she left with a don't-fuck-with-me look on her face. She wouldn't have listened to a word I had to say."

"And I will?"

"Maybe. Maybe not. Too soon to tell."

"Just spill it."

Vicki took her time doctoring her coffee. She added sugar, then creamer. Tasted. Added more sugar.

"You like to be in control," Logan guessed.

"You have no idea."

Logan wasn't sure any information she had was worth it. The woman was a pain in the ass. Self-assured beyond her abilities. Cocky, he'd call her, and she wore her background like a badge, and not one that shamed her.

He finished his bagel and grabbed another from the

basket. "I'm a patient man, sister to the mob, but you've reached the end of it."

"Fine. Mostly it's just an observation about my brother's habits. You see, normally he has multiple conversations a day with his second-in-command."

Sofia had said something to the same effect. "Sam Capadonna."

"The one and only." Vicki smiled brightly. "Thing is, not only have they not spoken, but I haven't seen Sammy C since I've been back in New York. That's news."

"Where do I find Capadonna?"

"If I tell you, what are you going to do with that information?"

"Verify it with a source I trust."

"Then there is no need for me to tell you how to find the man. That way, I haven't broken any rules, and you still have all you need to set your investigation on the right path."

"How do I know you're not trying to misdirect me?"

"Honey, you weren't on any direction but out."

He resented the truth in that statement. He set down the unfinished portion of his second bagel. "Lady, I still think you know more about this than you're saying. I don't trust you."

"Feeling's mutual," she assured him. "But I am equally certain that you care for Sofia, and since I would risk anything for her—"she shrugged—"our mutual protection of Sofia is all the assurance I need."

Logan needed more than mutual assurance. He needed solid evidence. The number one problem with this investigation was the fact that he'd been reacting from the second the bomb went off. That was about to change.

"One more thing," Vicki said. She'd set her bagel aside and added a lid to her coffee. "There's still a little boy out there. Be as mad as you want at Sofia. She can take it, but don't make Eli suffer for it."

"Don't try to push my buttons," he warned.

"Touchy," she said. "Can't blame a girl for trying."

"But I do," he said, because deep down, it worked. The same thing that got him involved was keeping him involved. Vicki manipulating him didn't change anything, because no kid deserved to die. Not like this.

• • •

The search for information took Sofia on a circuitous route through the city. Going from bus to cab to subway, paranoid backtracking along the route, all in an effort to avoid surveillance from a man who may or may not know she was in the city gave her the shakes. Sofia didn't need any help in that department. Thanks to a coffee shop on every corner, she'd had several hits of caffeine in the last two hours and far too much time to think.

She'd gotten, by her estimation, seven hours of sleep. Enough to think rationally, but logic didn't come easy. She spent her trip second-guessing every decision she'd made up to and including last night. If she were honest with herself, she would admit that she had been attracted to Logan from the moment she laid eyes on him, on the treadmill across the cardio room when he first joined the gym, but she made a point of never being honest, especially with herself.

Last night had been about sex. And sex never made things easier.

Today wasn't looking much better. Seeking Juliana was a risk. Nick had made sure Juliana knew what he would do to a woman who crossed him. Added to that, anyone who knew Sofia and Nick would seriously consider giving her over to Nick. Not because they hated her, Sofia tried not to take it personally, but because they feared him.

Turn Sofia in; get rewarded. Help Sofia; get the mother of all paybacks. Not a tough decision for most people. The risks made Sofia clench a fist so tight her nails drew blood on the palm of her hand, but facts were facts. She didn't have another option.

The blond wig gave her some comfort. The houndstooth pantsuit provided more cover. She didn't look like Sofia Capri.

She walked briskly past the front of Juliana's salon. No men loitered near the entrance, nor were any visible through the windows, but Sofia wasn't your average paranoid. After a single pass, she circled back, coming through the alley, making certain it was clear. Finding no obvious signs of testosterone, she made her way to the front. The moment the door closed behind her with a gentle *whoosh*, the outside world ceased to exist. No city sounds, no pollution, just cool air with a hint of eucalyptus, New Age music, and dim lights. The aura was calm enough that Sofia took a bracing breath that eased the nerves in her tight jaw. She gave a false name to the receptionist. "I have a nine o'clock with Juliana."

The petite brown-eyed girl smiled. "Have a seat. She'll be with you shortly."

As with anything she'd done in the past forty-eight hours, the risks in visiting a place she was known to frequent were harsh. If the FBI knew her favorite restaurant, then they knew this place. As did the Calvettis. She grabbed a magazine from the side table before her brain could conjure up a worst-case scenario that sent her running. It was as safe as it could get, which wasn't saying much.

The magazine chronicled the mini-dramas of celebrities Sofia didn't follow. She turned the pages, pretending to be engrossed, while every moment, she counted each person in the room, everyone who entered from the outside, and everyone who moved through the private spaces in the back. The slick pages of the tabloid shook with the combination of caffeine and nerves. She set it back on the table.

To her great relief, the receptionist called her alias and led her to one of the treatment rooms. Shortly after, Juliana burst into the room like a petite hurricane.

Without a word, Juliana grabbed Sofia into a whirlwind hug. "I was so worried," she mumbled. The last time Juliana had seen her, Sofia had needed more than a touch-up. She'd needed a complete makeover to hide the effects of Nick's cruelty. Sofia had been too mortified by her own weakness and concerned for her friend's safety to come back.

Yet here she was, in the woman's arms while she patted Sofia's shoulders like one might a child. Juliana leaned back and lifted her hands to embrace Sofia's face. She kissed her once on each cheek while her round eyes swelled with sympathy. Sofia didn't respond, not afraid of listening devices, a real threat, but afraid of collapsing. It would be so easy to relax in the comfort of a familiar embrace, but so much harder to walk away afterward.

Their gazes met, and Sofia saw her own fears mirrored in Juliana's expression. Both sets of eyes watered. Juliana, a petite brunette who barely reached five feet tall, was the first to blink. She led Sofia to a private room with a pedicure station. Once settled, they began a conversation on paper. Aloud she said, "Which color do you prefer?"

Sofia looked at the selections and chose a deep metallic purple before taking off her shoes, rolling up her slacks, and letting her feet soak in a hot soothing bath. Juliana began the pedicure, stopping at opportune moments to answer the questions that Sofia wrote on a notepad. It went against all she had learned to put questions like this on paper, there was a reason it was called a paper trail, but there was no other way to communicate in the small salon.

While Juliana scrubbed and polished, she painted a word picture that terrified Sofia. Shortly after Sofia returned to Colorado, the power structure shifted. Where once the Calvetti family ruled, now doubt fermented into something dangerous for all the families they knew.

Change. Someone was challenging Calvetti power. At first, it was a neighborhood here, a business there, suddenly under the protection of a new family. No one knew who ran it. Sofia leaned back against the massage chair. Change of this magnitude came with a price. Violence and bloodshed. Loss.

Eli.

The ache in her chest magnified. She still had another day, Sofia reminded herself. Despite the worries, and because she needed to think clearly, Sofia forced herself to relax in the routine of the familiar. Here she felt safe enough to think through the situation rationally.

Juliana was a friend. She had nothing to gain and everything to lose by talking to Sofia. It occurred to Sofia, too late to do anything about it, that the same was true of Logan.

He had everything to lose by helping her. Her behavior this morning had been cruel and petty and beneath her. She added it to her long list of transgressions. Guilt nagged at her.

She wanted to rationalize her behavior. Alleviate some of the guilt and place it back on Logan. Like all men, he thought guns solved problems. They did not. They created more than they solved. The first real lesson she'd learned when she'd tried to leave Nick was to never, ever, arm your enemy.

Logan had told her the first day that no one ever took his weapon. She wanted him to understand that that attitude could get him killed. That's what she had been trying to show him. If it took their minds off the sex, so much the better for both of them.

Juliana clucked as she buffed the calluses from Sofia's feet. The whirr of water and the smell of bath salts soothed Sofia. Being in this place where she'd once spent so much time showed her a small picture of normal, which was a million miles from her current life.

Since Eli went missing, it hadn't mattered to Sofia who she hurt or lied to or damaged in the process. All that mattered was Eli. She didn't regret anything she'd done to get Eli home safely, but there was no purpose for the gun incident. Sofia took a deep breath. Determination was important. It's how she'd escaped. What she had lost in the last two years was her strength. Anxiety kept her in line better than any threat Nick had ever made.

Her treatment of Logan was grounded in hideous, ugly, debilitating fear. She'd treated him badly because Nick had treated her badly. Suspicion and despair were a byproduct of her life with Nick, even after she'd fought so hard to free herself from him. It wasn't the same as the daily fear of living with him. It wasn't as intense, but it was insidious, affecting all her encounters and every action she took or did not take. It angered her that she still let Nick dictate so much of her life.

Making friends was complicated. Were they informants? FBI or mob? Take your pick. The truth was people did watch her. Living in a glass house left her close to shattered.

Juliana tapped her calf. "Just about done, hon." On paper she wrote, *You OK?*

Sofia shrugged. She was beyond the tears she wanted to cry. No one could survive living so isolated. If she made it through this, things would change. They would have to. Just as she'd reached out to Juliana, she could reach out to others and rebuild her life.

She couldn't live in fear.

Friendship was a necessary part of life. Maybe the watchers were as well. That didn't mean she had to be alone. She couldn't live a lie anymore. She would learn to trust again. Nick wouldn't take that from her.

Juliana led her to the drying lamps and Sofia slid her feet under the lights. She didn't have much time. There was one last question that needed an answer.

On the paper she scrawled a single word. *Who?*

Horror flashed in Juliana's eyes.

He has my son, Sofia wrote.

Still, Juliana resisted putting a name to the ugliness. Instead, she wrote a question.

Do you remember what they said that night they brought me to you?

Sofia remembered the night she desperately wanted to

forget. Nick's words were indelibly etched on her brain, but that's not what Juliana would remember. They brought Juliana later. That's when Eddie had pleaded, "*Don't provoke him, Miss Sofia*." The other enforcer in the room had muttered in anger as he walked out the door. "No one will do this to a woman," he had said. Sofia froze, her gaze transfixed on Juliana. "*When I'm in charge of the family*," Sofia whispered as she remembered what had been said. He had as good as admitted his plans.

Juliana nodded.

Sofia closed her eyes, feeling foolish that it had taken so long to figure out. Who knew enough about Nick's business to get to Vince? Who did Nick trust with protection? Who had as good as said that he planned to take over the family?

Chapter Twelve

Saturday, 10:00 a.m.

Who had the motive, the means, and the opportunity?

Sam Capadonna. Nick's right arm.

It made sick sense.

Sammy C had been Nick's father's second-in-command. No doubt he thought himself the best choice to take over the family business when the old man passed away. Add to that, Sam knew Nick well enough to know that Eli was a weak link. Eli wasn't protected and he wasn't in New York where Nick could keep an eye on him. Eli was vulnerable, and Sofia's plan to escape had given Sammy C the opportunity to put Nick over a barrel.

No one leaves the family.

When Nick had fought to keep Eli, Sam had misunderstood. He took Nick's determination as an emotional attachment. Sam didn't realize that Nick had no true affection for his son beyond ownership. Sofia's stomach rumbled with nausea. Sunday night, when Nick didn't cede, Sam would be enraged. He would kill Eli, and Nick would keep his precious honor.

Not. Going. To happen.

Sofia stood. She gave Juliana a hug. "Thank you," she said. Emotion choked her voice, narrowing it to a mere whisper. Juliana risked much to talk with her. Sofia would never forget.

Juliana grabbed the paper one last time. *What are you going to do?*

It's better you don't know, Sofia wrote.

But Sofia knew exactly what she was going to do. She was going to get her son.

Sofia chose her seat on the train carefully. Next to her was a man in a suit absorbed in something on his laptop. He looked up expectantly when she sat down. When she didn't engage in conversation, he turned back to his laptop. Next to and behind her were women a few years younger than her jabbering innocuously about their Saturday night plans. Just a group of single girls out for some fun. Nice, safe seat companions.

Where Sofia's plans went awry was a half an hour into the trip when her seatmate exited the train to be replaced by what she called a snorer. Within five minutes of sitting, the man was fast asleep, snoring at noxious levels. The women behind her giggled and gave her sympathetic looks. Sofia shrugged. The snores rattled her a little, but only in the way they would annoy the average traveler.

Snores and all, this was the most peaceful mode of transportation. Planes made her frenzied because she was trapped in a closed space for hours without possibility of leaving. A train, however, made frequent stops. If she needed to get off she could, but there was no need for the on-again-off-again antics this trip. Not a single one of Nick's associates bothered with the Long Island Railroad.

It gave her time to think.

Sam had been with the family for decades, which was probably why he felt entitled to lead it. His association with the family had made him nearly as wealthy as the Calvettis. He had several homes and businesses of his own. He owned a small construction company, interests in a garbage company, stables, a restaurant and more that Sofia couldn't remember and would never be able to track down in one afternoon.

Sofia was betting on Sam's house in the Hamptons. The reasoning was sound. He wouldn't keep Eli in the city because it would be too easy to be seen and too easy to lose control. By keeping Eli under guard in the country, he ensured that no one took them by surprise. The house had an excellent security system complete with motion detectors and video surveillance. There would also be plenty of armed guards.

Any attempt to extract Eli would lead to bloodshed.

So Sofia was betting what precious time she had left on Eli being on Long Island. Certain she had the right man and the right place; Sofia concentrated on the next part of the plan.

How to approach Sam? She couldn't exactly sneak onto his estate. Security notwithstanding, she was wearing a designer suit and Louboutin heels. She'd bought them as a form of camouflage, not for hand-to-hand combat. They didn't exactly give her freedom of movement.

It made the most sense to deal with Sam directly. He never had anything against her, except when he counseled Nick to kill her and be done with it, but that was business. As her defection had given him cause for his coup, he owed her the courtesy of a civil conversation.

The next problem was her disguise. No one save Logan knew what she looked like as a blond bombshell, and she intended to keep it that way. If she managed to get out alive, she'd need the blond-haired aristocrat disguise to do so safely. She looked back at the women plotting their weekend. They were dressed casually in everything from miniskirts to skinny jeans. Sofia got a rough estimate of their sizes before she turned in her seat. She twisted to face the women, knelt with her knees on the seat and her arms resting on the seatback.

"I don't suppose you want to trade?" she said, motioning to the snorer.

"He's all yours," one of them answered.

"Gee, thanks. How about a different kind of trade?" Sofia unbuttoned her jacket, removed it and turned it for the women to see. My suit coat for..." She pointed at a woman wearing a trendy denim button-down. "Your jacket."

The brunette rubbed her fingers on the label. "That's Armani."

Sofia smiled. "It's so last year."

The women laughed. "Are you serious?"

"Absolutely."

"You didn't steal it, did you?"

Sofia laughed. Not that she was above it, but no, she'd paid for it. "My ex bought me this suit. We just broke up. I can't stand to wear it a minute longer."

The woman whipped off her jacket and handed it over before Sofia could change her mind. Sofia traded the Armani without regret.

Emboldened by the feel of the jacket, the woman pointed at the other half of the suit. "What about the pants? He buy them, too?"

"As a matter of fact…" Then Sofia shook her head. "Better not. You're wearing a skirt, and where I'm going, that just wouldn't work."

"What about Gina? She's about your size."

Gina, the one wearing the skinny jeans, shook her head. "No way. I love these jeans."

The friend with the jacket gave her arm a whack. "It's *Armani*. I'll buy you new jeans."

"I do not want to wear half a suit."

"Oh, well," Sofia said. "It was worth a try. Thanks for the jacket."

She slid back into her seat and let the women work it out amongst themselves.

"Gina, don't be a jerk. Do you know how much this suit costs?" one of them whispered.

"I don't really care. I like these jeans. Do you know how much *they* cost?"

"I said I'd buy you a new pair."

"And what else?"

The other woman paused. "You really know how to piss me off."

"You know what I want," Gina taunted.

"Fine. I'll buy you a new pair of jeans *and* you can have my skirt."

"Deal."

A moment later, Sofia felt someone tap her shoulder.

Sofia turned to face the woman whose jacket she now wore.

"Um, I'm Denise, by the way. We changed our minds if you're still interested."

"Sure, why not?" she said casually. It was amazing what friends did for friends.

"How do you want to do this?" Denise asked.

Sofia glanced around the compartment. The snorer was still out and had driven everyone else forward in the car. Sofia gestured to several empty rows behind them. "It's just the bottoms. I think if we changed back there, no one will get a cheap peek."

Gina frowned. "Won't we get arrested?"

Sofia laughed. It would be her luck to escape Nick and avoid the FBI just to get arrested for flashing. "I'm sure women trading clothes in the backseat is the least this rail car has seen."

The logistics were easy enough. Between stations, the three women cycled through the back rows until Denise wore Sofia's Armani pants, Gina wore Denise's skirt, and Sofia wore Gina's skinny jeans. All in all, a successful trade.

The entire transaction lasted ten to fifteen minutes at the most, but it was more fun than haggling at an estate sale. It was hard to admit how much fun those few minutes had been for her. These women, only a few years younger than her, were so unburdened by life. It lifted her spirit just being with them. She also felt more at ease wearing jeans. She would have loved to kill the heels as well, but none of the women wore her size. It worked out as it was supposed to, she thought. She really did like the shoes. They just weren't practical.

As the train eased into a station, Sofia stood. "This is my stop. Thanks again."

Denise thanked her and they all waved. Sofia walked several car lengths as if she were headed to the station before entering another car. She liked the women, but it was no good giving them too much information. If someone asked what she looked like, they would merely say *blond, about my size*. If someone asked where she got off, they would mention this stop, not her real stop. That vague knowledge is what kept them safe.

Sofia had her choice of seats as they headed farther east. She picked one close to the front. There were only a few more stops until her final destination, and while she should have been fearful, the encounter left her feeling hopeful. She may have mishandled the morning with Logan, but she was back in the zone.

When she arrived at her station, she went directly to the ladies' room. There, she removed her makeup, the wig, and combed out her hair. Simple Sofia stared back at her from the mirror. There were circles under her eyes and the scrape had turned from pink to red as it healed. She looked dog-tired, but she was back. As much herself as she would ever be.

There were a couple more hurdles to this haphazard plan. There was still a risk that one of Nick's men would see her entering the Capadonna estate. Surely Nick knew of Sam's defection and was watching him, but it was unlikely the men were told to stop someone going in, so she would be safe, at least for a time. She'd worry about getting out later.

Then there was Logan. Sofia sighed despite her new-found optimism. Neither of them had called or texted since the incident that morning. He could have taken the first flight back to Colorado or a cab to FBI headquarters. That possibility hurt. It was no less than she deserved.

Still, if things went wrong, if she misjudged Sam's reception, she wanted someone to know where to find the body. Logan was the only one she knew who would follow through. Sofia pulled out the cell phone and stared at it for a moment. If she could walk in on Sammy C unannounced, she could send a text. Sofia forced herself to open a new message to Uncle Ernie.

The thing she wanted to say was sorry. There weren't enough characters in a single message to cover the explanation she owed him. In the end, she texted the address and nothing more. She was tempted to add *I'm going in*, but decided against it. Too melodramatic.

Then, like the coward she was, she turned off the phone and dropped it in her bag along with the wig. She tucked it into a locker and didn't look back as she went to find a taxi.

The drive to Sam's estate was too short to give her time to change her mind. The taxi stopped at the gate leading to the drive and before the driver could hit the call button, a voice over the intercom demanded to know their business.

Sofia rolled down her window. "Sofia to see Sam."

The camera whirred to face her. She waited while it captured her image.

"Just you. Not the driver," the disembodied voice announced.

Sofia stepped out, paid the driver, and watched him drive away. The gate swung open enough for a single body to walk through. Her heart pounded. There was no going back.

· · ·

Travel on the Long Island Expressway was inexplicably slow as Logan drove out of the city. He had spent the day working with another agent—one he trusted not to turn him in—to get as much Intel as he could without risking exposure. He thought back to what Vicki had said Friday night before the sniper hit. Who had the power to make Eli disappear? The answer was Sam Capadonna, but Logan was less certain of Vicki's involvement. There was no indicator that Vicki and Capadonna had communicated, but Logan was certain of a connection even if there was no solid evidence of it.

The New York office had begun hearing chatter of changing alliances in the Calvetti family business, but they didn't have anything on Capadonna. Yet. Logan and his buddy dug into Capadonna's finances, which were murky. When they moved on to known associates, however, they struck pay dirt. For all appearances, Sam remained a loyal Calvetti lieutenant, but he'd begun to meet outside the family circle several months back and had acquired two enforcers who weren't on the Calvetti payroll.

Logan wasn't a betting man, but he was betting all his chips that Capadonna had Eli. His gut tightened. He wasn't following procedure; he was following his instincts and that was new territory. Would it improve his odds or make it worse? Logan didn't know, so he put his doubts aside and reviewed what he had learned thanks to that stroll through

Capadonna's financials. The man had business interests throughout the city and on Long Island. Knowing what property Capadonna owned made it possible to form a calculated guess as to where to find Eli.

Logan rented a car with Sofia's bogus credit card and headed out of the city. If traffic picked up, he could be there within the hour. He knew how to get to the boy, but he was less certain how to handle things with Sofia. Neither had texted all day and Logan didn't want to be the one to break the silence. He wasn't sure he wanted the silence broken. He was mulling his options when the traffic cleared and resumed normal speeds. Moments later, a text arrived from Aunt Bertha.

It was an address Logan recognized from perusing Capadonna's assets. He cursed and eased the car into a left lane. He was going to be staying on the expressway for a few more exits. He texted Aunt Bertha and told her to stay put, but she didn't respond. He knew her well enough to know she'd gone without him. She had no idea how close he was. He got off at the exit nearest the address she'd sent and down a county road toward Capadonna's estate, hoping to intercept Sofia before she did something stupid.

Too late.

Logan's heart convulsed. The first pass in front of the estate confirmed his suspicions. The long drive to Capadonna's country house was blocked with a controlled access gate. A yellow taxi was pulling onto the county road as Sofia walked with a determined stride down the long drive. Gone were the wig and uptight suit. It was simply Sofia, open and exposed. Logan flexed his hands on the steering wheel and tried to control the knot of fear that settled in his gut.

His first instinct was to run the car through the gate and retrieve her from what was certainly a trap, but that act would get them both killed. His fingers knotted into a fist. Things had just gotten more complicated.

He picked up the burner phone and called back his friend. "I need another favor."

· · ·

Sam's city house was ultra-sleek and modern, a real show of wealth. Here on Long Island, the show of wealth was in the large section of land. The house itself, while impressive, was more homey than ostentatious. Wood floors and warm earth tones were meant to give a sense of comfort and ease. The click of her heels on the hardwood gave Sofia a sense of dread. Her heart pounded as she followed two bulky men in suits down the hall.

Sofia had been here once before on a holiday weekend when Sam's family had been in residence. The family preferred this laid-back home to the one in the city, but today, the wife and kids were nowhere in sight. Sofia hadn't expected them to be privy to the situation with Eli.

When they arrived at the door to Sam's study, a third man, his gun drawn, pulled open the door and shoved Sofia inside. The book-lined room took on a golden hue in the afternoon sunshine. Behind her, the door closed, leaving her alone with Sam.

The man was a class act in his dark suit and hundred-dollar tie. His silvering hair was cut short, over the ears, and his eyes were a startling blue that matched the chill of a glacier. He looked up from his desk like any overworked CEO and smiled as if he were genuinely happy to see her. "Sofia, dear, what a pleasant surprise. Not the Calvetti I was hoping for, but not a complete loss."

His voice was cultured, something that never ceased to surprise her. He told her once that in the early days, working with Nick's father, he'd studied the men they fleeced until he could pass for one himself. Something about his civilized air sent a shiver of dread through her, because she knew beneath the high-powered sheen, he was lethal.

"To what do I owe this unexpected pleasure?"

"I came for my son."

The smile that twinkled in his eyes made him seem approachable, but his respectable veneer didn't fool Sofia. "Just like that?" he asked.

"He doesn't belong to you. He doesn't belong in this fight you have with Nicky."

"Is it a fight?" Sam shrugged as he came around the desk. "It doesn't feel that way to me. It takes two to fight, and so far, there is only me."

She understood what he was saying. Nick wasn't fighting back. "He won't give in. Not for Eli."

Sam sat on the edge of his desk like a college professor giving a lecture. "I think you are wrong, but if not"—he shrugged—"he will still look weak for losing his son. Already he is losing the respect of his men."

The fact that Eli's fate was dismissed with a shrug terrified Sofia. "If Nicky is already losing respect, then you don't need Eli."

"But I do, to show that Nick is no longer the head of this family. It started when he let you go. Marriage is about power. I tried to tell him that, but he just toyed with you like he did that first night. Do you remember that night?"

Sofia shivered at the reminder of the night she tried hard to forget. The thing that kept her in line after that night wasn't the worry of what Nick would do to her. He had broken her to the point she didn't fear for her own safety. Instead, she despaired of what he might happen to Eli if she weren't there to protect him. Nick comprehended that completely. He used Eli to punish Sofia.

Sam was using the same tactic against Nick, using the child to restrain the adult, but Nick wouldn't bend as she had. "He won't give you what you want. Not for Eli. Not for anyone."

"Perhaps you are right." Sam reached back and pressed a button on the desk. "But I cannot capitulate as he did when you left. Respect is all we have in this business."

Sofia nearly imploded as the weight of his words worked their way into her thoughts. Neither side would give ground, out of pride, out of the need for respect. Eli would pay the ultimate price. When the door opened, it was the single enforcer with the gun who entered. Adrenaline fed her muscles as she prepared for what came next. If they killed her now, no one would save Eli.

Sofia was not the same woman who had escaped Nick's clutches and she had more to fight for this time. She had two years of confidence boosting and gun training and self-defense classes. For years, she fought a punching bag, knowing someday she would fight something that would fight back. While the guard moved into the room, Sofia quietly toed off her heels. She wished she had time to remove the jacket, which would give her more freedom of movement, but Sam gestured for the guard to take her away.

While the guard's gaze fixed on Sam, she went on the offensive. She kicked his hand to disarm him. *It worked.* A microsecond delay as Sofia processed that it actually worked. The gun skittered across the hardwood, but before she had time to celebrate, the man turned to confront her. He had a hundred pounds of steroid-enhanced muscle on her, but she didn't back down.

The man looked formidable as he prowled toward her. He didn't stop, but kept at her until she was within reach and then he jabbed with a right hook. Smaller and faster, she used that to avoid the punch. It went wide, but when he turned back to her, his face was enlarged with rage. This time, the jab caught her full on her left cheek. The force sent her flying back across the room to land in a heap on the floor.

Confident in his own success, the man approached without defending. She curled up as though defeated until he was within striking distance. She kicked out, catching the side of his kneecap with the flat of her foot. He twisted in agony and she repeated her attack until he collapsed in agony. She leapt up, searching for the gun until the hammer of a gun clicked back.

"That's enough," Sam ordered. He motioned for the other two men to subdue her. "Send the kitchen staff home and put her in the freezer."

Sofia was stunned silent as they waited for the staff to leave. She turned to Sam. "You said—" Her throat clogged with fear, but she swallowed it with the last of her will power. "You said no one would do that to a woman when you were in charge."

Sam's eyes narrowed. "I'm not the head of the family

yet, and I'll do anything to get there."

"Even abuse a woman?" Sofia countered.

"If it's any consolation, I'm sorry, but you have no one to blame but yourself. You came to me."

Sofia tried valiantly to keep her head up as they led her into the kitchen with her wrists in vise-like grips. The bruising pain was nothing. The cut and bruise on her cheek were nothing. Sofia was already numb. Terror squeezed the air from her lungs. She heard the *click* of the lock and *whoosh* of a seal breaking as they opened the commercial grade walk-in freezer.

Chapter Thirteen

Saturday afternoon, time unknown

The darkness didn't make it hell. The hell was in her memory banks. As the cold seeped into her skin, the memory rose like a monster. This prison was not so different from the last, the monster taunted. Sofia started to hyperventilate, her breath coming in loud and shallow huffs that echoed in the small room.

The prison might not have changed, but Sofia had. If she passed out this time, all was lost. No time for a panic attack. She hitched a breath through her lips, then another, forcing herself to breathe slow and deep. Once she had mastered her breath, she marched the perimeter, testing the boundaries for doors or another suitable escape. The only door was the one she entered. She heard them padlock it closed right after they'd turned out the light.

The terror of an enclosed space choked her throat

closed. The darkness amplified the terror until she wanted to scream, but she'd learned not the let them see her fear. No one would hear her, and those who did would take pleasure in her pain. Instead, she forced herself to move. The freezer wasn't as small as she thought. The space was larger than the one in her past.

She paced the rectangular-shaped room. At first she tripped over what she told herself were frozen foods. She prayed it was just frozen foods and not a dead body. In time, she automatically stepped around the obstacles, but she couldn't maintain the pace. She'd lost her shoes in Sam's office, and the cement floor chilled her toes until she could no longer walk.

Giving up wasn't an option, but if she wanted to survive, she had to be smart. She couldn't risk her feet. The next few minutes, she searched the shelves for something soft to use to protect her feet, but found nothing. The tips of her toes burned. Frostbite waited, the next step in her torment.

Sofia sat with her legs crossed and back to the door. Once settled on the cold floor, she tucked her naked feet into the opposite pant leg and let them curl against her calves. The warmth thawed the toes enough to stave off frostbite, but it only bought her a little time.

The bigger concern was her core body temperature. Sofia rubbed her hands on her exposed skin, trying to keep it warm, but it was a losing battle. She'd been here before. Not this exact place, but in the insipid cold of a freezer. Already her body temperature had dropped and an unstoppable shivering possessed her limbs.

She rocked back and forth. *Keep moving*, she reminded herself.

Time moved. It was impossible to know how much passed. She wondered if Logan got her text. He did, she assured herself. He would come, even after what she had done. She started rocking again. God, how she had messed up with him. If he came, it would be a miracle she didn't deserve. And he wasn't her only problem.

Eli.

Sofia didn't know what motivated people without kids. She only knew what motivated her. She could endure anything as long as she found him. He needed her. Not just because she was his mother—many mothers could do a better job—but because she was the only one who could save him. In another situation, she might give up to inevitable death, but she could never leave him alone and in danger. If she got out of this, she'd be a better mother and a better person, because the person her grandparents raised would never have woken Logan with a gun.

Seeing Juliana and her interaction with the girls on the train had shown Sofia how much she had isolated herself over the last two years. She had changed. For too long, she had ignored the terror of leaving Nick, the pain of losing her grandparents, the fear of raising her son in a dangerous world. She pretended they didn't exist and now that she was forced into her worst nightmare, she had nothing left to fight off the internal demons. The fears bowled her over and buried her in a pit as dark as her cell. Sofia closed her eyes and went to her happy place.

The mountains in her mind were just forest trails with a slight incline. She jogged along that mountain trail under the shade of piñon pines. She was alone. No watchers. No bodyguards. Just her and the mountain.

• • •

The hornets fled the nest at the first whisper of trouble. Logan watched Capadonna step into a dark sedan with a contingent of bodyguards and a driver. They left the gate open on their way out to make it easy for local police to enter. Capadonna didn't want anyone damaging the property, Logan thought bitterly. He waited until they drove out of sight before driving the rental down the drive and around the back where they had exited the building.

A house this big took more than a handful of people to run, but Logan was counting on the fact that only household staff remained. Still, Capadonna might have left someone to guard Sofia. Logan stowed the gun in a holster and took out the badge he hadn't left in Colorado.

"No guts, no glory, Stone," he mumbled to himself. With that, he marched up to the back door and banged with authority. "Open up. FBI."

A beefy bodybuilder in a black suit answered the door. The man had him by twenty pounds of pure muscle, but Logan pushed through to the kitchen with the energy of a man on a mission. The kitchen was empty except for the man and a pile of dishes and simmering pots.

"Where's the warrant?" the man demanded.

Logan didn't answer, but prowled the kitchen until he found what he was looking for. The guard paced after him, but by the time he reached Logan and grabbed his arm, Logan had his hand on an iron skillet. He brought it down on the man's skull with extreme force.

The man dropped like the dead. Logan reached down,

felt a pulse. Strong enough, Logan decided. He peered from the kitchen into the rooms beyond, but they seemed empty. Taking out his gun, he cleared the rooms on the main level before heading back to the kitchen. He should have kept the guard awake long enough to find out where they were holding Sofia.

As he stalked back into the kitchen, he heard her screaming with such horror it chilled the blood in his veins. The sound emanated from the freezer. "Sofia, step back," he yelled.

She continued to scream. Alive, but terrified. Logan's sense of urgency didn't leave time for careful consideration. There was no help for it. Logan pulled out his gun and aimed it at the lock. It shattered, the bullet lodging in the freezer door. He pulled it open and Sofia fell back onto the floor, her legs twisted and frozen into place. The scream died in her throat as she became aware of the warmth and the light.

The exposed skin of her face and neck was tinged a pale blue and her lips were leached of color. He never should have let her leave alone. Logan ran back to the living room, grabbed a blanket off the couch, and headed back to the kitchen.

Sofia had rolled into a ball on the kitchen floor.

His phone buzzed with an incoming text. Logan didn't stop to read it. It was a warning, the only one he'd get. *Get out while you can.* Logan wrapped the blanket around Sofia before lifting her into his arms. He ignored the twinge of pain in his ribs.

"Logan?" Sofia asked.

"Yes?" he choked the word out. It was the first time she used his name. Not Mr. Stone, or Fed or some other derogatory term. Just his name. It hit him deep inside as he carried her from the house.

"I knew you'd come."

Her faith in him battered him worse than any accusation she could fling. He'd failed her today. "I'm sorry this happened. I know better than to leave a vic."

The bite in his tone matched the hard set of his jaw.

"I'm not a victim," Sofia assured him. Her tone bit back. "No matter what else I am, I am most certainly not an innocent in all this."

But she had been, once upon a time, when she first met Calvetti. She was as much a victim as Eli, and just as vulnerable. That's what she hid behind the Ice Queen mask.

Logan set her in the passenger seat and buckled her before tucking the blanket around her shoulders. The chill emanating from her cooled the car by several degrees. He wanted to check her vitals, make sure she wasn't injured, but they needed distance from the scene before the cops arrived. Logan yanked the car into gear and eased down the long driveway.

The heater combined with the heat of the day turned the interior of the car into a sauna, but Sofia's skin still glistened with the sheen of death. "How long were you in?"

"Long enough to subdue me," she whispered. Her voice was hoarse, like a woman who had screamed until her voice had given out, but now she was emotionless. The anger, the bitterness, the control he had come to associate with Sofia Capri had been wiped clean by whatever had happened inside Capadonna's house.

The man would answer for his sins, Logan thought as he pulled onto the highway. He had been—

Hell, what had he been when she pulled a gun on him this morning? Mad as hell. Wary. Ready to walk. But he didn't. Couldn't. The woman sitting like a corpse in the front seat infuriated him, but she needed him. And in a sick part of his soul, he needed her. It wasn't just sex. If it had been sex, that scene at their adjoining door would have sated him. That's what she wanted. Had made it perfectly clear. Just sex.

Logan wanted more than that. He wanted to reach her, to dive deep into her soul and retrieve the woman she had been before Calvetti. He wanted a Sofia who could trust again. He wanted their mating to be more than sex. Instead, she sat comatose next to him. She didn't pull the mantle of control around herself as if she had nothing left to continue the illusion. She rocked lightly in the seat as if rocking an unseen child. She didn't look at him. She kept her focus outward, outside the window to the world beyond, as if to center herself in a space larger than the car. She curled her legs into her core, with her feet on the car seat and her knees pulled into her chest. Hiding, making as small a target as possible, she kept her gaze outside the window. Her thoughts held her captive.

"Sofia."

She didn't answer.

Shock. He knew the signs and didn't have anything in the car to help. He turned down the next county road and went another mile before he found a pullout surrounded by trees.

He walked around the front end and opened her door. She started before looking around like a skittish colt. Panic flared through her eyes. "Why did we stop?"

Logan reached down to calm her. The second he touched her shoulder, she snapped back as if he hit her. She scrambled across the seat, but the belt trapped her in place. "We have to go. We have to find Eli. We have to—" Her eyes frantically took in her surroundings.

As far as he could tell, she was one step away from a padded cell, and he didn't have time to be gentle.

Shaking her was a mistake, but Sofia would approve of the tactic as long as it got her back on track. "I won't take you to Eli until you look at me. Look at me, Sofia," he ordered.

The deep brown of her eyes was muddied, glazed and unfocused. He needed her back with the living. He bent down to her level and slowly reached forward to grab her shoulders. The fact that she didn't flinch was progress.

"Sofia." He choked back the soft words he wanted to say. Held himself from cradling her and giving her the comfort she desperately needed. "I know where Eli is."

Her eyes snapped into focus. She reached out and grabbed him until her fingernails bit into his flesh. "Where?"

He shook his head. "You're no good to him like this."

Her nails drew blood on his arm. "Take me."

"Not like this. Do you have any idea the impact you would have on him in this condition? You couldn't have been in there for more than thirty or forty minutes. Not long enough for this. You're acting—"

"Crazy?" The word was bitter. And closer to the Sofia he'd grown to care for.

"I will get Eli," he promised. "But I'll drop you at the nearest hospital first and let them straighten you out unless you start talking to me. What happened in there?"

She dropped her arms, looked away. "Sam reminded me,

that's all."

"Reminded you of what?"

"Of how truly powerless I am." She stared up at the tree, at the leaves dancing in the evening air. "I went to see my friend Juliana today. The boss's wife doesn't have any allies, not really, but she was a friend to me. It was through her that I got a gun."

Logan didn't understand what she was saying. "Today?"

"Not today." The look in her eyes kept him locked out of her thoughts and for a moment he thought she had retreated within herself again. "The day I realized I'd married a monster."

• • •

Sofia didn't remember Logan finding her. She couldn't remember anything after the door closed, leaving her in bitter darkness. The thing she held on to in that moment was Logan. He would find her. He knew where she was going and he would find her. Then she came-to with Logan at her side. It was the answer to the prayer she wouldn't say. She was sitting in a car she'd never seen, wrapped in a cream-colored chenille throw. She was out of her prison, thanks to Logan, a man with every reason to ditch her, but who saved her anyway.

"Sofia." His words were a plea, bringing her back to the present. Reminding her of the last time they had spoken. In a fit of insecurity she had pulled the gun on him. It was screwed up in so many ways there was no way to make it right. "I'm sorry," she whispered.

"For what?"

"It was wrong," she whispered. "What I did this morning. And I'm sorry."

"Yes it was, but it didn't work."

She looked at him, clueless.

He wasn't very good at hiding his emotions, Sofia thought, but she no longer considered it a weakness as he stared down, his soulful brown eyes ringed with concern.

He reached out and gently rubbed her cheek. "It didn't push me away."

The warmth of his fingers brought on a spat of shivering, or was it more than his touch? How could he forgive something so vile? Sofia had never been as close to tears. She coughed, cleared her throat, and did all the things she'd learned that kept the tears at bay. The cell had emptied her of all. Emotion. Hope. Fear. She didn't think she would ever feel again, but Logan's words thawed her as effectively as his touch. Curling her legs onto the seat, she wrapped her arms around her knees and wrapped the blanket tighter around her shoulders.

Trust would probably never come easy for her, but that was no excuse for bad behavior. Logan showed her another way. She needed to explain what happened, but she couldn't explain to him about today without revealing what she had never told anyone. What only Nick, Sam, and Eddie knew. The thing she ran from every day on the treadmill.

"Juliana helped me get a gun once. Before. When I'd decided to leave Nicky."

A gun. That one thing had made her feel powerful. She had dared to reject him for the first time, not allowing him into her bed. That night, she vowed that she would take a stand and recover herself. She would dig herself out of hell and rebuild, even if she had to use a gun to do it. "I woke to the sound of the hammer being pulled back. He wasn't gentle. I felt the gun gouge into my temple. The pain." She shrugged. "It was nothing compared to the terror when I looked into his eyes. I swear I saw the fires of hell reflected in the depths of his soul."

She squeezed her knees into her chest. "Before, I had never given much thought to evil. Never given much thought to demons. Until that night. He made me stand and strip."

Logan cursed.

"That's what I thought as well." But rape wasn't what Nick had in mind that night. "He didn't want me demoralized and humiliated as I would have been if he'd forced himself on me that night. I would have recovered from that. Women do." It would have built into anger and hatred of a very personal nature, and it would have fed her need and will to escape him.

"Nicky may not be book smart, but he is a strategist, as he proudly told me that night. He had been studying me, the enemy he called me." She looked at Logan then, at a loss to understand the psyche of a man like Nick. "Can you imagine calling the woman you married, the mother of your child, the enemy?"

A chill went through her that no heat could ever dispel. "If there's one thing the Calvettis know, it's how to deal with an enemy." Nick had been enraged as he forced her downstairs at gunpoint. The paranoid accusations flew out of his mouth like some sort of Old Testament wrath. "I thought he was taking me to the basement to kill me. I didn't understand yet how much he hated me. How badly he needed me to suffer. Death would have been too easy. That's when I learned the true depravity of the man I had married."

She swallowed, the picture vivid in her mind. "Behind generations of castoff furniture and dried paint cans was another Calvetti secret. A room."

Sofia tried to jump up, but the seat belt locked her in place. She jerked against it, but it wouldn't break free. Panic built in her chest and she started pulling against the seat belt like a horse against reins. Logan brushed her hand aside and removed the seat belt. The moment the belt was free, she brushed past Logan in an effort to escape memories of that room. She moved past Logan, but made it only two steps before the pain in the sole of her foot shot up the nerves to her calf. She stumbled, but Logan grabbed her and helped her to the tree. She leaned against it as if to find her roots and her balance, but the stab of pain in her frozen feet kept her from going to her happy place. She wanted to escape, but had to face the past and the horror of that sterile room with its stainless steel counters and wall of drawers.

"I never imagined such a place existed in the civilized world, but I had forgotten that I was no longer part of the *civilized* world."

The sun shone through the leaves of the tree and birds flew past, but Sofia wasn't seeing those things.

"What was in the room?" Logan asked quietly.

"Nicky's private morgue. *Can't have the bodies decomposing before we dump them,*" she mimicked. Nick managed to sound so reasonable at the most insane times. "Television shows make a morgue seem like a sterile place, with the cadavers cleaned and peaceful. No one had cleaned these bodies."

"Calvetti wanted to show you what he was capable of."

"That was only the beginning." She rubbed her arms. Some days she thought she would never be warm again, not after that day. "I must have passed out when he showed me the cadavers. Even now, I can't think of them as people. When I woke, it was cold and dark. The floor was hard, I thought he'd locked me in the room with the bodies and I started to panic, tried to stand—"

Sofia's knees buckled. She would have fallen to the gravel if Logan hadn't caught her. He pulled her close. "He locked you in one of the freezers."

Logan's body was warm against hers. Vital and strong, it pushed back the terror of that long-ago day.

"I don't know how long he kept me there. Until I'd screamed myself silent. Until my fingers bled trying to pry my way out that coffin-like space. By the time Sam and Eddie pulled me off the slab, I had given up." She had been thinking about Eli, wondering what would happen to her son if Nick raised him. If Nick was the only example he had.

"That's when Eddie asked you not to provoke Calvetti?"

This time, her knees did give out. She took Logan with her. They landed in a controlled crash next to the tree. She could still hear the tears in Eddie's voice.

Please, Miss Sofia, don't provoke him. He can be good to you. He has been good to you.

As if Nick's cruelty were her fault. A tear escaped and paved the way for the torrent that followed. Sofia wiped her tears on Logan's shirt. She couldn't tell him the rest. How after she'd been freed, they brought Juliana to tend to her, to clean Sofia and make her presentable.

It was a warning to Juliana as well. They never spoke of it. When Juliana left and Sofia was once again presentable, he came to her. He greeted her calmly, as if he'd been at work and seeing his wife after a long day. He bent, kissed her, and whispered in her ear.

No one leaves the family, except by way of a body bag.

. . .

Logan was certain Sofia didn't realize she'd said the words aloud. She mumbled as if in a trance. He cradled her and rocked as the sobs tore through her body like storm waves. He soothed her, but inside, a tidal wave of anger churned. Calvetti and his men deserved to roast in the darkest pit of hell for what they had done to her. He planned to be the one to put them there.

The tears subsided and Sofia relaxed into slumber. He continued to hold her, on the side of the road, thinking of what she had told him. It explained a few things. Why she didn't like confined spaces or guns. Why she would never so much as speak to anyone at the gym. Why she refused to speak to the Feds after her divorce. Divorce hadn't freed her from the psychopath she had married. Logan knew of only one thing that would.

One step at a time.

Logan lifted Sofia and returned her to the passenger seat. Her face was raw from the watershed tears, but her eyes were closed. Once he settled her, he wrapped the blanket back over her limp shoulders.

"Logan," she whispered. "Did you cover me that night at Vicki's?"

He thought back to that night, watching her sleep with her son's stuffed elephant in her arms. "Yes," he said, although he'd forgotten until now.

"I thought it was Vicki." She peered up at him with so much desperation in her deep brown eyes. "I'm glad it was you."

The words choked him up, but he couldn't say why. It was that look in her eyes, so like her son's. It was innocent still, trapped behind too many bad memories, and he wanted nothing more than to return her to a time and a place where she didn't have to hide her feelings. He looked away as he slammed the door shut and returned to the driver's seat. Wordlessly, he turned the car back to the highway.

He'd been running on adrenaline since the bomb at Sofia's house. Living on a fantasy of a woman he didn't understand until this moment. She was at once intensely vulnerable and fiercely strong, and he didn't have a clue as to how she'd survived. The only solution, the only way she could survive, was to remove Calvetti from the picture. Permanently.

• • •

When Sofia woke, the light had not faded much beyond where it had been on the country road where Logan had taken her. Not much time had passed gauging by their location on the Long Island Expressway. A lifetime had passed in her psyche. Sharing the trauma diminished its strength. She stretched her legs and let the past go, because living as she had lived the past two years was a tragedy. Her future hinged on escaping the fear. She lifted her gaze to Logan. The man had saved her.

"How did you get into Sam's?" she asked. "He had enough men to take you down."

"Thanks for the vote of confidence," he teased.

"I didn't mean—"

"I know," he said, the crinkle lines around his eyes turning up in a smile. "I had a little help. An *anonymous* source saw a fugitive enter the residence of a known mobster." He glanced over at her. "Christ, when I saw you walk down the front drive it was like watching an old west showdown in slow motion. I about had a coronary."

Sofia wanted to believe that he'd worried for her, that he had felt something for her that made the moment important on a personal level, but living in a fantasy world would not help her any more than living in the past.

The reality was that Logan never let the job go. He was FBI inside and out, day and night, day in and day out. He felt responsible for her and for Eli, because they were victims in his mind, like the little boy he had lost. She couldn't stand the thought of being diminished to victim status. Instead, she focused on the facts. "The anonymous phone call. Sam left because you had a search warrant. Someone tipped him off. He knew you were on the way, and you knew someone would warn him."

"Not me," he denied. "I'm a wanted man. I can't get a warrant."

"Then how?"

He tapped the steering wheel for several minutes while he considered his answer. "I called in a favor."

"Big favor." Sofia realized that he'd not only put his reputation on the line, but that of a friend. He was too good for her. That fact was never more apparent than now. She raised her head, her eyes momentarily bright. "Did they find Eli?"

Logan shook his head.

They were running out of time. Her heart clenched. "Did Sam take him when he left?"

"No. Eli was never at the house."

She'd made the wrong choice. Sofia closed her eyes, defeated. Sam had a hundred businesses, maybe more, and there was no way to run them all down before the deadline. "You said you knew where he was."

"I do," he said, concentrating on the road and his law-abiding driving. "And you're not going anywhere near it."

"What?" Sofia surged forward in her seat, knocking the blanket to the ground. "You have no right—"

"We can't go in alone, Sofia. I need to call in reinforcements."

"So it can become a standoff with my son as the bargaining chip. Not a chance in hell."

"Sofia—"

She raised a hand to silence him. Following his plan would be catastrophic. She closed her eyes and forced herself to focus on the facts. Fact, Logan had come to get her, but before her text, he'd been after Eli. Fact, it didn't take him long to find her after she sent the text. That meant he'd been close. What business or residence did Sam own in the area?

"Oh my God." Sofia let her head drop back against her headrest. "I had the answer from day one. Vince told Eli that he would be horseback riding soon. I thought Vince meant with Nick, but I should have known. Nick would never take Eli riding. Vince was talking about Sam's stables. He knew all along where they were going."

"We're not going," Logan insisted. "It's not safe to walk in there like John Wayne."

"I'm not a cowboy. I'm a mother." Sofia grabbed her door handle. "I'll go without you. Nothing will keep me from my son."

"Nice try, but that threat isn't going to work. You can't play me."

"It's not a threat." Sofia was dead serious. "Let me out of the car or I will jump. I have not come this far to stop short."

"It's suicide."

"I just survived hell," she said. Her heart thumped loudly in her chest. She was so close. She would not leave without her son. "What happened at Sam's? That was nothing compared to losing my son. Pull over."

Logan rubbed a hand over his eyes. "Be reasonable. I can't let you go in there alone."

"Yes you can." Sofia flexed her fingers into a fist. "You can. You should. You've taken me this far, now let me go."

At the next exit, Logan whipped across two lanes and pulled off the highway. He stopped on the shoulder and rammed the car into park.

The shock of it shut her down. No coherent thoughts coalesced. No words formed on her lips. By pulling over, he'd called her bluff. He was letting her go. He was giving her exactly what she'd asked for and it made her feel empty inside. Sofia cleared her throat, effectively silencing the tears that waited. "Thank you," she whispered. "For—"

"I'm not letting you go. Not alone." He released his seat belt and slid across the seat. "You make me crazy."

The man gave her no time to think. He wound his fingers into her hair and dropped a punishing kiss to her lips. She responded in kind. The fear of the past several hours, combined with fear for Eli and the ever-present attraction for Logan, meant she had too much adrenaline and nowhere to spend it.

Sofia wrapped her hands into his hair and pulled him to her. She kissed and nipped at his lower lip. The man made her angry, he pushed against her strong will and took charge when she wanted to control, but he was good and kind and trustworthy and she was no longer in danger of falling for him. She was in deep.

When their anger was spent, Logan released her. He slid back across the seat and put the car into drive. He turned back east on the expressway and drove two exits in silence.

A mile from the stable entrance, Vicki came running out of a copse of trees.

"Pull over," Sofia told Logan.

"Because you trust her?" Logan asked.

"No. Because she knows where Eli is. I'm certain of it."

Vicki raced to Logan's window. "What is wrong with you people? We expected you hours ago. We thought you were still sitting at the train station, which made no sense." She reached into her bag and pulled out an electronic device slightly larger than an iPod. "Where is Ellie?"

"The elephant?" Logan asked.

What made no sense to Logan clicked instantly for Sofia. "You put a tracker in Eli's stuffed elephant!"

"Back off your high-horse, sister. We needed to track you to make sure you were following the clues we left behind."

"Clues? What's wrong with *you*? You should have told me on day one."

"No. I should not have. One, you had this guy with you. Really, Sofia, a Fed? Two, if you had gone to Nick with that information, he would have come in, guys blazing, and someone would have gotten hurt. Maybe Eli. Maybe Vince. The only way to control the outcome was to string you along with just enough information to keep looking, but not enough to call in reinforcements."

"Why? Sofia asked. "I trusted you."

"And you still can," Vicki insisted. "Sam found out about your plan with Vince."

"I never said a word," Sofia swore.

Vicki winced. "But we did. We didn't think about it. My house seemed safe, but Sam must have bugged my house to find a way to get to Nick. If Vince had refused, Sam would have killed him. If he had gone to Nick, Nick would have killed him—and you—for plotting this in the first place. We had to move forward, let Sam think Vince was going along with it. But trust me, he would never let Eli get hurt."

"How many men can we expect?" Logan asked.

"What, are you just going to waltz in the front gate?" Vicki asked. The sarcasm oozed from her words. "I thought you were smarter than that, Logan No-Name."

"I thought you were too smart to betray your brother," Logan said. "What did you have in mind, sister to the mob?"

"Are you always going to be like this?" she asked. "Because I'm trying to play nice."

"*Now* you want to cooperate? You could have done that this morning in the city and saved Sofia another day in hell."

"And Eli would have had a full complement of guards," Vicki said.

"Stop it, you two," Sofia insisted. "Vicki, you've obviously had time to plan a way out."

"Yes, and you almost missed the window. Vince and Eli are out riding. The bodyguards are *not* in attendance. Can you see some of these jokers on horseback?"

"Where do we go?"

Vicki gave them directions to a back road that wound along the edges of the property where they would meet Vince.

"What's Vince's escape plan?"

"Take him with you. We'll meet up at the railroad station."

"What about you?"

Vicki grinned. "I'm just going to make sure they won't be able to go anywhere."

"Practicing Auto Shop again?"

"You know, it was always more fun to disassemble than reassemble."

"I bet." Sofia wanted to return her friend's saucy grin, but she wouldn't smile again until she had Eli in her arms. Instead, she gazed gravely at Vicki. "Be careful."

Vicki saluted as Logan turned the car toward the back road. He stopped a half mile from the rendezvous site, removed his gun from the holster, and checked to make sure the safety was off. Sofia wanted to believe Logan was being his usual overprotective self, but there was a very real possibility that Vicki was playing them.

If it looked like a trap and felt like a trap… Sofia sat up, prepared for the worst.

When she saw Vince and Eli galloping toward them alongside a white fence, her heart lurched.

Chapter Fourteen

Saturday, 10:12 p.m.

Eli drifted to sleep in the big hotel bed, his Ellie tucked into his side. Sofia smoothed his dark curls with a soft, soothing touch, her heart a jumble of emotions. Thankfulness, her heart filled with gratitude so great that he was alive, yet sick at the thought of what she would do to keep him that way.

Vicki had tried to convince Sofia to take Eli and run, to get on the Long Island Railroad and disappear. It was an intoxicating thought. She had been living in survival mode for years and the urge to run was high, but she would never make it out of the city. The FBI was looking for her in connection with Eli's kidnapping, thanks to Nick. Nick and his vast network were an even greater threat. The one remaining option sickened her.

Sofia's thoughts drifted to the man in the adjacent room. Against Logan's objections, they had dropped Vince at the train station while Sofia retrieved her go-bag with a disguise she would likely never wear again. It was a humbling realization. All the trouble she had started with her plots and plans had been for naught, and it had endangered everything.

The drive into the city had been silent for the adults. Eli had jabbered nonstop about horse camp and the airplane ride and he didn't stop until they reached the hotel. Logan made sure they had supper. Of course he had. Then Sofia had given Eli a bath and tucked him in for the night.

She and Logan hadn't spoken directly since they'd found Eli, beyond the "Pass the ketchup" or "Would you like more coffee?" At the moment, Logan was on the other side of the adjoining door, brooding. The look on his face had been closed to her. She wouldn't call it cold. How could a man who made sure her son had chicken nuggets be considered cold? No, not exactly cold, but definitely not open to conversation.

That had to change.

Sofia took the time to wash away the remnants of her disguise. Off came the makeup and the fake lashes and the polish that gave her a sense of invisibility. In their place, she put on the jeans and wrinkled shirt she'd worn that first day. Was it only two and a half days ago? Those days had changed everything.

She stepped to the adjoining room, trembling to face the man who understood her too well. He sat on the couch, his feet resting on the coffee table, watching a sports channel on television. He muted the sound when she came in, but he kept his focus on the TV. She closed the door, leaned against it as she had the first night, without the fear and exhaustion that had pushed her to seduce him. The need for him, however, still burned in her blood, despite the tension that arced between them.

His eyes were hooded as he watched the TV. His jaw clenched, the muscle in his cheek flexing beneath several days' growth. Water glistened in his dark hair from a recent shower and dripped onto a plain dark T-shirt that covered his solid chest and inviting arms. The man was... Sofia sighed and breathed him in. Logan was a fine specimen of man. No wonder she had been attracted to him from the beginning. Tall, muscular, with dark hair and eyes, he had the solid look of someone who could protect and defend, but the similarities to Nick had frightened her.

Those similarities did not define Logan. The man on the inside was the only man she trusted. He would be easy to love. She thought back to Vicki's advice. It was oh so tempting to disappear with Logan, to go somewhere and play house and pretend they weren't on the run from the government and the most dangerous man in Sofia's world, but Logan deserved better.

It didn't matter if Logan would leave it all behind for her. She'd never ask it of him. He had to act with honor and she had to face her past.

"I want to thank you, for everything," she squeaked. She cleared her throat. "I don't honestly know what would have happened if you hadn't been there. If you hadn't found me."

He looked up, his gaze intense. Not the hellfire of Nick's eyes, but solid, strong energy that brooked no argument. "Leaving you was never an option."

Sofia swallowed, went to the table that room service had setup. She poured herself another cup of coffee. It tasted like re-warmed sludge, but it gave her hands something to do. "I know you need to go in, file reports—"

"*We* need to go in."

She shook her head. "I won't press charges. I'm certain Nick will deny anything happened."

"Sofia, you can't cover this up."

"I'm not covering it up," she said, risking a glance in his direction. "I'm accepting reality."

He leaned forward, hands on his knees, his jaw hard.

Sofia was afraid of the thoughts he kept reined in. She didn't want to hear them because no matter how sound his logic, she knew it would never work. "It may not be what I want or what your honor demands, but it's the way the world works."

"I can see it in your eyes, damn it." He exploded off the coach. "You're taking Eli back to his father."

"What choice do I have?"

"That's the freezer talking."

The shock of it stopped her, cup midway to her mouth. In that second, she was trapped back in that cold, dark room. Alone. Terrified. Sofia couldn't think. Couldn't breathe. Couldn't focus beyond the sting of his words.

The freezer and all it represented tainted every move she made. The truth did not set her free. The illusion of strength she had built over the years washed away like sidewalk chalk. Nick still manipulated her, controlled her, the same way he had since that first night in the morgue, and she'd allowed it. She set the coffee cup down. "You have to admit, it was a damned effective tactic."

The regret in his tone was palpable. "Sofia, I didn't mean—"

"Stop." She closed her eyes, shook her head. "You're right. It is fear talking, but that doesn't change the facts.

According to the custody arrangements, this is Nick's visitation time with Eli. The FBI is looking for me in connection with Eli's kidnapping. Nick played it right. Remember, evil smart. I wouldn't make it out of the city with Eli, let alone the country."

"That isn't your only option. These past few days prove Calvetti is an unfit father. His lifestyle puts Eli at risk. I can testify to as much. No judge will give Calvetti custody after this."

"There is no judge on the planet Nick can't buy," she said softly. She didn't expect Logan to understand. He didn't live in her world.

"The man doesn't care enough about Eli to buy off a judge."

A soft snort left her. She opened her eyes, made herself look at Logan. "You and Sam, you just don't get it. It isn't about love. Eli is an object. *You can't have the clothes I bought you. You can't take the dishes. You can't take Eli. Because they're mine.*" She imitated Nick's voice. "He will fight for Eli because he won't lose anything. He won't cede anything, just as he wouldn't cede territory to Sam. His territory—his manhood—means more to him than the child he wouldn't let me keep."

"And you're going to send your son back to that," Logan snapped.

"Don't judge." She shook her head. No one else could make her feel so wrong. "I do what I do for Eli. Nick will protect Eli. Not for the reasons you or I would. He will protect him as he would protect his territory. *That* will keep Eli alive."

"Testify."

Sofia shoved away from the table. "That's a death sentence."

"Have a little faith in me, Sofia."

"I don't doubt you," she said sharply. She wanted to pound on the table. If only Logan would understand what was at risk. "Don't forget that Nick knows who you are and where you live. He'll chip away until he finds out who or what you love and destroys it bit by bit."

Logan looked straight at her. "He already has."

Holy hell. Sofia stumbled back as her heart imploded. She prayed that Logan wasn't saying what it sounded like, because that would give Nick one more piece of ammunition. Not that Nick needed much. The family Logan ate Sunday dinners with? They were easy targets in Nick's mind. Sofia's eyes blistered with unshed tears. "I won't let him hurt you," she promised.

"It's not your job to protect me," Logan said. "Respect me enough to do my job."

"I do." No man was as solid as Logan. "But I have a healthy respect for what Nick is capable of. His pride, his resources, and his determination. Long after the Justice Department moves on to the next big threat, Nick will be out there, and he will wreak vengeance on all of us. Why do you think I wouldn't let them through the front door when I left Nick? I won't risk Eli."

He rose to stand behind her, set a hand on her shoulder. "If you won't trust WITSEC and their witness protection program, trust me."

She did. What she didn't trust was her own determination against the feel of his hand on her. "You'd give your life to protect Eli, I know that."

He rubbed a thumb along the column of her neck. "Him. And you."

"The price is too high." The words came out a mere whisper as the heat of his fingers sent currents through her body. "I won't ask you to pay it."

"You didn't ask. Not once. You have some pathological need to work alone."

"Because I'm good at it," Sofia admitted.

Logan pulled her against him until her backside was nestled between his legs. He wrapped an arm around her waist to hold her close. "I'm falling for you."

Sofia's throat ached to say the words, but instead, she whispered, "That's why he would kill you slowly." If only she had met him five years ago, when she still believed that love had a power all its own. Sofia closed her eyes and wished the emotions away. It did no good to believe in fairy tales.

"Don't make this about me, Sofia. I can take care of myself."

"And me? And Eli? It's too much for one man, and someday soon, Nick will find your weakness and destroy us all."

Logan pulled her tighter against him and growled in her ear. "No."

Saying it didn't make it true. "You're bound by honor and a badge and the law. Nick isn't handicapped by that."

He turned her in his arms. "Honor isn't a handicap."

Not in his world. Sofia turned her gaze away, wishing she could explain. A man like Logan could hate a man like Nick—neither side had a patent on hatred—but Logan would still pause, even for a fraction of a second, to give Nick the benefit of the doubt. And in any fight, weapons or fists, Nick would use that moment to destroy Logan. Sofia couldn't allow it.

"I want to know how you can face Calvetti or Capadonna head on, fierce as I have ever seen a woman, but you can't look me in the eyes."

"Because they can only kill me," she whispered. And losing Logan would destroy her.

Everything she had done to escape Nick had endangered good people. No more. She let herself sink into Logan's embrace, knowing it would be the last time.

He tilted her chin so he could see into her eyes. "Promise me you won't make a decision without telling me. Trust me enough to give me that much."

Tears pooled in her eyes. She couldn't blink them away. "Promise," he said. "Say it."

She closed her eyes, felt the tear glide down her cheek. "I promise," she lied. Lied, because she already knew what she had to do.

Untouchable is what Nick had called her. Only now did she fully comprehend. Anyone who touched her would die. Logan had touched a part of her she thought long dead. The price would be his life. Not by her hand, but that did not make it less her fault.

"I want you," she said. It was as close to the truth as she could risk. Tonight was not about physical release. It was not about hormones or loneliness.

He brushed her tears away with the pad of his thumb. "Look at me," he whispered.

That was too risky. Instead, Sofia rose on tiptoes and planted a kiss on Logan's neck. The pulse beating in his throat doubled. She tasted him, nipped at him, and let her hands roam the body of a man she would soon leave. But before she left, she wanted one last memory to hold her. She wanted to know how it felt to make love to a good man.

. . .

"I know a distraction when I see one," he said, but he couldn't make himself care when Sofia nibbled her way to his jaw and her hands slid under his shirt.

"Is that a complaint?" she asked. She bit his lower lip.

Every muscle in his body flexed in response. "An observation."

The spark of her icy touch fueled the need in his soul. She kneaded and caressed her way up his stomach to his pecs where her fingernail scraped across his nipples. Desire burned from her cool touch. He sucked air into his lungs. He had no restraint when it came to Sofia. He looked down at her and wanted nothing more than to give in to the temptation. The bed was tantalizingly close—two steps and he'd have her where they both wanted her—but after the hell of today, they both deserved better than fast hotel sex.

Everything was a trade-off with her, Logan reminded himself. "We're in the middle of a conversation."

She ran her nails up his back and yanked the shirt over his head before he had time to breathe. "I think we're done."

His erection jerked against the confines of his jeans. The woman made him crazy. She turned every switch he didn't know he had, but if he had one more night with Sofia, he wanted it all. He wanted to brand new memories into her frozen heart, but that would only work if she opened for him. "You want the conversation to be over?"

She licked at his nipple and his restraint nearly melted in her mouth. "It is over," she insisted.

"Then I control this." He pulled her against his heat, showing her what she did to him, showing her what he wanted to do to her. "Look at me. No hiding. No running. No pushing to get your way."

She blinked. Wet her lip. "I wouldn't —"

"The hell you wouldn't." He laughed, but it ended on a groan. The way she licked her lip made him want to taste her. "You'd push me to the point of crazy, until I rammed you up against the nearest wall."

Sofia lowered her gaze; her pause so drawn out — so silent — Logan heard the rapid thump of his heart pounding through his skull.

"Maybe," she said finally, a mysterious smile tilting her lips. "But that worked so well last time."

"Not this time." He'd taken her hard and fast and it wasn't enough for him. He stepped back to illustrate his point. The draft from the air conditioner cooled the space between them. His chest rose and fell with each ragged breath from his lungs.

"You want me to give you control?" She stiffened in defense, building herself into the Ice Queen.

He didn't want to argue. The woman pushed him beyond restraint until he gave it all in one swift mind-blowing moment, but he wanted more and he was willing to fight for it using every dirty trick she had taught him. "Stay the night with me, Sofia."

She closed her eyes, but not before he saw the haunted expression. "You don't know what you're asking." Her voice quivered.

"I do," Logan assured her.

Emotion flitted through her ever-expressive eyes—fear, shock, desire—and he couldn't stop himself. He reached over and pulled her close, massaged the tension in her neck and tried to soften her fall.

The sigh on her lips was acquiescence. Logan bent to brush his lips across hers. "Trust me, Sofia," he whispered. "At least in this."

"I do, more than anyone, but—"

Logan kissed her quiet. "That's enough for tonight. That's enough."

The kiss spun out from slow heat to intense fire. He slid his tongue into her mouth and tasted her, sucked and reveled in the shiver that slid through her lithe body. He felt her up, over her clothes like a horny teenager, he flicked his thumb over her nipple and she moaned in his mouth, thrust her chest into his hand. He took what she offered, kneading her with one hand while the other reached back and unclasped the bra through the fabric of her shirt. He used the shirt to tease the nipples into hard pebbles.

"Please," she whispered against his mouth. "Touch me."

He flicked his nail over her nipple and it puckered like a piece of hard candy. "I am."

She grabbed his wrist and guided his hand under her shirt. It rested just under her full breast. "Touch me," she insisted.

He rubbed the tender skin around her nipple, teasing them both as his rough fingers stroked. He bent to taste her through the thin cotton of her shirt while his fingers teased the soft skin on the underside of her breast. She arched into his mouth and Logan couldn't go back, didn't want to. He lifted the shirt over her head, slid the bra down her arms so he could draw her fully into his mouth. Tasting slowly, he wanted to draw it out like a fine dinner with her nipples as the appetizer. He switched sides, suckling the other breast while his hands slid to cup her through her jeans.

She bucked against his hand, tilted, upset her balance and tumbled back on the bed where he had wanted her from day one. She righted herself so she sat on the edge of the bed and the look in her eyes was pure wicked. When she licked her lips, he thought he'd lose it in his jeans. "Nothing below the waist."

She arched a brow in response. The saucy look in her eyes challenged his order.

"I won't last, Sofia, and there's too much I want to do to you tonight."

A smile lit her eyes as her hand lifted to the waistband of his jeans. True to the rules, she stayed north of the line, but just barely. She touched and kissed and licked her way from his stomach to his chest and all Logan could do was grab on for the ride. When he couldn't take it anymore, he pushed her back onto the bed. Need glowed in her eyes and he was ready for the next course. He yanked off her jeans and explored every smooth inch of exposed skin. He nibbled at her hip, at the panty line, on the inside of her thigh.

Sofia squirmed; gasped each time his teeth lightly scraped her skin and moaned when his warm breath blew against the bundle of nerves he desperately wanted to pleasure. He nipped and licked through the lace until she arched into his touch.

"Please," she moaned.

Logan wanted to savor, but Sofia was wound too tight

to last. He slid off the bed, landed on his knees between her sweet thighs, and slid the panties off her. He licked and suckled and teased as he had her breasts. Sofia squirmed, yearning for what only he could give. Slowly, he slid one finger inside. Her eyes snapped open and watched as he slid a second finger into her wet heat. She arched into him as he suckled one last time and she shattered.

The taste of her still on his tongue, he rose to her, a starving man. He stripped off his jeans and Sofia opened for him, reached for him, as he slid his way home. He buried himself in her so deep she could never remove the memory of him.

• • •

Logan spooned her. He wrapped a strong arm around her waist and pulled her to him before he drifted to sleep. Sofia wriggled against his grasp to create enough space to turn and face him. The sparkle from the city cast enough light to distinguish his features. It was a lifetime ago that she had examined him in the coffee shop. He wasn't so different now. He had more stubble on his cheeks that made him a little rougher around the edges. Drop-dead sexy. He was naked, and in the light of the city, she made out the toned muscles of his shoulders, arms, and chest. He was solid. Not just in form, but in personality. Never in her life had she met anyone like him. She wished in that foolish heart of hers that things were different, but facts were facts. Logan deserved better than the untouchable ex-wife of a crime boss, and Sofia had every intention of making sure he got what he deserved.

But a secret part of her needed to say the words he would never hear. "Logan," she whispered. When he didn't answer, she brushed a finger across his lower lip. How had she ever thought it too thin? It was perfect. It fit her perfectly, just like the man. It seemed too soon for the depth of feeling bursting in her, but she felt what she felt. She didn't question it. She regretted that it came at a time when she couldn't do anything about it.

"Logan." Again, he didn't respond. "I've fallen for you, too," she whispered. Then she allowed herself to sleep in his arms.

· · ·

Logan did not open his eyes, but he had no need to. Everything about Sofia was etched into his very cells. She'd said his name, intentionally. It didn't matter that she thought him asleep. She loved him, not that she would admit it. Love was a weakness to Sofia.

And she sure as hell wasn't an easy woman to love. She had given herself to him in pieces, never wholly honest, she managed to keep a piece of herself back in every exchange. Everything she tried to do to protect herself just solidified the isolation that ate her alive. But now, as she drifted to sleep, she had given him everything.

Every piece, every fear, every cube of ice. She was his, and no matter what she thought, she was not going to face Calvetti alone.

When her breathing settled into a pattern of sleep, Logan reached for the cell phone on the nightstand and winced against the twinge of pain in his ribs. He really needed to get that looked at, he thought, but he had more important things to take care of first. He let his gaze caress Sofia. She was beautiful and intelligent and strong. And she would hate him for what he was about to do, but the only way to save Sofia and Eli was to call in reinforcements. He was battered and bruised and not above asking for help. Fantasy aside, he wasn't a one-man army.

. . .

The order, when it came, was to *deliver* Eli before the first mass Sunday morning. Word that Sam Capadonna had taken Eli had spread, so having the boy present at mass was a statement to Nick's world that he was still in charge. Sofia did not care about his precious honor. She followed his orders because he had the power to keep Eli alive.

She held Eli tightly in her arms while Eli held on to his Ellie. He was barely awake when they climbed into the cab, and the ride was lulling him back to sleep. The taxi drove straight to the cathedral, and if the cabbie thought it odd to arrive so early, he didn't say so as she paid the fare. He did give her a sidelong glance that suggested she was up to no good, which was probably true. They certainly weren't dressed for mass. They had not eaten or showered. Sofia had not wanted to wake Logan. She had left him in bed as she readied Eli and escaped out her side of the adjoining rooms. She had been tempted to take one last peek at Logan as he slept, but the danger of changing her mind was too great. She had already made her choice.

The cathedral was locked when Sofia arrived. She knew Nick had a key because he liked to come and go through the staff entrance. Sofia knew the way to the back. She eased around the building in the pre-dawn darkness, following the glow of recessed lights to the side courtyard. The old iron gate to the yard between the cathedral and the rectory opened without a squeak, which made Sofia wonder if the priests kept it that way or if Nick did. The night cast eerie shadows along the cathedral's stone walls the deeper she moved into the courtyard. Eli tucked his head into her shoulder. Stone statues stood like sentinels, guarding against her intrusion. She half expected Nick to jump out and kill her on the spot. Her heart pounded as she carried Eli farther from the street.

A few steps from the rear entrance to the church, a shadow separated from the wall and into her path.

Her heart hitched. The man was tall and broad. Even in pitch-black silhouette, she knew him instantly. "Logan," she whispered.

"Did you really think you could sneak from my bed two nights in a row?"

She had hoped, Sofia thought, feeling desperate. Unfortunately, all she had accomplished was to make him angry. She heard it in the clipped words and biting tone. She hadn't meant to leave this morning the way she left yesterday. It was not a slap done out of fear and uncertainty. She only wanted to avoid conflict. He had his job to do and she had hers. They were never going to agree. "I knew you didn't approve," she began. She shifted Eli to her left hip.

"You're right. I don't. But if you're going to do something this stupid, the least you can do is to take backup."

"Armed backup, I suppose," she said accusingly.

"Damn straight."

She narrowed her eyes, even though it was too dark for him to see her expression. Sofia didn't want Eli around guns. *She* didn't want to be around them. "I don't approve."

"That makes two of us," Logan said.

"Mommy?" Eli responded to the tension with a worried frown. He wriggled against her hold.

Sofia glared at Logan as she set Eli to the ground. She held tight to his little hand. "Agent Stone," Sofia gritted the words. "You don't belong here." He had no place in the hellish world in which she lived.

"You don't either," he insisted. He stepped closer. "This isn't your life anymore. You get to have a second chance. With me."

Sofia's throat constricted. She cleared it, pushed the tears mercilessly aside. "I don't believe in second chances." She looked up at him with glassy eyes. "I want my son to live. That's all the happy ending I need."

"You deserve—"

"Stop," she said. She didn't deserve this man. "You need to go before Nick gets here."

"I'm not leaving you alone with him. What kind of man do you think I am?"

A good one, Sofia thought, and that's how she knew he would never leave her to face this alone, as much as she wished it. He would be there to the end. Sofia swallowed hard against the knot of longing for Logan and the simple life he offered.

Eli's little hand flexed in hers. He fidgeted, getting agitated. She started back down the walkway. "It's your funeral," she said aloud, but she hoped that wasn't true. It was bad enough to worry about her son, and now she was risking the man she loved. They strode all the way down the walkway to the back entrance of the church, which was lit from a bright safety light over the door. Sofia was afraid to enter, especially with Logan at her side. Once inside, Logan wouldn't be allowed to leave. Nick was not a forgiving man. Sofia laid a hand on Logan's arm. "Please go."

"Isn't that touching?" Nick stepped from the shadows behind the doorway. His voice was caustic. "It's too late for that. Inside."

Sofia stood between the two men, too alarmed to move. When Nick stepped into the light, Eli recognized him. "Papa." Eli ran to hug his father's leg.

Nick grabbed Eli's hand and pulled him into the church. They didn't know what they faced once they got inside, but Sofia and Logan had no choice but to follow. Nick led them through the priest's door into the sacristy, the small room where priests prepared for worship. He passed through it like he owned it and followed a series of back hallways until they reached a domed doorway. They walked single file through the door and into the sanctuary.

They stood on a platform that was nearly as wide as the church and fifteen feet deep. There was an altar where the priests would prepare the sacraments and a tall podium where they delivered the sermon. At the edge of the platform was a kneeling rail for the congregants. The room was dimly lit from the exit lights and the flame of an eternal candle suspended from a beam. Nick treated the sacred as if it were his own, an attitude she considered sacrilege. Sofia wanted to retreat down the stairs and into the safety of the pews, but Nick motioned for her to stay close.

"I didn't bother to tell you to come alone, Sof. I thought it went without saying."

Sofia's mouth went dry. She was afraid to say the wrong thing. If she angered Nick now, he might follow through on his threat to take Eli forever.

"I'm here on behalf of the FBI." Logan flashed his badge, an unnecessary move that also showcased his weapon.

"What business does the FBI have in my sanctuary at six in the morning?"

Nick's reasonable tone sent shivers of dread up Sofia's spine. She knew an outburst was imminent and she didn't want Logan caught in what promised to be a spectacularly angry and violent tirade.

"Nicky," she said in a placating tone that occasionally worked to settle the demon.

Logan shook his head as if to warn her back. "I'm here to verify that the *misunderstanding* of your visitation has been resolved to the satisfaction of both parties."

The hellish roar of Nick's laughter boomed through the empty sanctuary, echoing off its pillars and hidden alcoves. "You really are a piece of shit," he said to Logan.

"Look who's talking." A tall man in his mid-fifties stepped from the shadows.

The tension inside her snapped. Sammy C's presence meant things would not end well for any of them. She stepped toward Eli, who was still at Nick's side, but Logan grabbed her wrist and held her to his side. She yanked her arm back, angry and terrified. No one would stop her from protecting her son. Not even Logan.

Sammy C stepped deeper into the light. He stood near the kneeling rail, out in the open and apparently alone. "You have no clue how many holes you have in your organization, Nick. No clue which informant told me of your *touching* family reunion." His derisive tone hinted at a rage he had kept hidden for years.

Sofia thought of the freezer where he had put her and knew he planned to make them all suffer. She glanced nervously around the church. Were there more men waiting in the shadows to finish them off?

Nick pulled a handgun from his pocket. From the corner of her eye, Sofia saw Logan do the same. He motioned for her to step back. She shook him off again. Nick disentangled himself from his son's grasp so that he could move closer to the traitor.

Sofia took that moment to race to Eli's side.

"The blood of the traitors is on your head," Nick told Sam in a reasonable, deadly voice. "Because I will kill every last bastard that thought they could double-cross a Calvetti. Son, come here." Nick motioned for Eli to stand beside him as he faced Sam Capadonna.

"You want him to stand next to you while you kill a man?" Sofia dug her fingers into Eli's shoulders. With a vicious shake of her head, she told her son no. "Absolutely not."

Nick kept the gun pointed as Sammy C. "Sof, it's time you accept the fact that my son is going to take over the family business one day. I will train him, starting today, to be the head of the family. Today, I will show him how to be a man."

"Eli," Nick yelled.

Eli shivered beneath her touch, his fear a palpable thing, but he responded to the command in his father's voice. He jerked from her grasp and raced forward. In the split second that Eli darted between Nick and Sam, Sam pulled a weapon and aimed it at Eli.

"No," Sofia screamed. Eli froze, either by the absolute terror in his mother's voice or the tension he was too young

to comprehend. He stood there, a pawn between two heart-
less men. For a brief second, the craziness stopped spinning
in her head. The fears, the instinctive response to avoid conflict, and the trust that was so long gone it needed its own
search party.

All of that stopped.

Sofia wanted to fall to her knees. God, she had been so
stupid. Even now. After the gym, and the self-defense classes, and the months of self-talk. All she had been through,
and she still made decisions based on fear. She thought she
had to do it alone. She thought she was the only one she
could trust. The only one who could save Eli. These were lies
she told herself. The biggest lie was that somehow, through
sheer force of her own will, she had freed herself. The truth
was, she was as much his prisoner now as she had been in
Nick's basement morgue.

Fear told her only Nick could protect Eli. No doubt he
could, but it would cost Eli his soul. She'd send them all to
hell before she allowed that to happen.

The standoff assured no one would walk away un-
scathed. Sam, two steps down from the platform, targeted
Eli, while Nick targeted Sam. Logan stood where she had
left him on the other side of the altar, his gun trained on
Nick, a psychopath of epic proportions. Her eyes pricked
with tears too late to change the outcome. She'd caused
this showdown because she refused to trust Logan. *Why?*
He'd done nothing but help and protect her from the moment they'd met. Logan risked everything for her son. Sofia
took a breath and stood up for the first time in longer than
she could remember. She straightened her shoulders and
walked between Nick and Sam, two men determined to kill

each other in the next few minutes.

And the only one who cared was Logan. He stood on the other end of the platform where she had left him and when she glanced back, she saw the look of horror that crossed his face when she placed herself in such a vulnerable position. He couldn't protect her from where he was and she'd never make it around Nick and back to Logan's side.

Sofia wanted to care that she had put herself in the middle of a gunfight, but her thoughts were on Eli. Logan would make sure Eli was safe. No matter what happened to her, her son would live. That's what mattered. Her heart pounded furiously. "You can't have my son," she told the men.

• • •

Logan watched the scene unfold and hoped that reinforcements would get there soon. He couldn't protect Sofia if she kept putting herself in danger. He angled to the left, so focused on the tense scene that he didn't notice the third man until he had a gun in his side.

Eddie had moved in behind Logan, using the dim sanctuary as cover. The older man seemed to intentionally ram the weapon into the bruised area of Logan's ribs. "Lower your weapon," he said in muted tones. "If you shoot now, you'll get her killed."

Logan nodded his understanding. Eddie hadn't told him to drop it and he'd kept his voice low. Neither Calvetti nor Capadonna had seemed to notice Eddie's presence. Logan had no idea what side Eddie was on, but it didn't matter when he had a gun in Logan's gut. Logan lowered his weapon, but kept it tucked at his side. He waited for the right moment to use it.

In front of them, Nick and Sam glared at each other. Nick called to Sofia. "Get the hell out of the way."

She ignored him and turned to face Sam. "You can't use me. Or Eli."

The older man shrugged, his gun aimed at the small body in front of her. "Whatever motivates Nicky…"

Sofia caught Logan's gaze. Her eyes widened when she saw Eddie at his side. Her shoulders drooped as if she'd recognized the hopelessness of their situation. He wanted to swap places with her, to put himself in harm's way, but they were both stuck. She looked away, but not before he saw the shimmer of tears in her eyes.

Sofia shifted Eli behind her, turning herself into a human shield. "You can't use us because Nick would kill either one of us to get to you," she told Sam. "You can't use something he doesn't care about."

"Sam," Eddie yelled. As he did, he rammed Logan in the ribs with as much force as the assassin at Vicki's had done.

The force of it pushed Logan back into the communion rail. He flipped over it as Eddie ran across the small space and tackled Sofia and Eli to the ground. The first report of gunfire rang through the empty chapel, followed by a series of shots between Sam and Nick. The sound echoed as Logan rolled to his feet and aimed his weapon at the men who had mercilessly used Sofia and Eli. Neither man was walking out alive, Logan vowed, but they fell to the ground before he could take aim.

The smell of gunpowder seared his nostrils as Logan stepped to where Capadonna had fallen at the base of the kneeling rail. The man's eyes were wide in shock and his bleeding body was still. Logan kicked the man's weapon out of reach and checked for a pulse. There was none. Logan did the same with Calvetti and felt relief flood him when he realized Calvetti was dead, but the relief was short-lived when he turned to find Sofia.

The dog pile near the altar was not a pretty sight. Sofia's and Eddie's legs were tangled, blood spatter marred the altar vestments that had fallen during the scuffle, and Eddie was unmoving. The bulk of his weight landed on Sofia who also didn't move. Blood dripped from Eddie's shoulder onto the floor and Logan heart squeezed in panic. Eli was hidden at the bottom of the pile, his grunts and groans the only sound in the chapel.

Logan pushed Eddie aside to get to Sofia. The older man was pale and appeared to be unconscious. Beneath him, Sofia's eyes were squeezed closed but her breathing was rapid. She was alive. Logan dropped to his knees beside her.

"Are you hurt?" he asked. He ran his hands along her body as he searched for wounds.

She didn't answer. Eli whimpered beneath her. She lifted her body so her son wriggled free. The boy tried to run to his father, but where Nick had stood, a body lay. Logan grabbed Eli before the boy could run, then pulled both Sofia and Eli into his lap. He held them there, in the silent chapel, his breathing ragged. Once their breathing normalized, Logan bent to whisper roughly in Sofia's ear, "Do you have any idea what could have happened?"

Sofia leaned against his solid frame and he took comfort in the feel of her in his arms, but as the adrenaline left his body in a rush, the realization that they'd lived—that they most surely should have died—flowed through him until it bubbled out in anger. "I almost lost another child. Do you realize?"

Sofia nodded. It would have destroyed him as surely as it would have destroyed her. He'd lost one kidnapping victim. Everything that led to today had been to prevent that singular tragedy from repeating.

"I'm sorry," she mumbled. "I didn't think."

"No. You didn't. You took off like a damned cowboy. You are not John Wayne." He balled his hands into fists. "I'm not even sure why you're still alive, and I was here. I saw the whole freaking thing and I still don't understand how you're alive."

She grabbed Eli into her arms and held him like a talisman in front of her. The shakes started then and her skin chilled. She was going into shock.

He rubbed her arms. "I almost lost you today," Logan whispered.

• • •

Sofia soaked in the warmth of the man who held her and the scent of the little boy in her arms. She couldn't believe she had them both. "I almost lost everything," she whispered.

He leaned his chin against the top of her head. "Do you know what that would have done to me?"

She shook her head no.

He angled her head so she could see him. "Then you haven't been paying attention."

His eyes had aged since Thursday. They were bloodshot, the lids hooded, and he stared at her with mixture of dismay and agony. No one had ever cared for her that way. No one in a long time had cared if she lived or died, but Logan did. It was in his eyes and in his soul. The rest of the world ceased to exist. It was just her and Logan and the controlled strength that hummed through his body. Sirens punctuated the silence. They didn't have long before the world of law enforcement descended on them.

"WITSEC will take you somewhere safe. I promise. You will be safe. Eli will be safe." He enunciated every word. "But I need to know something first." His gaze stabbed into her soul. "Was it all a game?"

The knot in her throat choked her words. Friday morning had started as a game, a plot, and Logan knew it. He knew she was capable of almost anything to save her son, yet he cared for her. She wanted to tell him that she was too raw to fake all they had shared, but she barely whispered the word, "No." What she felt for him was not a ploy.

He closed his eyes. His chest rose and fell against her back. When he opened his eyes, he was Agent Stone as solid as his name and just as cold. "Paramedics will be with the first responders. I'll send you and Eli out so you won't have to—" He nodded toward the bodies.

Sofia nuzzled Eli closer to her chest. After all she had been through, she thought she could survive anything, but this might well do her in.

It was time to say good-bye.

It hurt, the sting in her eyes, the ache that reached to the empty pit of her heart, but she didn't have it in her to fight.

Logan stepped back before the hoard arrived. Sofia felt her body give out. She hugged Eli and fell into a fetal position on the floor of what had once been her spiritual sanctuary. It wasn't like the movies. There wasn't a happy ending.

. . .

Logan protected the scene. He set up a perimeter, guarded Eddie who had regained consciousness, and yielded his weapon when the first responders approached. And watched the woman he loved prostrate on the floor with her son.

She was a contradiction. The most-strong and the most-vulnerable woman he had ever known. When she'd stood between two men intent on killing each other, he'd been certain she wouldn't survive. Had been certain of his response.

Logan called his boss who was five minutes out. As he waited, he ran the checklist. Paramedics took Sofia and Eli away from the scene and out to a waiting ambulance. Alive.

The body bags carried the bad guys for a change.

Logan sat on a nearby pew, let his head fall back as the adrenaline drained from his blood. He had another five days of administrative leave coming while they investigated the deaths of two known mob bosses. Five days wouldn't be enough. Had they not done themselves in, Logan knew he would have done it. Because the only way to free Sofia was to make both men disappear.

He'd told her he wouldn't lie on his report, but he didn't know the truth. His actions were situational and his ethics questionable.

He took a deep breath. He could live with that.

Sofia and Eli were alive. The ends justified the means. Logan relaxed against the pew until he realized that Sofia could disappear from the ambulance outside. She could disappear into the labyrinth of witness protection and he would never see her again. He didn't have access to their records and no knowledge of the safe house or the agents involved.

No living person could disappear like Sofia. She'd have a go-bag stashed somewhere. Money and passports and disguises, with just enough ice to evaporate. He would never find her, unless she wanted to be found. Did she want him to?

Logan didn't know the answer to that question.

He grabbed Eli's gray elephant from the marble floor.

"Agent Stone." The disapproving voice of his boss addressed him from the far end of the sanctuary.

Logan shifted his gaze down the aisle to the narthex where his boss stood without his usual entourage. Time to face the music, Logan thought. "One moment, sir. I need to get this to WITSEC." With a quick flick of his knife, he opened a seam of the stuffed elephant to remove the tracking device and headed into the street.

· · ·

The red and blue lights of emergency vehicles lit the early morning sky. A crowd gathered outside the yellow perimeter tape as parishioners assembled for seven o'clock mass. Mass would have to wait until the NYPD, the FBI, WITSEC, and the county coroner finished their respective jobs.

Sofia hadn't believed so many rival authorities existed within minutes of the cathedral. Like most of her assumptions in the past several hours, she had been wrong. From what she gathered, Logan had called in their location as soon as she left the hotel room, and even though they hadn't needed the backup, she was glad that he had done it. Glad to be out in the cool air while the coroner arranged for body bags.

At least the blare of sirens had long since extinguished, although Eli's cries did not. A paramedic had taken him into the ambulance to examine him. Eli was healthy enough, but inconsolable. The sound of his cries, the helplessness of it, damaged her more than the time in the freezer and all that had preceded it. A boy deserved a better father. A better mother. A life free of what had just transpired.

What started as minor tremors turned into near convulsions, and the blanket they had given her couldn't stop the shakes that rattled her body. An agent who identified himself as WITSEC approached. "Ma'am, if you and your son are stable, I'd like to move you now. It's not safe in the open."

A mass of bodies waited behind the yellow tape. How easy it would be for any one of them to finish her off and escape into the anonymous crowd. She nodded. "We're ready."

She had hoped to see Logan again, to say good-bye and to thank him for saving them, but maybe it was better this way. She would never be able to say what needed saying in front of a swarm of law enforcement. Maybe it was better to have a clean break, so that neither of them felt it necessary to make promises they couldn't keep. Maybe it was better to disappear.

Eli's cries softened to whimpers as she lifted him from the ambulance and followed the agent to an unmarked blue van. The sunrise lit the cold stone cathedral into a tower of pink and gold. Today, life had given her two of her three most fervent wishes.

Eli was alive and she was with him. She wanted to be grateful for what life had given her, but she yearned for more. Sofia let the van door close behind her. The only other thing she wanted in life was Logan, and he deserved better than the morally challenged ex-wife of a crime boss. She wanted to be a good enough woman to let him go. She twisted and belted Eli into the waiting car seat, jabbering at him to keep the tears at bay. She didn't look back at the scene, didn't look for the tall man with wide shoulders that she would never forget. She kept her eyes on Eli. He was the only prize that mattered, she thought, and tried to believe it as the van slipped through the empty city streets.

An ache formed deep in her chest where the fear once resided. Would she ever see Logan again?

Chapter Fifteen

Two weeks later, 6:50 a.m.

Sofia made it two blocks before checking the rearview mirror for a tail. Progress, at least, to have made it two blocks without checking. It would take time before she stopped expecting trouble and the nightmares faded and the fear subsided. Eli sat in the back eating goldfish crackers and babbling. He was doing better than her, having more memories of horse camp than of the morning in the cathedral. He had spent so little time with Nick that eventually all memory of his biological father would fade and he would have no memories of a dark night and his mother's scream, or so the WITSEC psychologist had assured her.

Her own issues would take longer, but she planned to face them this time. No running, no matter how much she wanted to start over with a new identity in a new town, Colorado was home. It was where her grandparents had raised her. She moved back to her now-repaired house, with its suspicious neighbors and hidey-holes, and planned to hit the gym this morning as she did every morning before the kidnapping. She wouldn't be held prisoner any longer.

She glanced into the mirror before making the last turn into the gym. Old habits, she thought. The road was empty, but the parking lot nearly full with the pre-work crowd getting a workout before the day began. She checked Eli into the daycare, whose security measures had been updated so that no one save Sofia could spring Eli. She walked past the weight benches with only a slight temptation to look for an out-of-work bodyguard who was no longer there.

The path to yoga was less ominous, but she did a double take when the man on the adjacent mat smiled at her. He looked familiar. Average. That's what clued her in. The target she'd selected for her ill-fated plan. The man had no idea how lucky he was that he left without sharing a cup of coffee with her. He'd probably saved both of their lives. She smiled back and eased into the first asana. Two weeks in protective custody had knotted Sofia's entire body into a tight ball of tension. It took the whole hour to stop her brain from running through the past, but when she settled in to quiet meditation, she almost achieved relaxation. Almost.

It was nothing a few miles on the treadmill wouldn't cure. WITSEC had released her the night before after ascertaining that no threat existed to her or her son. There would be no trial. Both men were dead and buried. She pushed the treadmill into a sprint.

More than anything, she wanted to run away from her thoughts. The treadmill didn't help. She hadn't heard from Logan since the morning Nick and Sam had died. Several times she'd nearly sent a text to Uncle Ernie on the burner phone the Feds didn't know to take from her, but she was afraid. Afraid he wouldn't answer. Afraid he might. She had known from the beginning that they were bound together until they found Eli, but now that Eli was safe and found, where did that leave them?

Maybe a friend, a family member, his *boss*, had convinced Logan to stay away from Sofia Capri, the untouchable who would destroy his career. And that friend or family member was correct. She was wrong for him. It hurt to admit, but Sofia was trying a new approach. Honesty.

At least parts of her life were better. The weight room below was free of bodyguards and the gym free of watchers. Or not, Sofia thought as she noticed a hefty man in a dark suit and polished shoes step into the foyer below. Mid-forties, with a slight paunch, everything about him screamed Fed. Her assessment proved correct when he flashed a badge at the front desk. The man looked straight at her as he headed for the stairs. The world tilted a moment before righting itself, and Sofia realized that until this moment, she had hoped that Logan would come to her now that WIT-SEC was finished with her, but the sight of another Fed where Logan ought to be told her she was being unrealistic.

She hit the stop button and the treadmill jolted to a halt. The pounding in her chest had nothing to do with the run. Whatever business the Feds had with her, Logan wouldn't be the agent assigned.

The suit stopped in front of her. "Sofia Capri?"

She nodded, her throat constricted with feelings she couldn't name. Regret. That's what she felt when he handed her a white envelope and returned the way he had come.

Her hands trembled too much to open the envelope.

Logan wasn't coming.

The ache in her heart cracked open and a wave of pain spilled through her bloodstream. She hadn't realized how deeply she wanted things to turn out better. Coming to the gym had been a mistake. It was too soon. Sofia raced from the cardio floor, uncaring of the people that stared as she passed. She grabbed her things from the locker room and retrieved Eli. She was running again but didn't care.

Logan wasn't coming.

In the parking lot, she blinked back tears as she strapped Eli into his car seat.

"Nice car," someone said behind her.

Sofia spun to face him. He'd snuck up on her again.

"It's just a car," she said. The ache turned to panic, sending her pulse racing.

"On that, I disagree." Logan rubbed a hand along the sleek lines of the red T-bird.

Sofia stared at him, gripping the white envelope in her fist.

"It's just a debrief," Logan said softly, pointing to the envelope. "A formality."

He wore jeans and a dark T-shirt. He looked solid, as always, but the circles under his eyes suggested he hadn't slept much lately. His gaze was wary and his eyes unfathomable.

Despite the uncertainty of his stance, Sofia had a strong urge to jump into his arms, an impulse she ignored. She was just as wary as he. It had been two weeks since they had seen each other. Two weeks for him to realize that she was bad for him. An imagined friend giving him sound advice.

"Debrief," she said casually. She cleared the knot from

her throat. "I can't imagine what more I can tell them."

"A few loose ends they need to cover."

"And you couldn't get that information while I was with WITSEC?" She straightened her shoulders to counterbalance the weak accusation in her voice.

"No. The WITSEC safe house was off-limits."

A car drove past looking for a spot. Sofia's throat convulsed. "Even for a Fed?"

"Protocol."

"Oh." Sofia closed her eyes. That's what kept him away? She wondered if he'd wanted to contact her. Did he dream of her at night, as she dreamed of him? The question she really wanted to ask seemed too big, too much to ask in the gym parking lot. "You mentioned loose ends," she said, opening her eyes.

"For instance, the person who arranged your fake passports has disappeared."

The official questions gave her the distance she needed. That's all the FBI wanted to know? She felt her lips curve into a slight smile. "I can't imagine why the passport people moved."

"Hmm." He moved a step closer. "And then there's the mystery of who provided the handgun in the hotel in New York."

"Well, really, you're the one who saw him. I only had a phone number."

"Disconnected." He stepped to within a short pace of her. "You wouldn't know anything about that?"

"Not a thing."

"And then there's the missing person." Logan stepped up and snatched the white envelope from her hands. "Vince.

Can't find a trace of him."

Her trepidation faded into anger. "Now wait a minute. Vince didn't do anything but—"

"Kidnap Eli."

"He protected Eli. That was his job."

"He kidnapped—"

Sofia grabbed the envelope and crumbled it at Logan's feet. "A dead man coerced Vince. He did everything in his power to keep Eli safe, and—"

"I agree," Logan interrupted.

The anger faded as Logan pulled her close. She closed her eyes, took a deep breath, and absorbed the feel and scent of him. God, he smelled good, a mix of man and strength and infinite possibilities. She leaned into the embrace, remembering the comfort of his strong arms. "Are those all the questions you have, Agent Stone?"

"Those are all questions the agent in charge will ask. I'm off the case."

Her eyes snapped open. "They fired you?"

"No, but I'm no longer an objective observer. I've been reassigned."

"So they'll send someone else to keep an eye on me." The taste of her words was bitter on her tongue. She hated the surveillance nearly as much as she'd hated Nick's bodyguard.

"No, Sofia. You're no longer a person of interest."

More tension unwound from her gut. "How long did you push for that?"

"You didn't deserve to be under the microscope. It was obvious when they reviewed the case. You're free now."

Free? Did that mean free of him as well?

"What do you want, Sofia?" he asked.

What she wanted more than the breath that came naturally to her lungs was a man who knew all her sins. Sofia Capri had a dark side. Some days, it defined her. For the seventy-two hours they were together, it had ruled her world. Logan knew the life she'd lived with Nick. He knew how naive and stupid and just plain blind she'd been. He knew her moral flexibility. He knew lies came easy to her lips, and that she would break any law to protect herself and her son.

Logan didn't even break the speed limit. Could someone like that want to stay with her?

"Sofia." He squeezed her close, no longer gentle. It was hard and deliberate and strong. Like the man. "Look at me."

Look at him? That's all she'd wanted to do every day for the past two weeks, so it was no hardship to peer up at his handsome face. He was day one Logan again, with a little scruff on his cheeks and crinkle lines around his eyes and too-thin lips that fit her perfectly.

"What is it you want?" he asked.

Him. She wanted, Lord knew, but Logan deserved better than a mobster's wife. What she wanted crumbled under the weight of reality. She was an untouchable and he was a Fed.

"You don't have to do it alone, you know?"

That was the last bit of advice from the WITSEC counselor, and somehow the words thawed the fear that immobilized her. Old thoughts and habits died hard. She took a deep breath and ignored the hiccup halfway through. She didn't have to do it alone. "I'm working on that."

"We could start slow," he suggested. "I could find a better way to store your comics."

She smiled and looked into his never-ending eyes.

"You'd like that, wouldn't you?"

The lines around his eyes deepened with his smile. "It's a place to start."

"When did you have in mind?"

"Now works."

Her heart skipped a happy tune. "Don't you have to get to work, Agent Stone?"

"I thought we'd worked our way past the Agent Stone thing," he said.

"Don't you have to get to work, Logan?"

"Thank you." He dropped his forehead to hers. "I don't have to work today. All week, actually."

"Administrative leave? Shoot someone else while I was gone?"

He laughed, a warm sound that thawed the chill that cooled her blood.

"Not much need with you gone. You were a one-person crime wave," he teased. "You know, I never said no to that vacation. It looks like I have the time after all."

The nerves that gave her the shakes were soothed by the thought of time with Logan. She relaxed into his embrace. He wasn't telling her good-bye. That was enough, for now. "What did you have in mind?"

He brushed a hand along her cheek where the scrape from the bombing had long since healed. Her heart did that awkward flip-flop of longing. He made her crave so many things. Normalcy. Family. Logan. "What did you have in mind?" she asked again.

"As much time with you as I can get. Time to get to know Eli."

"Chicken nuggets and Bert and Ernie?"

He kissed the pulse at her throat. "Especially Bert and Ernie," he said. "And hiking and driving your grandfather's T-bird and playing Scrabble."

"You want to drive the T-bird?" she asked skeptically. "Not going to happen."

He grinned. "Sunday dinner at my mom's."

She rested her head against his chest. "That all sounds" — she took a deep breath — "normal."

"I just want to be with you," he said in a husky tone.

Relief coursed through her and she finally had the courage to look up at him. No one had convinced him to stay away. Sofia's heart pinged through her chest. She pulled his head down and let her lips say what she could not say with words.

After a moment, she broke away. "I'll mess this up, you know."

"We both will. We don't have to be perfect."

Not perfect. She closed her eyes and tried to picture it. "I'm a mess. I have trust issues. I have baggage. I have a son."

"And you love me," he prompted.

"And I love you," she admitted. She peered up at him. "Logan, don't give up on me."

"Never." He relaxed by degrees. The stress left his shoulders and his jaw unclenched. "I love you," he said. "We can figure out the rest."

It was the best offer she'd had in years.

Another car came through the parking lot, slowing when it neared them. "If we keep hanging out in the middle of the parking lot, people will notice," he said.

"Let them watch." But she eased back, content to stare at his bewhiskered face. "What happens next?"

"That's up to you. You're a free woman now."

Freedom had exacted its price. No one would ever know what it had cost her. No one, save Logan. He had paid the price with her. Risked it all for a little boy who was no more than a stranger to him.

They were off the hamster wheel, running free.

Free.

Such a beautiful word.

Acknowledgments

No creative act is conceived in a vacuum, and so it is true of this novel. First, I want to thank those who have nurtured and mentored me on the journey. Especially, I want to thank the loopies. Time and distance have not diminished my connection to each of you. You ladies were the foundation of my writing life, and I will always cherish you. Second, I want to thank Lucy Clark for understanding my vision of Sofia and Logan. It's a gift when someone connects to your writing, so thank you for that connection and that belief (and for pushing me to make it better). All fairytales begin with a fairy godmother, and for me, that's Entangled Publishing. Thank you for turning my writing dream into a fairytale. Finally, I want to give a lifetime of thanks to my children, who gave me the time and space that I needed to create. If I had it to do all over again, I'd choose everything that led me to you.

About the Author

When they told her a woman could do anything, she thought they meant everything, and decided to give it a go. Cindy Skaggs holds an MA in Creative Writing from Regis University, is an MFA student at Pacific Lutheran University, works three jobs, is a single mom to two of the most active kids on the planet, pet owner, and child chauffeur extraordinaire. When she's not writing, she's trying to prevent the neurotic dog from either chewing the furniture or eating whole sticks of butter (often still in the paper). She's beginning to think maybe she can't do it all. At least not all at once. Connecting with fellow readers and writers is one of her greatest joys in life. Contact her on her website: www.CSkaggs.com